# THE BLITZKRIEG CASINO SCAM

*David Noble*

# THE BLITZKRIEG CASINO SCAM

## D. R. D. ROLLO

**To order additional copies of this book, contact:**
Xlibris LLC
0-800-056-3182
www.xlibrispublishing.co.uk
Orders@xlibrispublishing.co.uk
307270

# CONTENTS

For family and friends and those gone too early, including:

Brian Ferguson, Stirling University

Peter Rogerson, Sun City

Keith Rickman, Sun City

Paul Templer, Sun City

Marty Evans, Sun City

Dave Linley, Sun City

Gordon Nichol, Sun City

Dave Mackrill, Greece

Nick Mandalakis, Greece

and

David and Elaine Rollo.

# Chapter 1

## LAS VEGAS, SEPTEMBER 2013

Morris sat at the dimly lit bar, drink in hand, looking dead ahead at himself in the mirror behind the optics. On the radio 'Misty', by Johnny Mathis, started to play. 'Look at me,' he sung forlornly, the words resonating with Morris's mood. 'Jesus Christ! What a crazy few days! Had it only been a couple of weeks?' he thought and saw his head moving quickly from side to side—although he was barely conscious of it. He was trembling with nerves but was also feeling the exhilaration of still being alive. His old friend Cain, on the other hand, was in a coma—shot in the head. Morris had another gulp of beer, picked up his other glass, and let a mouthful of malt slide slowly down his throat. An hour ago, he had twenty million dollars at his feet, stuffed in suitcases and bags under a table at a local diner. Mad! Now, he had nothing save a killer's promise of a million dollars. He considered the casino scam that had gripped the casino world during the previous month. It had been a simple, but ingenious, cheat manoeuvre, which had led to all the madness: investigations, an international manhunt, and in the end, murder and mayhem, and now it seemed to be finally over. He hardly believed that it could be—but the transaction he had just completed should mean that it was. He hoped everything could slow down now and he could get back home to see Linda, as well as his kids. He ordered another malt whisky, the second of what would be many that night, and pondered the case, yet again, of what had become known as the 'Blitzkrieg Scam': teams of young, brilliantly capable, and previously unknown Italian roulette cheats, who had invaded casinos en masse and escaped with millions before anyone had even an inkling that they were being fleeced. 'And I was there at the start, the middle, and the bloody end,' ruminated Morris. His head was still darting from side to side, as if in denial that it could all have really happened. But it had . . .

ONE MONTH BEFORE . . .
ITALY, AUGUST 2013

In the small town of Tolo, in north-west Italy, resting below the Apennine Mountains, the church bells could be heard in the distance as people ambled through the quiet streets towards the old and now closed casino. They wore expressions of keen anticipation. As they entered the casino, they were greeted individually and by name by the local mayor, Marco Capone—a small, but powerfully built man, confident in himself. His hair was short and black, which matched the colour of his glasses. He had once been the general manager, before the casino had been shut down four years before. He still visited the casino every day, but for a different purpose.

Sitting around the covered blackjack and poker tables, small groups were busy with paperwork, intermingled with cash and colour chips. The roulette tables were uncovered, with cash and colour chips still lying on the baize. Around one roulette table, a group of older men burst into applause, as three young men and a makeshift dealer acted out their well-rehearsed moves. Other youths were tidying up the floats and talking excitedly among themselves, a few of them stretching their muscles after what had been a hard physical session.

The older men congregated and sat talking amongst themselves. Some of them were fathers of the young dealers they had been training that day and for the last two years. The locals often referred to them simply as 'The Trainers'. All were, in fact, retired roulette past-posters from Tolo itself or surrounding areas—happy to live a quieter life and pass on their famed cheating skills to a younger generation. That day's training had come to a close, and collectively, they had informed Capone that the boys were ready to hit their first casino. The mayor had immediately called a meeting to announce the great news to the people of Tolo.

Once everyone was seated on the assembled chairs, which had been placed on the periphery of the main pit, Marco Capone cleared his throat, adopted an upright posture, and spoke in a clear and simple voice. The workers at the tables put down their papers and directed their attention towards him. The mayor had their respect and trust. Capone himself was feeling unusually carefree, realising he enjoyed these moments in the limelight—especially when imparting good news.

'Welcome, welcome. Today is the final day of preparation before a group of you young boys leave us for a few days. It has been a long, hard road. Most of the young men amongst you have been preparing for this day for nearly two years, and now it is time to go and make . . . some . . . money!' The last three words were uttered slowly and loudly for added emphasis. It went down well with the audience. 'Little Tolo is our own special village. I hear the Chinese have towns to make only socks or shoes—Well, Tolo produces the world's best roulette cheats,' he said with a smile. The assembled crowd nodded their approval.

Behind him sat his elder brother Ernesto Capone—known in the casino Surveillance world as 'Calm Capone', for his emotionless demeanor when being interviewed for suspected cheating. He was the most notorious roulette cheat in the world. He too was smiling broadly, nodding in pride at his Tolo connection.

'We are going to attack the world of the casinos!' continued his lively brother. 'Greece will be our first destination. The casinos are rich and we are poor—We will take just a little of their money, enough for us, but a pittance for them. We have no choice—We must survive—We must feed our children,' he said, lowering his tone and looking at the floor.

'Don't overdo it,' thought his brother, cognisant of Marco's occasional dramatic tendencies, even as he was thinking of his impending trip to Greece the following day with a couple of the other trainers.

'Now the future may hold some danger,' the mayor continued in a grim tone, 'but we are all in this together, every man, woman, and child. We have discussed the importance of discretion in our work, the importance of silence with strangers. While our young men are away, we shall remain calm and await their triumphant return. But it will be worth it in the end—for all our families' benefit. Now we will share some wine. For those selected—the desks are ready with your instructions, new passports, flight details . . . so enjoy yourselves, for tomorrow, you leave—and we will see you back in a few days from Greece, rich and with fabulous stories to tell of how you broke the back of the Greek casinos and left them wondering where their money went. And for those not selected—don't worry, you will be on our next trip. Tolo will survive—long live Tolo!'

The crowd stood and roared their approval and enthusiastically moved towards the bar, or desks, as instructed.

Tolo was about to explode on to the world's casinos—unleashing new unheard of cheats, who the mayor believed were so adept that being detected barely entered his thoughts. After all, they had been trained by the greatest cheats in the world—his brother and colleagues! The repercussions of the town's actions would have dramatic consequences for the casino industry and lead to a worldwide manhunt for the men from this little town in northern Italy. Marco Capone knew what the effects of a successful raid would have on the casino world. He could sum it up in two words: 'absolute panic'.

### GREECE, AUGUST 2013

The day after the mayor had given his rousing speech, Sam Morris left the lift on the second floor of the Greek casino where he worked and walked the few steps to his office door. He swiped in and immediately felt the cool flow of the air conditioner on his slightly sweating brow. He enjoyed that feeling immensely, as it always reminded him of a fresh Highland wind. As was his daily ritual, he removed his black slip-on shoes and placed them at the foot of the wall. He moved them

11

a few times until he was content that they were exactly in line with each other, a habit he had—compulsive something, they called it. He went to his desk, stretching his toes under the teak table. Morris felt a warm content. Things were going pretty well for him at the moment, mainly due to the fact that the pain of his marriage break-up was receding, although he still wished he could see his kids more. His thoughts drifted away for a few minutes as he looked out of the office window. Morris remained pretty fit, was 100 kg, 1.85 meters tall, had broad, straight shoulders, and still had all of his sandy hair, which for a fifty-four-year-old was not bad going. 'Shame about my drinking and smoking,' he shrugged, reaching for his cigarettes.

For then, for a few minutes, it was good to get away from the casino floor. There were nearly 5,000 people down there, and the atmosphere was humid and chaotic, but as always, it excited him; he just wanted a break and to catch up on his statistics. The chase to get their money, he loved it—it was like a sporting event—who was going to win? The casino or the punters? It was not true that 'the casino always won', a phrase he had heard many times, normally by a disgruntled player. He had experienced plenty of losing nights, and it always irked him when it happened. He took it too personally. He had often been told this by his friend and employer John Cain—but he just didn't like losing—never had.

But that day was going fine. He looked at the consolidation sheet, which was updated every hour with relevant statistics. So far, 4,850 visitors, 10 per cent more than the day before at the same time. 'Probably due to tonight's car draw,' he concluded. The estimated win was €163,000 and the customers' dropped cash was €600,000—a good percentage win was always nice to see. It was seven in the evening—the casino was doing well and there were still a couple of high rollers in—which could be dangerous, but that was the risk you took with these players. He was hoping for a €300,000 win by six in the morning, when the casino closed. With a similar slots win, the casino should make in the region of €700,000 once the drop boxes were collected in the morning and the real drop was calculated—adding on another 3 per cent or so to the drop and resultant win. He was glad inspectors missed some cash being put down the cash box by the dealers and thus failed to 'click' the money, making the estimated win less than the actual. In his mind, he extrapolated that day's win and added it to his yearly bonus.

'Very nice indeedy. Not bad for a day's work, my son,' he nodded slowly, stretching his toes again and inhaling the cool air. Yes, things were looking good. In fact, Morris had about five minutes left before his whole world would be turned upside down.

He ordered a coffee and started to concentrate on one of the four monitors sitting on his desk. 'Decent game,' he thought as he saw the number of cash chips being played on American Roulette (AR) 6. Mr Kapitanis was playing—a regular big player—but not too dangerous. He made the mistake of covering nearly the whole layout in chips—he would get a small payout nearly every spin, but the casino's edge would get him in the end. He looked at Mr. Kapitanis's player tracking in the relevant programme. He had had 142 visits in 2013. He had lost €76,000 that year alone, and by adjusting the settings, Morris saw that he had lost €286,000 since he had joined four years ago. But he still came back, day after day. And he was only an average loser. 'Where on earth did they get the money?' he pondered, not for the first time. Despite the six years of recession, there were still some very rich people in Greece.

He looked at the dealer for a few spins—it took him a few seconds to find her name via the computerised table allocations. Stavroula Filippakou, very pleasant looking, with a good smile to greet the customers. Opening another programme, he saw that Roulette 6 was winning €12,300 and Mr. Philipides was winning €5,000.

If he picked up another €2,000, he would leave. Philipides was one of the few disciplined players who could get up and walk out the door when winning, despite the adrenalin shooting around his blood caused by the lucky streak. Morris's concentration returned to the dealer. He took a pen lying nearby and then printed off a dealer assessment sheet. It was a basic sheet for simple quick analysis. When dealers were suspected of wrongdoing, it was an altogether more complex process—involving a full investigation and sometimes days of all-out work.

Morris watched the dealer for fifteen minutes, ticking off the rating boxes as he watched: 'Game Speed', 'Procedure Adherence', 'Attitude', 'Appearance', and so forth. She was an excellent dealer, but she had a small habit of touching her trousers each time before she spun the ball. 'You too,' he thought and wondered if she had to straighten her shoes like him or touch a door handle ten times before entering a room. He made a note for her to be informed to stop her habit or at least swipe her hands clean before doing so—so that there could be no suspicion that she was trying to place chips in her clothing.

Just as he had finished the summary, his office phone rang. 'Morris,' he said firmly, as standard as his signature. It was 7.30 p.m.

'Mr. Morris, I think something might be going on,' came the message from the gaming director, Peter Ware. 'Can I come to the office?'

Now, Morris knew immediately that it could be serious. If someone wanted to be absolutely sure no one could eavesdrop, it was standard practice to come up to the general manager's office, rather than converse via the pit phone.

'Come up,' he replied, resisting the temptation to ask for further information.

He put the phone down and, muttering an expletive, went over to the wall to get his shoes and hoped some bastard was not stealing from him. It had happened before, and he took it personally. He gulped the last of the coffee and waited patiently, but with his mind suddenly spinning back to Sun City in the early 1980s—the Vegas chip cup scam.

Most of the staff involved had been sent to a Bophuthatswana jail. Another had presumably fled the country and was never heard from again. The rumour was that he was lying low to avoid extradition, but Morris had heard a whisper that he was 'lying low' under a Johannesburg shopping mall, along with the scam's ringleader—the real ringleader—not the guy caught at the tables. Maybe it was just a rumour intending to scare off those whose heads could be turned by possibilities of collusion. But Morris sometimes wondered if casino owners ever did get angry enough to consider violent justice. The Vegas cup scam had been a simple but clever operation. A hollowed-out aluminium tube with a real ten-rand chip glued to the top of it, and the remainder painted to look like ten-rand chips would be placed as a bet on the Punto tables. When it won, it was simply paid. When it lost, it was collected by the bent dealer and placed over hundred-rand chips. The customer then passed over fifty rand and asked for five by ten-rand chips but received the tube back with four by hundred-rand chips concealed in the hollow tube, which was slightly wider than the standard thirty-nine-millimetre casino chip width. He then subtly removed the high-value chips to be cashed out later. The scam went on for several months and involved pit bosses, inspectors, dealers, and cashiers and was only caught when the staff started spending too much on luxury goods, before one of then spilled all in an attempt to avoid the Bophuthatswana jail time. The casino result trends suggested that the equivalent of 3 million dollars was stolen. Morris had started work just after all the arrests had been made. He remembered the casino manager at the time. A decent, good guy, Marty Block—who always did all he could for the staff. He was heartbroken that his staff would do that to the casino and to him. He was never the same again. Morris had been strangely fascinated by it all and the things it told him about human nature: loyalty, greed, how far clever people can go in organising a scam, and how much could sometimes be made.

'Scams,' he thought, 'the bane of my life. You can't trust any bastard!' And since South Africa, he never had.

Ware knocked on the door and waited. He knew how personally Morris would take the news that he was about to impart. He slowly let out a deep breath as the door was opened and rehearsed his lines a few more times.

'Hello, Pete. Come in. Coffee?' said Morris, looking him in the eye, trying to gauge the gravity of the impending news.

'No thanks.'

'What's up—bad news?'

'Yeah, I think we have another situation on our hands.'

They both sat at the table and Ware continued. 'Greg, the pit boss, told me he was passing Roulette 32 and he thought he saw the dealer double-changing a customer. He didn't say anything straightaway but moved to the corner of the pit and he saw it again—with the same customer. Surveillance confirmed it. They are waiting for your call. They have already called in all the staff and are treating it as a full-blown investigation. Greg has been told not to say anything at the moment. The dealer is on a break.'

'Who is it?' asked Morris, dialling Surveillance on the phone.

'Yiannis Kontis, but there may be more . . .'

'What have you got?' he asked curtly on the phone to the Surveillance director, William Connolly.

'Yep, it's bad,' came the reply. 'Kontis has double-changed that same customer five times today, as far as we have established so far.'

'How much did he take us for?'

'Six hundred and fifty.'

'Any idea how long it's been going on for? Do we know the customer?'

'Just identified him. Markopoulos.'

'And . . . ?'

'His visits show that he was an old member from 2004, but he stopped coming in 2006 until this year, and he is now coming in every day at the start of the 14.00 shift. That's when Kontis always works.'

'How many visits since he started coming in regularly?' Morris asked, hoping against hope.

'Ninety-three,' Connolly almost whispered.

'Jesus Christ! Maybe a 1,000 plus a day for 100 visits. And maybe there's more than one . . . ?'

'We think there is,' interrupted Connolly. 'Haven't confirmed it yet, but Reception shows that Markopoulos enters every day more or less at the same time as two other players. We are looking at the footage now.'

'Keep me informed immediately of any developments,' Morris said to Connolly before hanging up.

Morris walked around the room, trying to collect his thoughts. Ware did not say a word.

Five minutes later, Connolly was on the phone again.

'At least one of the other guys, Spiliopoylos has been doing the same thing.'

'With the same dealer?'

'No, another two dealers.'

'Bastards . . . sorry, this is bad! I'll have to call Cain soon.' He drew the phone from his ear. 'Call the tables a little early,' he stated to Ware, who had a serious frown on his face. 'But don't draw suspicion and keep it quiet until we know more.'

'Right,' Ware replied, already leaving.

'So, what do we have so far?' Morris said, exhaling slowly, looking straight at the wall and concentrating, while still on the phone to Connolly. 'Probably three customers and three dealers. Three to four thousand a day for nearly 100 days.' He let out another sigh, trying to remain calm, but the veins on his neck were pumping. 'Up to half a million total.'

'Hopefully they didn't start on the first visit,' Connolly suggested.

'Perhaps. But they all start suddenly coming in every day. No. They were already prepared. Been practicing with the dealers for weeks, no doubt.'

'I doubt that our staff missed it for three months,' Connolly offered.

'You think? Four operators watching seventy roulette tables. It could easily be missed. You told me yourself that you were understaffed and that the operators didn't have enough time to monitor the games. I even told Cain that at our last meeting.'

Morris was still staring and nodding methodically. Now he had to collate everything and, as soon as possible, make the call to Cain. He wondered when he would get home.

# Chapter 2

At the same time that Morris and Connolly were discussing the details of the scam, Tommy Byrne, the gaming manager, sat on his chair in the corner of the ubiquitous Mama's Bar and contemplated another drink. He had finished his shift a couple of hours ago. His head was already pleasantly light, and he felt another drink would set him up nicely for the rest of the night as he slowed down from what had been a busy shift. 'Couple more, maximum,' he thought. 'Get some food and watch the rest of the DVD and then sleep.'

Byrne was by himself, as he usually was. He was fine with that, most of the time—time to think about things, make some decisions, analyse. His old boozing buddy had got a job in Cambodia. He missed talking about work with him and having a laugh. But the barman, Chris, a large, jocular character, was always there when Byrne felt like talking.

He became aware of a man who entered the bar and sat two chairs from him. 'Tourist,' he initially thought and sipped his whisky. However, looking at him again, he realised that it could well be the guy he had been told by Morris to look out for. There was some similarity to the old photograph Morris had shown him.

The newcomer ordered a beer and shuffled around his stool and beamed at everyone. Byrne knew he was about to speak.

'Nice bar . . . yes, very nice. What time do you close?' he asked Chris, the giant barman.

'When the last customer goes, or there is an earthquake,' he thundered.

Everyone smiled, including Byrne, although he had heard it many times before. The new guy sounded American, but with a European twang to it. 'Possible Italian,' Byrne considered.

'Are you on holiday?' he asked the man.

'For a couple of weeks.'

'Travelling around?'

'Not much actually—thought I'd come relax and maybe visit the casino, one or two days. The taxi driver told me this was the famous, wild Casino Bar.'

'On occasion, it is. I work there—at the casino,' Byrne commented, trying to remember everything the stranger said.

'Really? Don't Greeks work there?'

'Mostly, but there's a few expats left.'

'I heard it's a pretty big casino,' the stranger said.

'Biggest in Europe, but nothing like the ones in America, or Asia.'

'I was in Singapore two weeks ago,' came the reply, 'at the Marina Sands. Huge goddamned place—mostly baccarat—the Chinese seem to like that game better. Roulette's my game—do you have tables at your place?'

'Yeah, plenty,' Byrne commented. 'Greeks like roulette—We only have one Punto table.'

'Punto?' asked the American.

'Same as baccarat basically,' Byrne said. 'Have you been in Greece before?'

'No, first time—I like it though. I'll like it more if I win tonight.'

'Oh—you're going to the casino tonight?'

'With my buddies . . .'

'Where are they?'

'Had a few too many wines this afternoon at the taverna, having a lie-down.'

'Good luck tonight. Remember, the odds are against you!' Byrne smiled.

'I'm normally quite lucky—What do you do there?'

'Inspector, but we do quite a lot of dealing these days as well. I enjoy the dealing and the job, but our pay was cut recently—things are a bit tough all round. I could do with a boost, I must admit. Anyway, I'm in here most days. Tell us how you got on sometime.'

'I sure will,' came the reply and the American thrust out his hand. 'Bill Wiseman—nice to meet you. Right, I must be off, and by the way, I may be able to offer you some way of making money.'

'What would that be?' Byrne enquired.

Mr Wiseman didn't reply as he stood up, briefly holding direct eye contact with Byrne, then walking briskly out the bar door.

'Jewish name?—Didn't look Jewish,' Byrne thought, although he was unsure exactly what characterised such people. He was pretty sure that it was an alias, which only added to his growing belief that it was the man Morris had told him to be on the lookout for, Ernesto 'Calm' Capone.

Halfway home, he phoned the casino and asked for Morris. It took several minutes, but eventually, he was put through.

'Tom? Is it important, mate? Something's come up. Can you be quick?' his tone was terse.

'I'm in tomorrow and will speak to you then, but just wanted to say, I was approached at the bar,' Byrne replied. 'I'm sure it was Capone—looks close to the photo you showed me. He said he's visiting the casino tonight with some pals. He's using the name Bill Wiseman and has a bit of an American drawl, but with what sounds like a bit of Italian too.'

'Wiseman? Great! I'll call Surveillance and get them ready for a visit, but doubt they'll do anything on the first night, probably walk around looking like innocent tourists. Are you going to meet him again?'

'We didn't make any specific arrangements, but he looked me in the eye and said that he had a way that I could make more money—possibly trying to set me up to ignore his cheat moves. He mentioned Singapore—if that's any use to you. I told him I was an Inspector who sometime deals, so you can use me as bait if needed.'

'Never know, but this could be a real feather in our cap,' said Morris, growing more enthusiastic. 'One, if not the biggest, international roulette cheats is coming to our casino, and we are going to get him. By God, we're going to break his balls, and I wouldn't mind doing it personally. Good work, Tom—See you tomorrow—We'll talk about what happened today then. Got to go.'

'A few busy days ahead . . .' Morris muttered to himself, feeling a growing excitement within. Two loads of cheats at the same time. 'Handle it, man,' he thought to himself.

Byrne knew better than to ask what had happened earlier, but it sounded interesting. Morris had sounded almost fatigued at first, which was unlike him, but he had definitely perked up after the Wiseman news.

Byrne went home, sipped a beer, watched the news, and drifted off on the couch. He dreamt of spinning wheels and a layout of stars and stripes and grubby hands holding stolen casino chips.

After alerting Surveillance to Capone/Wiseman's impending visit, Morris went back and analysed the casino results again. He had already thought it strange that if half a million had been stolen, nobody had noticed the drop in profit. The roulette hold for the time the crew had been coming to the casino had only dropped to 18.76 per cent from 18.88 per cent. If half a million had gone, he would have expected a lot more, somewhere nearer 18 per cent. He phoned Connolly in Surveillance and put this discrepancy to him.

'I was just going to phone you,' Connolly replied. 'I have some very encouraging news. The group didn't cash out the extra chips they got—They carried on playing, and it looks like in most cases, they lost. So it doesn't look anywhere as bad as we thought. Could actually be less than fifty grand. The team's been working on it non-stop, and we have all those involved now. When shall we make the move? Tomorrow? All the dealers are on at 14.00.'

Morris clenched his fist tightly. 'Let me speak to Cain first and I'll call you back. Looking good, though. Yes, yes, yes, and thank God! Are you set for Capone? Remember, he'll probably come in with at least two others, although not likely to be exactly the same time.'

'Yep. We are on full alert,' Connolly confirmed. 'But as you said earlier, doubt he'd move tonight—would want to get a feel of the place first. I'll give you a call when he comes in. Can I ask, how did Byrne know Capone would be in the bar?'

'Afraid you can't at the moment,' replied Morris. 'Make sure you call when Capone enters.' He put the phone down, a little annoyed. Connolly shouldn't have asked him that. Everyone had sources they needed to keep quiet about, and Morris was the same. Only he and Cain knew who had given them the name of Ernesto Capone, and the supplier of the information had not revealed his own name—stating he had worked in Surveillance in the past and had heard a comment in the bar, that Capone was going to hit their Greek casino in a couple of weeks. Morris knew that his usual method was to initially try and isolate a member of staff who he had become familiar with and where better to meet one than in the local casino bar. If subtle hints of collusion were not reciprocated, then he fell back on his past posting abilities. So the guy at the conference informing them of Capone's visit had the correct information. He and Cain had been a little skeptical at first but arranged for Byrne to be ready after coming to the conclusion that there was no reason for the guy at the conference to give them false information. Forgetting Capone for the moment, he summarised all the Greek scam info on a piece of paper, re-read it, and phoned Mr Cain, one of the three owners of the casino and his closest friend for twenty years.

Cain and Morris's friendship had lasted thirty years, and they both had absolute trust in each other. Cain was a couple of years older than Morris. Slim, with a long Viking nose and green eyes, he had worked hard to get to where he was and was quietly proud of what he had achieved. Morris had worked with him in South Africa after they had finished their casino training at the Royal Chimes Casino in Edinburgh in the capable hands of Tim Hunter.

They had moved on to other casinos around the world, both moving up the ranks as they got more and more experience.

Cain had struck gold when he used his savings and a small inheritance to open a casino in Moscow in 1992—one of the first. He had hoped to make 5,000 dollars a day from his eight tables. After a month, he had twenty tables and was making 50,000 a day. After kickbacks, Mafia protection, rent, and other bills, he was clearing not far off 20,000 every day and he paid Morris, as the general manager, 25,000 dollars per month in pay and bonuses—which was more than twice the going rate for a similar job in one of the other casinos which were suddenly springing up everywhere by 1993. Cain was smart enough to know that things wouldn't last forever in Moscow, and he pulled out just as the government was coming round to the idea of closing all the casinos. He put his money into a consortium, buying one of the licenses for Greece, and he had seen his fortune grow further—although that year's figures were disappointing, as the economic problems in Greece started to affect the casinos. Cain was basically retired now, living in Lochinver, in the Scottish Highlands, but he kept a close watch on his investment. Lochinver was Morris's childhood holiday destination, and it was he who had introduced Cain to the village. 'The best thing you ever did for me,' he often told his friend.

After a few rings, the phone was picked up, and a female voice identified herself.

'Hello, Magda. It's Sam Morris here—How are you?'

Magda was a quite beautiful Indonesian woman that Cain had met in Bali.

'Oh, hello, Sam! I'm fine—Hope you are doing well. I'll get John. Are you coming to see us soon?'

'I may be there in a few days,' Morris replied.

Morris waited on the line for a few minutes. He thought of Lochinver and imagined looking out over Enard Bay, watching the black-backed gulls swirl around the sky, and he could almost hear their high-pitched squeals as they echoed round the hills of the village. He thought of his old girlfriend, Linda, who he believed still lived there and of his own son, now in Italy.

'Hello, Sam. John here,' Cain said. 'You just got me. I'm just off for my walk over to the pub for a couple. Care to join me?'

'Wish I could, mate,' Morris replied. 'John, I'll be quick. We found a fairly extensive scam today—but it doesn't look like it has caused us too much damage—somewhere around 50,000.'

'How many involved? And for how long?' asked Cain tersely.

'Pretty sure we have them all now. Three players and three staff. They were getting the money by the dealer double-changing them.'

'Exactly how was that able to happen?'

'Surveillance reviews showed that they mostly did it on a busy roulette table. They just looked for a table where there were a lot of cash chips being thrown over for change and of course with one of their dealers in place. You know, if there is a lot of people throwing over chips for change, the dealers place them on the wheel and deal with them one by one. Well, with these guys, the dealer changed their money, but instead of placing the chip into the float, they placed it back on the wheel and later changed the chip again. Then . . .'

'Where were the inspectors—What the hell are they getting paid for?' Cain blurted out.

'That—I wanted to talk to you about, even if this hadn't happened. I don't think the company's idea to have one inspector for four tables is a good one. It's easy to see when they are not looking and place a cash chip on the wheel rather than into the float. Our Surveillance Department cannot cover that amount of tables properly.'

'We had to cut back a little—Greece is struggling and so is the casino—You know that!'

'Granted, but this sort of thing will continue to happen if we don't secure our tables.'

'I know, I know,' Cain grudgingly acknowledged. 'What about Surveillance?'

'They missed it for three months. It was the pit boss that picked it up.'

'Impossible!' declared Cain.

'That's what I initially thought too', said Morris, 'but again, we expanded the number of casino tables and didn't expand the Surveillance staff. So we have three or four staff sorting all the disputes and all the other stuff they do, while we have 150 tables with games on them. With five to ten cheat incidents a day lasting a few seconds, the odds are that you would be unlikely to catch it. And I've seen a bit of the footage—the moves were well disguised. Obvious, once you know what you are looking for, but quite hard to see in the middle of a busy game.'

'Send a disc of the footage to me and I'll judge for myself. Right how much did we lose? What did you say, about 50,000? And when do we sack the bastard staff?' Cain said in anger. He shared Morris's hatred of employee betrayal.

'It doesn't seem too bad. From what we have calculated so far, the group received an extra 300,000 to 500,000 in chips, but instead of cashing those out, they mostly played the chips till they lost. Daft bastards—must have thought that they could get away with it forever—or chasing a million-euro win or something. I'll phone the final figure tomorrow and get the disc sent by courier. You'll get it in two days at the latest. About the staff, we will move in tomorrow—get them in the office, threaten them, etc., get all the information, and see if we've missed anything. I informed the Legal Department earlier. I would really like to take them to court this time, John. I know it's a pain, but it would send out a good message to the staff—cheat and you'll go to jail.'

'OK, OK, I'll think about it,' replied Cain. 'And by the way . . .' he waited.

'Yes?' Morris asked.

'Give the person who spotted it a wee holiday and for his family, if he's got one.'

'Right. Enjoy your pint,' finished Morris and put the phone down.

'That didn't go too bad,' he thought, letting out a deep breath. He deliberately hadn't mentioned Wiseman/Capone's impending visit. He wanted it all wrapped up and presented as a nice present, but there had to be no mistakes. 'Wouldn't mind a pint myself,' he mused. 'First, let's see what Capone does tonight. We are going to get you, and I'm going to serve you up on a silver platter at the conference,' he thought, referring to the annual meeting of the International Casino Surveillance Association being held in a week's time in Durban, South Africa. He was keen to visit the country again, and a big catch, such as Capone, would give him the perfect excuse to head down there.

Capone entered at 00.30 in the morning. He used the name Bill Wiseman, date of birth 10/08/1954. Morris, who was in his office watching the Reception intently, recognised him immediately. He was a little fatter than his blacklist photos suggested. 'Things change,' he thought, thinking of Cain's favourite quote.

Wiseman did not match any of Capone's sixteen listed aliases. The most notorious of the many Italian cheats, he hadn't been heard of for a while, Morris noted, looking at his file. Since 2007, in Switzerland, in fact. 'Possibly done some jail time,' he pondered, although it was unlikely. Most of the time, casinos usually just threw cheat teams out and circulated any new information to the other casinos. That is why the casino association was so important. Every day, numerous emails were sent, detailing customers who had been caught, explaining the modus operandi, and requesting if any other Surveillance departments were aware of the individual or group—or could provide any further information. Morris was also sent the emails and was in close association with the Surveillance Department regarding such matters. He had extensive Surveillance experience and had already been given the go-ahead to go to Durban in two weeks, if he wanted to go. He often wondered what sort of life these cheat teams had. Travelling the world, trying to find casinos which were lax in gaming security or had a weak CCTV operation, they especially favoured casinos that had newly opened, probably figuring that their past posting would be less likely to be picked up by the mostly inexperienced staff. There must be a certain excitement to it all, Morris had to admit. Sitting by the pool during the day and cheating the casino out of thousands at night, before rounding it of with a nice meal in the casino's top restaurant, sipping a glass of the finest wine, knowing it was all being paid for by the casino they had fleeced. 'Not for me, though,' Morris found himself saying out loud. 'In the end, they are all thieving bastards.' Basic honesty was very important to him—at work and at home. Ironically, in Surveillance, it was sometimes necessary to deny knowledge of something that could threaten the integrity of the department. That had been one of the hardest adjustments he had had to make when he had moved from the gaming floor to Surveillance, before moving up the ladder to the Number 1 or 2 job. He understood that there would be times when even Connolly would not be able to tell him everything—or tell him everything at a particular time. Almost paradoxically, Surveillance departments could be the least forthcoming with facts, or the truth of a matter—trusting no one save themselves.

Everything had been arranged for the scam bust at 14.30 the next day. Just then, he wanted to concentrate on Capone. He could have, of course, barred him immediately. But as in other Surveillance departments, blacklisted cheats were often allowed to enter a casino—as it was felt that since they were already known, any cheat move would be detected without loss to the casino. In addition, any new associates could be determined, and if truth be told—catching any cheat, even if one previously known, made the Surveillance Department look good, both in the casino it operated in and internationally; looked good when budgets were discussed too.

He took the lift to the Surveillance Room and went in so that he could watch the operators following Capone's movements around the casino. Connolly joined him as Capone moved through the pits and headed towards a seat at the bar overlooking Pit 3—the roulette pit.

'See him there,' said one of the operators. 'Had a quick look upwards to see the camera positions.'

'Anything at Reception yet?' asked Ware, joining them in the room.

'No,' another operator replied. 'No more American or Italian registrations.'

'Do you think there will just be the two or possibly more?' asked Connolly.

'There could be more,' replied Morris. 'But he did only mention two friends when he met Byrne at the bar. Maybe tonight will just be a trial run.'

'Yeah, I would think that is more likely,' agreed Connolly.

'Another Italian member,' called out a third operator. There were only two other operators in the room, and they were left to deal with the normal day-to-day stuff that was still going on in the casinos. The exhausted operators who had been collating all the footage for the Markopoylos team had been sent home—their work done for the day.

'I'll speak to you tomorrow of course, but do you have a final theft amount from the cheat team?' Morris asked the Surveillance director.

Connolly went to his desk and brought over a full report to Morris. 'All up to date,' he said. 'I'll complete it as soon as we deal with them. We've seen all the footage and are satisfied that we have seen all the incidents, and we make it €65,550 actual loss to the casino. The disc of every incident will be burnt tomorrow and a copy sent by courier to Mr Cain, as you requested.'

'We were lucky—the whole thing could have been a lot worse,' replied Morris. 'I've already told Cain that it would be about fifty grand.'

'Did he say anything about Surveillance?' Connolly said quietly.

'He was a bit incredulous at first, but when I told him the chances of catching a move with so few operators who are doing so much other work . . . think he was still a bit skeptical, but I think he will be OK.'

'Thanks a lot for that,' Connolly nodded.

'Look—I'm not saying there won't be repercussions . . . but I think if we can give him good news tonight, or tomorrow, I can swing it so you won't be shot at dawn,' he smiled.

'Fancy a good drink tomorrow night when hopefully this will all be over?' Connolly replied with half a smile on his face.

'Damn right, I do,' said Morris, as it was confirmed a third Italian new member was filling in the casino registration forms. Wiseman had entered with an American passport, with birthplace written as Chicago. 'Capone and Chicago,' Morris had smiled. 'Let's hope you get syphilis too, you bastard,' he said to the screen, which was showing the beaming Italian sitting on his bar stool.

Capone got up and walked quietly around the casino, looking relaxed and happy. He walked around each of the pits, smiling to the staff with the air of a new, excited customer. 'Busy place!' he called to one inspector. 'Nice uniform,' to another. Eventually, he headed back to the bar and ensconced himself in the same bar stool.

Morris was still in the Surveillance Room, watching eagerly. Sometime later, the other two Italians came near the bar, but showed no sign of recognising Capone. The names and dates of birth they had given at Reception had no matches on the blacklist. Giuseppe Nino and Frank Mara—definitely Italian—not American passports, like Capone, which Morris found interesting. Both of the guys looked about the same age as Capone, and he was sure they knew each other, but as with their names and dates of birth, their faces did not match any of Capone's associates. However, Connolly believed he had seen the faces of Nino and Mara somewhere in the blacklist database and was confident of eventually finding their true identity. The three Italians each took separate turns to walk around Pit 3 before returning to their same bar stools. After an hour or so, Morris was becoming increasingly sure that they would do nothing that night. In fact, he hoped they wouldn't. It had been a long day, gathering facts, reviewing footage, and generally running around organising things. He wanted to get a couple of ice cold ones down his neck, get a nice steak, and sleep well—for the next day was going to be another tough one. But he was quietly confidant that after that, he could relax for a few days, maybe even get some time off. He was thinking of Lochinver—a walk up the river Kirkaig perhaps—a bit of fishing. He thought of his kids too—it would be nice to be walking and talking with them at Inverkirkaig Bay, as they had done so memorably two years before. He could remember it as if it was two minutes ago—the smell of the sea and Kevin reaching down to pick up a stone, like a photo in front of his eyes.

His drifting thoughts were interrupted by the sight of Capone stretching his arms out, looking around, and heading for the exit. Never once did he appear to make eye contact with the two other guests sitting near him. Capone left the casino and was seen entering a taxi at 01.20. The other two both left a few minutes later.

'I'm off for a beer and a steak,' Morris declared to Connolly and Ware. He turned to the operators in the room. 'Look, guys, I know you will feel disappointed at not catching Markopoylos sooner than today, but I know you are understaffed and I think the big boss will be fine about it. And thanks for the amazing job you did today, in getting all the footage found and finalised. Good job. 'Night, all.' He could see the staff appreciated his comment.

Passing Connolly on the way out, he said. 'Tell the supervisor to wake me if they come back in—any hour. Get yourself home now as well—You look buggered.'

Connolly was visibly more relaxed than he had been for most of this hellish day. At one stage, he thought it would be his last day's work.

On the way out. Morris passed Reception and asked how the visitation was.

'Seven thousand three hundred so far—pretty good,' the Reception manager, Chrisoula, suggested. 'A lot of new members as well. What happened today, Mr Morris?'

'Goodnight, all,' was his only reply. Then he turned and spoke to her, not wanting to appear rude. 'Look, I'll tell you all about it tomorrow—hopefully.'

'Over a drink?' she suggested, keeping eye contact for a brief moment.

'Yeah, that would be nice,' he said, walking towards the casino exit and enjoying the possibilities of the suggestion. Morris caught one of the taxis waiting at the casino Reception. He just got a last glimpse of Capone as he got into the taxi in front of him. The drivers were always friendly towards Morris, even though they had missed out on a lucrative Athens fare and would get only €4 for Morris's local trip instead of the €100-plus trip to the capital. Pre-crisis, the taxis would often get up to half a dozen €100 trips to Athens per day—now, perhaps one a week, and even the local fares had dried up, as even €4 was now needed for less 'luxurious' spending.

He saw a taxi up ahead stopping at the Marko Hotel and noticed that it was Capone getting out of it by himself. Morris stopped his own cab about 100 meters further on and thought he'd have a quick look around the foyer, not really believing he would find anything useful, just telling himself that it was the right thing to do. He entered the foyer just as Capone's frame squeezed into the elevator, room key dangling from his hand.

Morris watched the floor button indicators stop at '3' and then left the hotel. He wandered over the road, stretched out his hands against the railings, and took in the night sea air. The sea was nearly flat and the waves fell gently across the shore, a peaceful night in sharp contrast to the day that he had just had.

A few minutes later, another taxi pulled up at the hotel, and Mr Nino appeared, going straight into the Reception area. Morris nonchalantly followed him in. Another few minutes passed and Mara arrived, following the same course of action and heading to the third floor. This all backed up Morris's belief that the group was together. He turned towards town and headed for Mama's, time for a beer and steak. He was glad that he had done that little bit of extra work and could confirm that the three were in the same group. Morris liked a beer—In fact, he enjoyed drinking but had given up the hard stuff when a friend had fallen down some steps and smashed his skull in after drinking a couple of bottles of wine. He had been a long-time friend—gone, just like that. 'RIP, Mr. Mackrill,' Morris muttered, remembering his friend. After that, Morris only drank beer—normally about four pints a day—a few more on his days off, and yet a few more with some malt whisky when on holiday. He could get slightly merry but would always be able to perform at work or take a call after work hours and be lucid.

It was fairly busy in the bar, but his seat was free.

'Working today?' asked Chris.

'Yeah—just finished. Long day . . .'

'Must have been,' Chris said, looking at his watch without actually reading the time. 'What can I get you? A beer, big one?'

'Thanks—you must be psychic!' and they smiled together. Chris knew that Morris never drank anything but beer, never soft drinks or coffee, and he always had a half litre. He gulped down half of the beer and let out a slow sigh of appreciation.

'Boy, I needed that,' he said.

'I could drink twenty beers a day—no problemo,' Chris laughed.

'I bet you could as well,' Morris replied smiling, looking at Chris's large girth.

Chris was a big guy—maybe 140 kilos and two meters tall, a good bloke.

'How come you were so late today anyway . . . ?' he asked.

'Some problems at work—hopefully, it'll all be sorted by this time tomorrow. I'll probably be along with Ware and Connolly about six or seven, depending on what happens. Could be an interesting day at work.'

'Good—I'll order an extra barrel of beer!'

'You may need it,' laughed Morris. 'Another beer, thanks,' he said, sliding his glass forward.

'Coming right up. Same glass?'

'Same glass. I'll probably get a steak later, in about half an hour. Want to get to bed early—I'm knackered.'

'You look buggered,' Chris confirmed.

'Cheers, Chris,' Morris replied with a smile.

They engaged in friendly banter, while Morris had another two beers and collected his steak on the way out. Getting home, he ate his steak while watching the news. Another EU Summit meeting had been completed with only vague solutions to the problems engulfing the continent. 'Don't they know how bad it is? What the hell are they up to? We need stimulation not stagnation,' Morris thought in frustration. He could hardly see a viable future for Greece—or indeed Europe. He thought of the rise of the Fascist Greek party, Golden Dawn. 'Cockroaches, mosquitoes, and Fascists— kill them immediately, without thought or regrets,' he had read somewhere before and it came to mind then.

His angry thoughts soon drifted back to work. 'Was everything in place for the scam bust and for Capone'? He went through each small detail one by one, considering deviations from the expected course of events. Surveillance were ready, Security was ready. The police had been forewarned that they would probably be needed around three in the afternoon. The report and all the footages had been completed, just to be updated with the final details of when the staff and cheat team were engaged the next day. Then, hopefully, when that was all wrapped up, Capone would come in the evening, try to cheat, be caught, and handed over to the police. Satisfied that everything was covered as best as it could be, Morris went to bed. Feeling quite relaxed, he fell asleep easily. He'd been involved in many similar situations.

# Chapter 3

Despite having little sleep, Morris woke early, immediately anticipating the excitement that the day would surely bring. He turned on the hot water heater and had a coffee and a smoke, while watching the news and waiting for the water to heat up. Greece was making the headlines again. This time, the group of international inspectors who had come to Greece to check on reform implementations were expressing their exasperation that the said reforms were still not in place. 'Welcome to Greece,' thought Morris. 'No responsibility.' The Greeks actually thought they could get out of the mess by doing nothing and waiting for the storm to pass. After all the crisis in the country was nothing to do with them. It was the international bankers, or the Germans, or the Greek government. Taxes were still not being paid.

'No money,' shrugged the people he met. 'Why should we pay taxes when the government is corrupt anyway?'

'Fair point,' Morris thought, contemplating the future of Greece with pessimism as he had his shower, even though he loved the country immensely. 'Back to the real normal world,' he thought as he headed out the door on the way to work.

He arrived at work at ten. Byrne came in just after and Morris talked to him just outside the staff room. Byrne had popped into the bar where he had met Wiseman the day before, but he hadn't appeared that morning.

'He'll probably approach you at one of the tables,' concluded Morris. 'Anyway, I've arranged for you to be dealing today,' he mentioned to Byrne. 'Just act normal, like you would to any other customer. We'll be watching. Don't worry about that.'

Byrne nodded and headed up the stairs to collect a dealer's uniform. Morris had made sure he was rostered for Pit 3, the main roulette pit. Morris himself headed up to the Surveillance Office to check on preparations. Connolly was standing outside the room, smoking and drinking a coffee.

'Morning,' Morris said. 'All OK?'

'Yeah, yeah,' Connolly replied. 'Staff are in and assigned. There are five operators on. Four will be watching Markopoylos and his group and one doing the rest of the stuff. Security will move in on our radio call, and the police have been warned to be ready to come to the casino at short notice. Footage for Cain is done and is on its way. Kontis and Makris are the two bent dealers working today—Kontas only is in the roulette pit—easier for us to handle.'

'Good, good,' said Morris, pouring himself his third coffee of the day.

'Right, now we wait. Probably Markopoylos will come at the usual time. First, we haul him and his cronies in—maybe get some useful info and hand him over to the police. The dealers are questioned separately and then sacked with a threat of court action. Then hopefully, Capone should be ready to make a move tonight when it's busy. We'll get him and be in Mama's with a double hit by midnight if all goes well!' Despite his experience, he could feel the excitement thumping away at his heart.

The next few hours seemed to drag by. Two o'clock came and went with no sign of Markopoylos, and in fact, he arrived just as one of the Athens buses arrived full of people at 16.45. Morris watched the cameras intently. He soon picked out his accomplices checking in at Reception five minutes after. Reception was unusually crammed at that time—the bus and tourists, loads of guests. 'Could be a good day again,' he considered.

Then something caught his eye—about twenty people behind Markopoylos was Capone and a bit further back were his friends.

'Shit,' said Morris, calling Connolly over. 'Double whammy. This makes things a bit complicated. How many operators are in or coming in?'

'Four, including the Security operator and another one in at six,' Connolly replied. 'We can put two on each and Panos can do any disputes.'

'I hope all the bastards go on one table—or two at the most,' Morris cursed. He had not anticipated both groups arriving at exactly the same time. He should have thought of the possibility, unlikely as it was to happen.

'Right, put two guys on Wiseman and his pals and the other two on Markopopylos. Weisman, the priority. He can take us for a lot more, a lot quicker. Where are they headed? Pit 3 looks like? Tell the security manager to get the office ready and to make a warning call to the police and send a text to Cain saying that the Greek team have entered and that we have things under control. We should have got more staff in—shit!' His brain was now in overdrive.

Wiseman and his pals walked around the roulette pit until they saw Byrne at an empty table. They joined him and bought in for €2,000 between them.

'You see the three of them are together,' pointed Morris at a monitor. 'They must be getting ready to make a move soon—here we go . . .'

Wiseman started betting, just placing a few chips on the layout while he talked to Byrne.

'Distract him, if you can,' whispered Morris, leaning close to the screen. 'He's not so daft.'

Meanwhile, Markopoylos had sat down on Ar 4, where Kontis was dealing a busy game. The inspector was busy at another table.

'Plenty of scope for your scam—last time though,' Morris thought.

Ten minutes passed, nothing had happened. Morris and Connolly were sure of that, both concentrating intently on the monitors. Another few minutes passed, and then Kontos received a €100 chip from Markopoylos, gave him the correct amount of coloured chips, and then placed the €100 on the wheel, looked round slowly, and then quickly gave Markopoylos another stack of chips before putting the chip in the chip bank.

'Got him live!' Connolly jumped from his chair. 'Office now?'

'Yes, let's get it over with, and we can concentrate on Wiseman,' replied Morris. Capone was still playing a few chips at a time and betting well before the spin. It was clear to Morris and Connolly that he was biding his time.

'Connolly, come with me!' He phoned Security with the instruction to meet them at the entrance to the pit. There, he met Paul Mandrakis, the security manager, along with a couple of bulky security blokes.

'Right, Paul, the guy we are taking is the bald fat guy at the end of the table. See?'

'Yeah, I see him,' replied Mandrakis. 'Is he by himself?'

'No, with the other two guys on each side of him at the table. Just throw them out. It's Markopoylos we want, for the moment. Get one of the security guys to take Kontas down to personnel. Take his access cards from him and tell him we will definitely be in touch, and then chuck him. And then get the other dealer out.'

They approached Markopoylos and let him finish his bet, before taking him off the table and marching him towards the security office. He offered no resistance. Several customers were staring at the scene, guessing what the problem was. His associates were approached and marched straight out of the casino.

The dealer, Kontos, had a look of resignation on his face as Security walked up to the pit to escort him to the HR office. He thought of making a run for it, but there was nowhere to go, and he frantically started inventing excuses while he thought of his son, who he was supposed to be picking up from the park at the end of his shift. He hadn't been told it would end like this.

Just before entering the office, he asked Connolly to check with CCTV that Capone had still to make a move. The answer came that he had not done anything yet. Morris was getting an unsettling feeling. Things were not going entirely as he had expected. He instructed Connolly to tell the operators to watch Capone and his friends very closely, reiterating that these guys were good and their moves would be very quick. He entered the office. 'Time to play the hard man,' he reminded himself.

'Ah, Mr. Markopoylos. Sit down . . .' he ordered rather than requested.

'Thank you,' replied Markopoylos in surprisingly good English.

'You speak English,' Morris confirmed the fact with him. 'Good,' he said. 'Well, I don't have much time. Just want to tell you that we know about you and your pals and your cheating and that we plan to call the police.'

'Police?' queried Markopoylos. 'What have I done? I am a good customer, I believe. I have lost thousands over the years. Check your records.'

'Oh yes, very good—especially when you get double the amount of chips compared to everyone else! We know all the dealers you cheat with. I would like to know everything, and maybe, I can not make that call to the police if you tell me something useful . . . ?'

As he finished speaking, the phone rang. It was Ware.

'Sam, we have taken some big hits in Pit 3 . . .'

Morris interrupted him.

'Sorry. I should have informed you. I'm in the Security Office with Markopoylos. I'll phone you back. I'm busy now.'

'I know, I know. We all saw you go in, but we've dropped a 180,000 in the last ten minutes!'

'What!—Bloody hell! Who has . . . listen, I'll deal with it in about fifteen minutes.'

He wanted to get out of the office quickly then; things were happening. He did not feel in control. He turned again to Markopoylos. 'Look, you are barred and will probably go to jail along with your friendly dealers . . .'

'Listen,' replied Markopoylos. 'I noticed a few months ago that a dealer always seemed to give me extra change. Why? I don't know, but most of the time, I just carried on playing and lost. Is that the truth or not?' He seemed to be relaxed and was enjoying telling his story. He sensed that the guy questioning him was becoming uneasy.

'It doesn't matter . . .' stated Morris.

'This dealer, I bought him a few beers once in the taverna over the road. Just being friendly, I don't know. I guess he just wanted to pay me back!' Markopoylos smiled.

'To the amount of half a million!' Morris felt the temptation to hit Markopoylos very hard indeed. 'Look, how much did you pay Kontos and the others?'

'The others? I don't know any others.'

'Your friends did!'

'What friends? I always come to the casino by myself. Check the cameras.'

'Enough, enough!' Morris was getting stressed. His phone rang. He ignored it, and when it didn't stop, he silenced it. A thousand thoughts jumped into his head at once. 'A lot of new members, losing 180,000—four operators glued to two customers . . . no one else watching anything else. No, no,' he thought. The guy who had approached him at Earl's Court with the news that Capone was coming—he hadn't checked him out. Capone walking around, practically asking for attention to be placed on him . . .

He suddenly made for the door, shouting, 'Paul—get this piece of shit out now! Get him out right now!' he yelled. The Security manager looked amazed but grabbed hold of Markopoylos's arm and hauled him from his chair.

There was a thumping on the door, very hard and determined. He could hear Ware shouting. 'Sam, Sam, we got screwed!—They took us for more than 800,000 in an hour and they've gone!' Morris flung the door open.

'They, they? What do you mean they?' Morris almost screamed. 'Eight hundred thousand? What are you talking about?!' He was told later that his voice could be heard at the casino's Reception.

Peter Ware's brow was gleaming with sweat. He was struggling to keep control.

'Listen. Seventy Italian members entered in the last two hours. They played roulette and took us for more than 800,000 and they have gone. No one noticed. Surveillance didn't even notice till we were losing four hundred. The little bit they saw just now was two cases of young guys who must have added 100-euro chips on the winning splits. But they were very, very good. We can't actually see the past-post move. We have been well and truly screwed. Every Italian has gone—the last one just before you came out of the office. They are probably on their way to the bloody Bahamas. Somehow, they all must have been cheating—at the same time . . .'

'How did they leave?' Morris said vaguely, hardly hearing the uttered words.

'A fleet of taxis pulled up at the casino entrance and they all pissed off— probably to the airport or Patra.'

Morris asked for a cigarette. He was aware that his shirt under his armpits was soaking wet.

'This is as bad as it gets,' he thought and immediately started to play the blame game, but there was no one to blame but himself. Everything was fitting into place. Capone had been planted to distract them. 'Was Markopoylos in on it as well?' he thought. He felt his world collapsing around him. 'What sort of scam was this?' There had been nothing like it before. Scores of cheats at the same time! This is going to change everything, he started to realise. And again, Cain's words came back to him. 'Things change,' and he realised it had been meant as a warning against complacency as much as it had been uttered to give hope in times of despair.

# Chapter 4

Morris spent the next two days in his office, liaising with Surveillance and taking and making calls. He forced himself to sleep on a chair for three hours when his mind got so numb he found he couldn't even remember Connolly's name when he went to ask him something. Connolly too, had never left the premises—calling in every available member of Surveillance to review all the scam incidents, log them, save the footage, and start to compile the report. An initial e-mail had been sent out to the other casinos in the ICSA group. Photos of those identified as cheating (fifty-five people was the latest total) were circulated and so was a summary of how the team had worked the scam.

By the end of the second day, they had determined eighty-one cheat moves, with a total amount of nearly 900,000 euro. It truly was as bad as they had feared. It had been an incredibly efficient and well-planned rip-off—skilled cheats, with, it seemed, some pre-knowledge of the CCTV's limited resources and the distraction of an international cheat to create the diversion. At times, Morris tried to look at the whole thing from an external perspective—almost hoping that he could find something that would let him off the hook, but he knew he would be out. He had phoned Cain an hour after the Italians had left and Markopoylos had been thrown out. He had not given any excuses—just the facts. Cain had listened silently; Morris just heard him let out his breath slowly. He knew Cain wouldn't panic, but there was no doubt of the seriousness of the situation and the potential threat they, and indeed all casinos, now faced.

'How long before you get the final amount?' he asked tersely.

'Two to three days,' Morris had replied quietly.

'Phone me back as soon as you know, but Sam, you know I don't think I can help you on this one.'

'Aye,' said Morris. 'I'm finished. I know. Look, I am going to sort this out. Even if I never work again, I'll catch the bastards—I mean it, John . . .'

'Look, Sam, you have enough money saved up. It's bad for the company, but you'll survive. The company will too, but the owners will want heads to roll for sure. Didn't you notice all the new Italian members flooding in?'

'Reception told me the night before that there were a lot of new guys but didn't tell me that they were Italians. It's so long since any Italian coming in was a threat to us, and I guess we all got a bit blasé . . . I should have asked though. The Markopoylos thing was on my mind. And I know there were other signs I missed.'

'What about that guy that gave us the heads-up on Capone? Did you check him out at the time?'

'No, but why should I have really? He had nothing to gain by telling us we were going to get a visit, or so I thought at the time.'

'What about the meeting with Byrne. He didn't actually ask him to collude with him and didn't go back to the pub—strange?'

'No, he knew staff would be likely to be there, but if he had actually asked Tommy to let him cheat, he probably figured we would not have allowed him entry, and that was not part of the plan. He was part of the diversion, a back-up sort of thing. Visiting the pub was to deliberately alert us to his visit.'

'The timing of the Greek and Italian cheats seems a bit too much of a coincidence, don't you think?'

'We don't think Markopoylos was part of the Italian group—Remember, he had been doing his moves for a good while before. It was just our bad luck that they happened to come in together.'

'So two different cheat teams in the casino at the same time—Jesus.'

'Mind you, even without Markopoylos, I have to admit that I don't think we would have spotted the Italians—They were bloody good. You know, even after all the footage we have reviewed, there isn't one verifiable past-posting incident that we could prove in a court. When the chips go on, there is always a hand or something obscuring the coverage.'

'Wiseman, or should I say Capone and his pals?'

'Oh, I'm certain he was connected to the Italians. Coincidences can only go so far.'

'So, who the hell were they?' Cain said, his voice exasperated.

'All Italian, young males with a few good-looking girls too. As I say—well bloody planned—another distraction for the pit bosses and inspectors. The girls were going around the tables asking inspectors if they knew where there was a topless beach and if they could show them when they finished their shift. The others could have walked out the door with the roulette tables under their arms, and the inspectors wouldn't have noticed. Best bloody scam ever, and I've fallen for it! Jesus! Time to put me out to seed, John.'

'Yes, it's a bad one, and I thought we had seen it all. Things change. I told you,' replied Cain. 'Look, the way you've described it, I can't see that you could have prevented it, but the owners aren't that casino-aware. They'll just look at the fact that you didn't pick it up. Look, Sam, if it does all go wrong, come up here to Lochinver, stay in the guest house, and we'll talk and figure out something. Get some fresh air, do a bit of fishing, bring the kids if you can get the wife to let them go. I want you clear-headed, mate. Don't worry. We'll sort it out.'

On the other end of the phone, Morris nodded, suddenly remembering why he had always had so much admiration for Cain. 'John,' he said slowly, 'I truly appreciate that, my friend. Let me finish up here, but I'll be there as soon as I can. Thanks again.'

He put down the phone and went back to his desk, freshly invigorated. He didn't feel entirely alone any more . . .

Another day and a half passed before the full scam details were finalised. No feedback had been received from any casino about a similar type of scam, and no one had been able to identify a single member of the team.

'We were the first,' Morris surmised, although he had already believed that would prove to be the case. He was still amazed at the numbers involved. All of the males had registered the night before—the girls on the day of the scam. After registering, the men came in and did nothing, save walk around the casino. Many had been watched by Surveillance, and the general consensus had been that they were members of a tourist group. Morris had seen all the footage by then and begrudgingly admired the skill of the table distracters and the speed of the hand movements as bets were placed after the winning number was known. The pit staff had done courses on cheat training, and there had been a few roulette cheats caught in the past, but nothing like this and certainly not on this scale. Morris was convinced that the scammers had come up with a new strategy—a quick all-out raid involving many, not a single group, of cheats.

It was dawning on Morris that if this was going to be the new way cheats operated, Surveillance departments around the world would have to change. 'But what could they do?' he thought. Employ dozens of extra employees in the expectation that one day your casino would be hit? No owner would go for that. Refuse entry to Italians full stop? Racist and impossible. Refuse to let then enter until they had all been checked against the blacklist? Not practical, if dozens were arriving at once. Refuse bets on roulette once the ball had been spun? Customers would rebel, as it was part of the game's excitement to bet as the ball was spinning. 'Who the hell had devised this strategy?' he kept thinking over and over again.

Examining the passports which were scanned as the Italians registered showed that several had identical official signatures and that they had all been issued in one place—Milan. Morris had no doubt they were very good fakes. They didn't even need to be that good—just enough to get in the casino, do the cheat moves, and then be thrown away after.

Once everything had been collated, a full report had been sent out to all the casinos in the ICSA group, and the news spread around the casino world like lightning. He was receiving nearly fifty emails a day—many expressing deep concern.

Probably the press would pick up on it too, and Morris grimaced as he anticipated the headlines: 'Greatest casino scam ever! General manager helpless as cheats take a million!' The emails from the other ICSA Surveillance directors and also from some non-aligned casinos were showing that some of the biggest casinos in the world appeared to be very worried, well aware that their very size made them open to a 'Blitzkrieg scam', as one of the emails had referred to the way the Italians had operated. 'A dramatic, but apt description,' Morris thought. The casinos in Macau, Singapore, and Vegas were asking for a general casino strategy to combat the threat, and after a few days, a general consensus would emerge that an urgent meeting of casino owners and Security and Surveillance departments had to be convened as soon as possible. There was agreement that the quickest way to facilitate this was to have the meeting at the ICSA conference in Durban. The wheels started frantically turning, as all casinos worldwide internally debated how to stop a possible 'Blitzkrieg' attack.

Morris had completed the final report of the scam by the end of the third day. A total of €921,100 had been stolen, 139 cheat moves had occurred in around an hour, and fifty-four different cheats had been identified—quite incredible figures. They had been divided into groups of three for a bit of cover and to spread themselves around the tables as much as possible. Nearly all of the moves had involved a push of four by €100 chips on to the winning split, with the chips being placed on the split line below the number. All had been third dozen splits and the vast majority had been on the splits in the last column, involving numbers 27, 30, 33, and 36. Number 24 in the second dozen had also been used on occasion. Even in slow motion, the hand movements at the time they knew the additional chips must have been placed were incredible. On average, each team had managed a successful past-post move about once every eight minutes or so. All of them—for an hour! 'How had so many people learned to cheat so well?' thought Morris, and how did they get so good? He knew skills at that level must have taken hundreds of hours of training. 'Where did they train? Who trained them? Why have we never seen them before? Did all of then train together? Was it possible that they hadn't been in other casinos, waiting years for the opportunity?' His head was spinning.

The Surveillance technician, Stratos Kidonas, had completed the footage, and it was forwarded to head office along with the full report and CCs to Cain, after his request. Morris only felt deflated when he handed in the report. It was probably his last ever useful casino act. He had not tried to blame anyone. In fact, he had attempted to make sure that none of the Surveillance staff would be blamed by truthfully emphasising the skill of the cheat moves and the lack of Surveillance resources. He really didn't care much if they prosecuted Markopoylos for fraud or tried to jail the dealers involved.

He said a few words to close friends and colleagues, who obviously sensed that his job was on the line. 'On or two would be pleased,' he thought, 'the ones who always saw an opportunity for themselves in others' demise. Good luck to you as well.' Unless this thing was sorted out and quickly, casinos' Security and Surveillance departments would change forever, with paranoia reaching new heights.

Outside the building, he paused and looked up for a few moments. 'Jesus,' he thought, 'fifteen years! I was married when I started here.' Memories of walks with his wife, tavernas, his son running to him one day when he had finished work . . .

He headed home, but after a few minutes, despite his exhaustion, he had opened the door to Mama's bar. 'Time to get wellied,' he had decided. And he did.

# Chapter 5

He received the expected call from Cain two days later. He was relieved of duty pending head office's final accountability report. He was pleased to be told that no one else had had to take a fall. He had looked at the Surveillance Department's roster, and there had not been any particular operator who could be matched up to the time of Markopoylos's cheat moves with a suspicion of deliberately ignoring them. Could have been a few of them at it, but he knew collusion involving several members of a Surveillance Department at the same time was scarce.

Cain informed him that it was very likely that he would be sacked in the next few days and again asked him up to Lochinver.

'Booked the flight to Glasgow for tomorrow,' Morris replied. 'I'll probably stay there a couple of days, sample the local delicacies, and meet a couple of pals. Then, I'll be up. Thanks again for the invitation, John.'

'Listen, Sam,' Cain said, 'I want you to come to Durban for the conference—We can travel together.'

'I'll be sacked by then. Why would the company want me to go?' said Morris confused.

'It's not so much the company,' replied Cain, 'but everyone wants to meet you to get the inside story. I want you to present a report and maybe a solution. What do you think?'

'I don't know,' said Morris, exhaling slowly, 'would feel a bit of a laughing stock—can imagine all these smirking executives . . . as for a solution, at the moment, I can't come up with anything except mass murder!'

'I think you're wrong about giving a talk,' replied Cain. 'Most people hold you in high regard. The casino owners are all shitting themselves—you wouldn't believe it. They want to sort it out. You may be offered a job as well. Some of the big shots will probably be in Durban. Kruger and Ling will definitely be there.'

'Serious players,' agreed Morris. 'Look, can we discuss it in a couple of days? But I guess if I can swallow my pride and shame, I may take you up on the offer, but only if I pay my own way!'

'Agreed,' replied Cain, sensing Morris's pride, even though he had already bought the tickets for both of them.

Morris took a flight from Athens to Glasgow, with a quick changeover in Amsterdam. He arrived early evening, got a taxi to his flat in Park Road in the West End, unpacked, and had a shower. He felt surprisingly good after the depression of the last few days. He was home and out of Greece, and the disassociation perked him up. He was determined not to worry for the next week and then take it from there. Anyway, there was something about Glasgow. It was home.

He was in the Doublet Bar at seven-thirty in the evening, which was a bit late for the regulars that he remembered, but two or three of them were still there, on the same seats, as if a change of position would herald some calamity. Morris could appreciate this urge; he too liked familiarity—it felt safer. The last week had had a distinctly unfamiliar feel about it. The regulars had not expected his visit at all, and there were a few nods and offers to sit down and an offer of a pint from old pal Gavin Steele, who put his crossword down for a moment.

'Here's a surprise,' he said, bringing a pint over. 'Just decided to take a holiday?'

'Nope. I got sacked, or I will be in a day or two,' said Morris.

'What?' Steele said, sounding incredulous.

'Yeah, we had a huge scam, and I, as the boss, had to take the fall. Anyway, I deserved it, made some mistakes.'

'I saw something in the paper,' said Steele. 'Your casino—shit! They got away with more than a million?'

'Not far off it, but it was less.' Morris couldn't bring himself to quote the exact amount.

'How did they do it? The papers were a bit vague but said there were several people involved.'

'Yes, it's starting to be known as the Blitzkrieg scam. It was like a lightning attack—they just poured in for an hour and wiped us out while we were interviewing some other cheats.'

'So you had to take the blame?' Steele extrapolated.

'Maybe I'll get back. I may be off to Durban, as there is going to be a conference to try and sort it all out. I'm supposed to give a speech telling everyone how I failed to see what was happening—bit embarrassing . . .'

'A few days in Durban mind wouldn't be so bad. Remember that night on Marine Parade?' said Steele, memories coming back.

Morris took a long gulp of his pint, nodding and smiling a bit. Marine Parade on the Indian Ocean coast and the night of the 'three and a half girls', as they had retrospectively named the group of girls they had met up with. Three of the girls looked exactly the same height, and the other seemed to be exactly half the height of the other three. They had joked about who was going to get two girls and who was going to get the one and a half. It had been a strange night indeed . . .

Such banter made him feel good, and the night passed by in pleasant conversation until tiredness started to seep through him. 'Fish and chips and a nightcap in the house?' asked Steele.

'That sounds great,' replied Morris. All his life, on his first night back in Glasgow, he always had fish and chips from the Philadelphia on Great Western Road.

They reiterated the story of when Morris was about eighteen. He had once come from the Pewter Pot pub in the winter after a last round of six Drambuies and accidently dropped his gloves into the deep fryer while trying to place his order.

The lady preparing the fish suppers had said dryly, 'So it will be fish fingers and chips to go then?' She still worked there, and on each of Morris's visits, she reminded him of the incident. She did so again as they collected their suppers and headed up to Wilton Street.

They sat at Steele's bamboo bar and had a last beer before having the fish and chips while watching the news. Immediately after eating, Morris headed down the road to his house—a little tired and tipsy but feeling much better than he had been during the last week. He fell asleep in an instant. He did not dream of casinos at all, falling asleep to the thought of three and a half girls in Durban . . .

Morris was up at five minutes before seven—just in time to get a coffee before the news. Scotland seemed to be in the midst of financial problems. 'Go and have a look at Greece,' he observed. Morris went out to the shops, bought the papers, and some square sausages, eggs, and rolls and spent the next couple of hours watching TV, reading and eating his Scottish breakfast, unhealthy—but tasted great.

Steele was working that day, and Morris had arranged to meet him in the Doublet at about four. Morris walked down Byres Road, got some money from a RBS machine, and then walked over to Park Road, and then continued into the town centre. He had more or less decided to go to South Africa and found himself buying some new clothes without thinking about it too much. He had a pie and walked back up to Park Road, having walked about five miles in the course of the day. He pottered around in his house, checked his e-mails, had a wash, and then walked up the stairs and the few yards to the Doublet.

At that time, many more of the regulars were in, many of whom he had not seen the evening before. He sat and chatted with them and bought Steele a pint when he came in.

At about 6 p.m., he got a call from Cain. It was the news he expected—He was glad he received it when still sober. Sacked. It had never happened in his life. A wave of self-doubt came over him. He felt unsure about Durban again; suddenly, the thought of making a speech seemed impossible. 'Get over it,' he chided himself. 'You got a good pay-off and you haven't suddenly become a bad GM.' But the words felt hollow.

He thanked Cain and confirmed his arrival time in Lochinver the next day and ordered a 'Malt of the Month', along with the next pint. He bought drinks for half a dozen folk sitting around him and informed them of the news. There were a lot of nice things said—they were good guys. Suddenly, though, he wanted to be alone for a while. He informed Steele that he needed a break and said he wanted to go up to the Halt pub for a while. 'I'll be back in an hour, at most,' he stated. 'Just need to figure some things out.'

'I'll still be here,' Steele said in understanding. 'We'll have a curry next door later—OK?'

'Aye, fine,' said Morris, rising from his chair.

The Halt was just up the road. His father used to go there during his university days, and there was a rumour that the stone of destiny had been kept there for a while when it was stolen from Westmister Abbey. He had remembered his father saying that he had had a ring made with a tiny piece of the stone, but had lost it somewhere. Morris knew the son of the Halt's owner, whose father had known Morris's father, but he wasn't in that night. 'It would have been nice to see him,' he thought.

He got a pint and a malt and sat at the near-empty bar. The TV was on—about the only noise that could be heard—but the smell of malt and stale air was strong.

'What was he going to do?' He had money, but not an infinite supply. He was too young to retire and had no desire to do so in any case. Perhaps he would be offered a job if he went to Durban, but he again suddenly felt a strong draining away of his confidence. Would he be OK at work again or permanently paranoid and panic stricken of any possible scam situation? This drinking wasn't helping, he realised, but sometimes, you needed a good session to get some things out of the system, he quickly reasoned. He had another drink—suddenly thinking that he would like to speak to his kids. On impulse, he phoned.

'Hello, Son,' he said when Kevin picked up the phone.

'Hi, Dad,' came the reply, the same response that he had always given.

'How you doing, Son? Everything OK? I'm actually in Glasgow now. Guess what? I got the sack from the casino.'

'What happened?'

'There was a big scam. Quite exciting really, except muggings here didn't manage to spot the buggers, and they cheated us out of nearly a million euro.'

'A million!' Kevin responded, suitably impressed.

'Yes, a lot of money, so the big bosses thought it would be better to get rid of your old dad. So here I am in Glasgow, having a pint in the pub and drowning my sorrows.'

'What are you going to do now, Dad? Will we meet you soon?'

'For sure, Son. Can't wait to see you, Son. At least now that I am not working, I will be able to see you and Margaret more often.'

'Yeah!' Kevin replied.

'Thanks for that, Son. I needed a wee boost. It's not much fun getting fired, I can tell you that.'

'Did they give you a lot of money?'

'Enough for a while. Don't worry. I can still send you and Margaret to school, but stick in and work hard, OK?'

'I'll try, Dad. So when are you coming?'

'Well, I'm going up to Lochinver to talk to Mr. Cain, you know, my old friend from way back. Then I might go to South Africa for a few days. Maybe someone will give me a job there.'

'Can you bring back some biltong?'

'Biltong, forget you like that stuff. Sure, Son—if I go.'

'You'll go, Dad, now that you said you would get the stuff for me.'

Morris laughed. 'You know me too well. Anyway, I'll come and meet you and Margaret straight after I go, or in a week or so if I don't. OK?'

'That would be great, Dad.'

'How's your mum?' Morris asked.

'OK.'

'Is the new guy OK with you?'

'I suppose.'

'Try and get along with him a bit. I'm sure he's not too bad.'

The conversation was coming to a halt, and Morris was aware that he was getting a little drunk.

'Right, Son, I'm off home soon, and I'll phone you soon. Bye then.'

'Bye, Dad.'

As Morris ended the call, he realised that tears were forming around his eyes. Morris ordered the same drinks as before and sat thinking painfully of his kids and how much he missed them. His life was in a bit of a mess, he concluded, as the drink started to get a hold of him. Without being aware of it, his drinking speed had increased rapidly.

Morris had ups and downs before, and he looked at the floor, determining that he would do something positive to sort it out. 'Last night on the heavy booze till I sort this out,' he determined. He gulped back his pint and headed back to the Doublet. Now that he had decided to lay off the drink for a while, he deserved another drink as a reward, his drunken logic was telling him.

Back in the Doublet, he found the weekly quiz night was in full flow. He was too late to join one of the teams, and in any case, the regulars kept to their same teams in the serious effort to win the thirty pounds of free drink, which was the winners' prize. The teams huddled together at each question. 'Too much university challenge,' thought Morris, who was back up in the clouds at that moment. 'Drink—took you up and down like a yo-yo.'

There were two teams who normally won, and both had very clever members, as the Doublet could be described as an intelligent man's pub. Good beer and no TV. Many of the regulars were teachers or professors, some lawyers, media guys, actors: mostly clever folk who liked a drink. 'Funny that,' thought Morris, 'the strain of being smart—how did that work?' His mind was all over the place then.

Morris nodded to Steele, who was in one of the top teams huddled around one of the tables. Morris sat at the bar. Alistair, the owner of the bar, did not come in too regularly, but always read out the questions on quiz night. The standard was high, although some celebrity and football questions were always included to keep the less cerebral teams involved.

'Question 4,' Alistair cleared his throat, in an official, serious manner. 'Which production team was responsible for the film Toy Story?'

There was a sudden huddling among the teams, and Morris heard one young student whisper to his teammates, 'It's Disney Wizney . . . I mean, it Wiznae Disney . . . it was, I know, I know . . .' He looked as drunk as Morris felt. That was one good thing about Glasgow: When you were steaming, it never took too long to find a sympathetic accomplice.

Morris gave himself one point as he ordered a double malt. 'How many was that?' he tried to recall. He got Steele a drink and settled down for the rest of the show. After each category of questions, Alistair read out the answers and Morris heard a few 'I bloody told youse' or 'I knew that . . . !'

'Why didn't you say so, then . . .' he answered to the non-hearing team member.

To add excitement to the proceedings, Alistair always added up the scores prior to the final set of questions, which were a mixture of the previous categories. As usual, the Top Hats and Doubleteers were neck and neck, with the Top Hats a mere point ahead. Morris was enthralled and ordered another pint (to wash down the malt, you understand). In the end, the deciding question was how far the sun was from Earth, and the Top Hats' answer was a mere million less than the Doubleteers' correct answer, and so a draw was declared. This outcome seemed to be acceptable to both teams. Less drinks for each team member, but they had both still 'won', sort of.

Morris moved to the tables from the bar and managed to spill about half a pint as he did so. He was aware enough to know that he had drunk way too much, but at the moment couldn't care a damn. 'I need a re-tox,' he declared to himself, 'and I'm doing a damn good job,' he thought, a demented smile on his face. He sat next to Steele, but he left soon after, as he was working the next day. They could both see that a curry in a restaurant would not be a great idea at the present time. Morris sat by himself, in no hurry to go home as he ensconced himself in his little corner with drink in hand. All his troubles seemed so far away . . .

He picked up on the conversation at the next table. One guy was out of the game. Judging by his nose and general appearance, he'd been there for a very long time. The other guy, smartly dressed, looked pretty sober but was maintaining pub etiquette by pretending to believe that what he was hearing was interesting and pertinent. This skill required few words, only an occasional 'Damn right', 'I agree', or an angry look in sympathy. Best to keep on the good side of someone who had had too much. The drunk guy, who Morris did not know, had been talking about the Second World War. Why? Morris had no idea.

'You know, Churchill is the only Englishman in history that I truly admire. If it wasn't for him, you and I widnae be here having a pint. Do you know that!'

'Damn right,' came the immediate reply, accompanied by severe nodding from the well-dressed gent.

'Did you know that Churchill lost an election in Dundee to a pro . . . proa . . . bitpissedionist?' continued the drunk guy.

'Yes, I think I heard that somewhere. Good man, that Churchill!' the other replied. 'Best Englishman ever,' he added diplomatically.

'F'damn right, but can you imagine losing to a teetotaller in Scotland!' He whacked his hand on the table, causing some of his drink to jump out of the glass. 'Can't believe it! What was the guy's famous speech again?' frowned the drunk man. One of his eyeballs looked like a lead weight was pulling it downwards, while his lips reminded Morris of a broken elastic band. 'Never in the field of human history has so many beaches (he hesitated) . . . so much . . . been so owed by so few to so many . . . people.'

'That's right! Pretty close,' replied the sober man with a wry smile on his face.

'We shall fight them on the beaches. That's what I wanted to say before, on the hills . . . all the way . . . We shall never surrender . . . f' brilliant stuff, man. He won the war. I tell you, without him, we would all be speaking German. He liked a good drink too. Here's to Winston Churchill!' he shouted, raising his glass and then hitting in on to the table. 'Do you know that I share his first name, me? Winston McGinally,' he said in a somewhat pompous manner. Big mistake in Glasgow. Arrogance is never welcome there.

'Shut the fuck up!' one of the regulars said. 'Fucking Churchill!'

One of the bar staff, Dawn, came over and told the drunk to 'cut it down a bit'.

'All right, all right . . . don't I deserve a drink? . . . Work all f'ing day. I pay your wages, hen (said after she left). Take my money all night and then . . .'

'Hey, Winston!' somebody called out as the regulars warmed to the theme. 'Got a Marlboro?'

Winston started muttering and drifted quietly away to a destination that Morris could not fathom or follow. He caught the eyes of the sober guy and they both laughed, making sure the drunk guy was unaware. McGinally suddenly lurched from his chair and weaved his way to the door of the pub.

'Winston, Stalin just called. Said he's meeting up with Roosevelt at the Yalta and do you want to have a pint with them?' another regular called out.

McGinally did not reply as he went for the door, opened it, and then tried to turn back, which almost sent him to the floor. He boomed out to the whole pub, 'Let's not say goodbye—Let's say au revoir.' Then he was gone into the cold Glasgow night.

'What a place!' Morris laughed. 'What a great, bloody city!' He started talking to the more sober guy and a few more drinks were ordered. The rest of the night was forgotten. He did end up ordering a curry, but it was unappreciated and unremembered, evinced only by the stains on his carpet the following morning.

When he awoke, it took him several minutes to realise that he was in the land of the living. He felt exactly as he had anticipated. 'Pure shite.' The last time he had drunk so much was on his fiftieth birthday when the police had found him lying in the street, a victim of rubber legs syndrome. They had kindly given him a lift home, although Morris, in his confusion had tried to pay them, believing he was in a taxi. He looked at his bedside desk. There must have been twenty pounds in change spread across it, always a sign of a heavy night. Opening his wallet, he found a solitary five-pound note—all that remained from the ninety pounds he had started the night's drinking with. He knew what he had to do. Calvinism was kicking in. He made it to the kitchen walking like a zombie in his sleeping shorts.

He poured himself a pint of water, then drank it all. The hangover routine was in full swing. Then he made a coffee with two large spoons of Nescafe and no milk nor sugar. He then had another pint of water and sipped the coffee with a cigarette in hand. He felt the bile forming and retched. He went to the sink and got rid of some liquid, which he presumed was a mixture of water, coffee, and bodily chemicals and some remnants of booze. He sat down again, finished the coffee, and had another cigarette. 'Why the hell do humans drink anyway?' he pondered, as he had done on countless previous occasions.

He sat there staring at the wall for about twenty minutes and then headed to the bathroom and remained there for half an hour, completing various essential tasks. He then ventured round the corner to get a newspaper. There was another strong coffee while he read the paper. Still feeling bad, he packed up his swimming gear and headed down to the local swimming pool. It was nearly eleven in the morning. Ten o'clock till eleven was booked for Muslim ladies to have a swim in private. 'Good touch by the Council,' he thought. Dead on eleven, he paid to go in and then swam a hundred laps of the thirty-metre pool. By the end and after his long, hot shower, he was feeling quite a bit better. Although not particularly hungry, he bought a cheese sandwich and a pie and swallowed it down with an Irn Bru.

He walked home and packed for the trip up north. It was one o'clock when he set off. The trip up to the Highlands via the west coast was one he had always enjoyed, especially once getting past the stretch of road bends around Loch Lomond. He drove slowly, thinking of a lot of things—his future—his kids. There was a lot of pressure on him for sure. 'Things change. Be strong.' He started wondering again about the scam team and determined that once up in Lochinver, he would attempt to try and figure out where they were from and how the hell they had organised the thing so damn well. There would be a clue somewhere, he thought. There nearly always was, he had found. Perhaps he would meet up with his old girlfriend in Lochinver too. He was longing for company, which always happened after a heavy night, he had found.

He stopped for a while and had some delicious sea food at Kishorn Seafood bar, but wanted to push on, and by six o'clock, he had reached Ullapool. From there, it was a lovely run to Lochinver of about forty-five minutes, passing lochs and mountains, with few cars in sight. As he had always done, he started to look out for Suilven, the magnificent mountain of many shapes. Spotting it near Elphin, he slowed down for a moment and then pulled into a lay-by as many memories came flooding back. Lochinver had always been the holiday destination for his family since he had been a small boy in East Kilbride. His father used to give sixpence for the first member of the family to spot Suilven, and Morris and his two sisters would be stretching and peering over their seats to try and claim the first prize. The poet Norman McCaig was friends with his father and had taught Morris how to fish and, on their long walks to the lochs sprinkled around Suilven, had also given him an insight on how to look at things with a different perspective. McCaig was a great poet and man.

Morris had seen and been up Table Mountain, but to Morris, Suilven was the greatest mountain that he had ever seen. It had been named by the seafaring Vikings and translated meant 'pillar mountain'. It appeared as such from the sea. However, it was actually quite a long mountain with a myriad of shapes, depending on one's viewpoint. From the north-west, it looked to Morris like an Egyptian mummy lying flat on its back. Suilven's base of Lewisian Gneiss was some of the oldest rock in the world, at somewhere near 3 billion years old. The mountain stood proud and firm. Morris felt a powerful surge of connecting emotion. 'Do not give in—be strong.'

He started the car again, and after heading left at Ledmore Junction, slowly drove the last few miles to Lochinver and Cain's magnificent lodge, holding a sense of renewed vigour within. The hangover had dissipated to near non-existence.

It was about eight o'clock when he drove up Cain's gravel drive. He saw the door opening and Cain's figure appearing and walking towards the car. He looked grim and friendly at the same time.

'How does he manage that?' Morris pondered.

'Hello, mate,' Cain said, opening Morris's car door for him.

'Welcome back to Lochinver. How was Glasgow?'

'Same as ever,' replied Morris. 'Honestly, I'd be dead if I lived there, but nice to see the Doublet and the guys again.'

'I'm sure. Are they all OK?'

'Yes, fine, and how are you doing? Looking good—all that fresh air . . .' Morris said.

'Yes, I'm feeling pretty good. Anyway, let me take your bags. You are carrying enough weight on you at the moment as it is.'

'Must admit . . .' replied Morris as they headed into the house.

Cain took Morris's bags into the room that had been arranged for him and then left the latter to take a shower, saying they would head over to the Culag Bar when he was ready. He hadn't asked if he would like to go and it didn't matter. On each of Morris's numerous visits, the bar had been the first port of call whatever the circumstances, a bit like the fish and chips routine in Glasgow.

After a shower and a change of clothes, Morris actually felt pretty good. The morning haze felt like a couple of days ago. A pleasant walk and talk around Enard Bay and a beer or two at the Culag Bar, where he might meet a couple of old friends too. Perhaps Linda would be there. However, he knew enough to know there were a lot of serious questions to answer before the night was through.

As they walked the two miles to the Culag, Cain made no mention of the scam and they talked about family, Lochinver gossip (always plenty of that), and the economic problems in Greece and Scotland.

The bar was not too busy, but a couple of regulars, or some would say inhabitants, were sitting at the bar, talking quietly and mouthing generous greetings when they recognised Morris. 'Alistair! How are you doing? OK, pal?'

'Hello, Pele,' he called out to another customer, who came over to shake his hand. After a few minutes spent ordering the drinks, Cain and Morris sat themselves down at a quiet corner of the bar. Linda was nowhere to be seen, Morris noted in disappointment.

'Right,' said Cain immediately. 'Tell me the whole damned story.' He of course knew all the details, but there was nothing to compare to being told by the person actually involved.

Morris had already prepared the way he was going to approach his explanation. He wanted to ensure he did not start rambling from one connection to another. Cain appreciated facts and clear connections, not opinion or rumour. It took about half an hour, with the very occasional succinct question from Cain, who hardly moved or drank his pint while Morris was talking.

'. . . so they all left together. As I said, they all had Italian passports. It is definitely some sort of new method of cheating. There has never been a "Blitzkrieg" scam before—I've searched all the blacklist files and all the emails are telling me the same thing. This is new and very dangerous. To coordinate such a scam and to organise it all and to train, they must have some sort of base somewhere. And they must have access to forged passports on a large scale. Some clever guy thought of the whole thing—the distractions were brilliant. I was all over the place, have to say.'

'Understandable,' Cain commented, turning his head slightly in sympathy.

'Capone could be the key to it all. He definitely has been to America, and we may be able to drag something up about him from somewhere. Once we have a lead, I think we can find them. I really want to do that.'

'The name he used, Wiseman, is a Jewish name—not like all the other Italians . . . ?'

'Despite his name—he's Italian, all right, or of Italian extraction. Probably if he is an international cheat, he prefers a non Italian name, knowing that most casinos automatically watch new Italians coming in, such is their reputation. Quite a few of his other aliases are similarly non-Italian sounding.'

'So why did the scam team all have Italian passports?' asked Cain.

'Safety in numbers. If you think about it, what better way to screw up Surveillance than by having dozens of new Italian members coming in at once and sending them into a panic? That way, they knew they would be watched on the first visit, when they did nothing—leaving it clear for the next day. The thing that gets me is that most of the cheat moves were done by the younger ones—and they were bloody good. We've searched through the alias file and they are all new. Where have they been and why have we never seen or heard of them before? It takes years to develop the hand movements required to past-post a bet within a millisecond of the ball dropping. You know—not one member of the pit staff, or Surveillance come to that, noticed a single move. That is phenomenal in itself. Well, I seem to be out of the loop now, but you guys still operating should be very worried. It could happen again, no problem. And I think it will, and soon.'

'We have the, albeit fake, names and photos that you circulated around the world,' replied Cain. 'Believe me, they are on every casino's blacklist.'

'They will know that though,' replied Morris with a frown. 'And I'm sure they will have access to more forged passports. And again, what do you do if they all start arriving at once? Even the best and biggest Surveillance departments need time to check the names, organise observations, or interviews. All these guys need is half an hour. By then, you may have matched half a dozen names with our cheats, but there may be another fifty inside by then!'

'I know,' said Cain. 'I've discussed this with numerous top owners already. Legally, we can't just stop Italians from coming into a casino. We can't stop the games while we check them out. And maybe next time, they'll all come as Swiss nationals or something. It's a bloody awkward situation . . . I'm starting to think losing nearly a million was not too bad!'

'Oh, they could have taken almost as much as they wanted, but the table result dropping like a stone would have alerted us that there was something wrong, and we could then have maybe isolated a few cheat moves and taken some of them into custody. For them, that would have been too dangerous. Possibly, we could have got all their real identities. No, "Blitzkrieg" is very apt. In and out very quick with what they wanted and no one got caught at all.'

They both paused for a while.

'Anyway,' Cain stated, 'you really need to come to South Africa. Look, there's no way you will get hostile treatment—or be made to look ridiculous. I told you before. You are held in high regard. And I want to tell you on a personnel level that my own opinion of you has not changed one iota.'

'Thanks again for that,' replied Morris. 'It's just that my confidence has taken a big knock. You know me well enough, John. I'm not the most confident type. I can pull it off sometimes, but only when I'm feeling totally comfortable in my job and with my colleagues. When I get a setback, I start questioning myself in all areas of my life. I'm hard on myself, which I know is daft, but . . .'

The talk drifted away from the scam as they had a couple of more pints and talked about old times. They even managed a couple of laughs over some favoured old stories. Later they mixed around the bar for a while. Morris hadn't noticed, but his old girlfriend had entered, and as he looked around the bar, he caught her eye.

There was that eye-contact moment, so brief and yet full of promise. Linda! Still looking marvellous. Cain was talking to someone, so Morris went over to where Linda was sitting and asked if he could buy her and her friend a drink. They said yes and he ordered for them as well as one for Cain and himself.

'Great to see you, Linda. You're looking great . . . !' he said with an easy familiarity.

'Hello, Sam. This is my friend, Sandra.'

Morris rose and shook hands. He remembered Sandra as well—bit of a wild one if the stories were true. Although, there were always wild rumours in a small town like Lochinver. They talked for a while, and Morris felt the stirrings in his body. It was a pleasant rush and he realised it had been a very long time since he had been with a woman. He felt no hostility coming from Linda. In fact, the opposite. There was considerable eye contact and the occasional brush of her hand on his arm. She started talking less and less with Sandra, who looked mildly annoyed and eventually moved off to talk with other friends. Morris felt himself merging with Linda, his attention now totally on her and visa versa. A warm contented glow was pumping through his body, and he had to remind himself that he was with Cain.

He asked Linda if she would like another drink, but she shook her head and looked at him directly as she said slowly, 'We could have a drink at my place . . .'

'That would be great,' he replied, smiling nonchalantly as his heart felt like it had suddenly trebled in size. 'Look, I'll just go and tell John that I will be late getting back to his place.'

'Tell him you'll be back in the morning.'

Morris had a sudden thought flash of dollar signs rotating through his eyes and almost ran towards Cain, so keen was he to return to Linda.

'John, do you remember Linda . . . ?'

'Sure,' said Cain 'your old girlfriend. You two look like you are keen to re-introduce yourselves to each other. Enjoy. I think you could do with a bit of comforting. I was just off anyway. You have your set of keys. How about a walk up to Suliven tomorrow, not too early? Bit of fishing and we can talk a bit more about what we are going to do about these damn Blitzkriegers—or whatever we should call them.'

'That would be great,' Morris replied. 'Now, if you'll excuse me . . .'

'Off you go, you randy bastard,' Cain replied, briefly putting his hand round Morris's shoulder.

Linda had not taken her eyes of him and started to stand up even as he walked towards her again. 'Encouraging sign,' he thought. She had a car but had had a little too much to drink, so they decided to walk the mile or so to her house.

He slid his hand across her waist and leant slightly into her as they walked. It was a still night, with a little moonlight reflecting off the sea water. 'Must be fate,' thought Morris. 'It's really, really, nice to see you again Linda. Sometimes, I think I should have stayed here with you. You look gorgeous . . .'

'You look good too, Sam, and don't worry,' she said, turning and placing her hand at the top of his thigh and rubbing gently. 'You can have me tonight, if you want?'

'Oh, I want, I want! Thanks for saying that, Linda. Must admit I was getting a bit nervous. Felt like I was going to say something stupid that would put you off!' They stopped, reached towards each other, and brought their lips softly together.

He held her close and it felt just right. She responded and then they sort of staggered to her house, through the door, and up the stairs. There, the animal instinct took over, as old desires were re-enacted and frustrations extinguished.

# Chapter 6

At that moment in Tolo, Marco Capone had just about finished his business for the day. And it had been a long day. They had to move quickly. 'The second attempt was sure to be harder,' he thought. But he felt good. The raid on Greece a week before had been successful. Not one member of the team was caught. He shook his head in amazement at the skill and hard work that his boys had put in. The years of training had been worth it.

Tolo had once been a thriving town with a canning factory, spa, and a casino situated among beautiful mountains and a river. Everyone worked and tourists from Italy and beyond game to gamble and spend their money. Nearly a quarter of the town's workers had worked or been connected to the casino in some way. Another third had worked in the canning factory. Those were the good days of full employment, laughter, and security.

However, in 2009, the head office in Milan closed the factory, with only two weeks' notice, and then the news came through in 2011 that the casino was due to close after a slump in business due to the economic downturn. Just like that, the town was ruined. Capone had been elected mayor in 2008, while still the casino manager, and was a popular figure. He prided himself on honesty and kept a clean and anti-corrupt town hall. He was paid the same as the average councillor, taking a 30 per cent cut in his salary to do so. He insisted all the town's inhabitants learn English 'to give us a better chance in this global world,' he had said.

When the casino had closed, he had called a crisis meeting with the townsfolk to try and figure some way of saving the town from complete collapse. The meeting had been fiery and noisy and was almost out of control as the desperate inhabitants aired their opinions and possible solutions. Then, a young croupier had spoken up.

'Mr. Mayor, as you know, your brother and many of our relatives are famed casino cheats. Some of them were very good and got a lot of money. We have many croupiers here, and we could choose a few to go out and try and get some money for us.'

'I don't think a few thousand dollars would save us, Salvatore,' Capone said sympathetically. 'We need to get jobs for everyone and work every day, not just once in a while. But thank you, but stay within the law next time as well!' he admonished the boy with a frown.

More ideas were discussed, including opening their own casino, as well as some ideas to increase tourism, but the meeting ended without any firm decision made.

It was later that night, while he was sitting in his garden drinking a glass of wine, that he remembered Salvatore's remarks. He had seen a documentary a couple of hours before where thousands of marching ants had killed a prey thousands of times their size, by pure force of numbers. He thought wildly of the whole town invading a casino and running away with all its money. Suddenly, this crazy idea changed form, and he started to concentrate on the subject very seriously indeed. 'What if . . . what if a bunch of highly trained people hit a casino at once? What would the casino reaction be? Could such a team be created and trained and organised?' He imagined it in his mind, and the more he thought, the more excited he became. Damn it! It could work. His brother and his past-posting friends could train the croupiers! In and out, in a quick attack. A disciplined offensive. Like an army team. He got of his chair and started walking around his garden, oblivious to his dog following his every footstep. He went inside to get a paper and pen and spent the next two hours writing and rewriting his burgeoning plan.

At the end, he was convinced it could be done. 'My god,' he thought, 'it could really save the town. Even one hit could keep us in food for months. Two or three, and we could build our own damn factory and tourist hotel . . .' He slept little that night and was in his office by six o'clock in the morning. He was about to cross the line, but he had no qualms in doing so. After all, his job was to look after the people of the town—that was what he was elected for and that was what he was going to do.

He met the town councillors at eight-thirty and, after various points of business, introduced his idea slowly. After running the town on a ticket of anti-corruption and legality, he knew there could be some opposition to his plan. He needed to be at his most convincing and persuasive.

'I would now like to talk about a plan I have been thinking of to try and save our town, because we have to think of something, and believe me, if we don't, the town dies and your jobs with it. We all love our little town, and I have had to consider all possible solutions. I believe I may have the answer. But, I have to tell you that it is on the wrong side of the law, not in the sense of robbing banks, but more of, you know, the story of the Englishman, Robin Hood—taking from the rich and giving to the poor. All the money collected through my scheme will be distributed among the townsfolk on an equal basis, even those not directly involved in my plan. This is fair and will make sure everyone benefits equally and also that no one has anything to gain by informing anyone else. So, I have to say, this plan could be considered criminal. Although, I have to say I doubt any one of us would ever go to jail if caught, but you have the chance now to leave and resign now if you want. Consider it and we will meet back here this afternoon at two. I must admit that this is the only plan I can think of that will save the town—so think very carefully before you decide . . .'

The councillors left, some by themselves; others in groups, talking wildly amongst themselves about what this master plan could possibly be about. At two, they reconvened and Capone asked if anyone wanted to leave, because once in, they would be expected to stay in.

'Can't you tell us what it's all about?' said one councillor, obviously disturbed at the prospect of breaking the law.

'All I can say is no harm will come to anyone except in a financial way, but for the people who lose this money, it will not be a serious thing for them and will soon be forgotten.'

This seemed to reassure everyone, and they all stated, when asked, that they were ready to commit themselves to the plan.

'Thank you for your support. Now let me explain . . .' Capone continued. It was not until nearly ten at night that he felt that they had covered everything: training, identity documents, travel, operational matters, buying some new casino roulette tables and wheels, organising secrecy and discretion. All were discussed and analysed over and over again.

'Regarding the training, we have many old ex-croupiers, but they are too old now to learn new tricks. We shall train the young men who had just started in the casino before it was closed. The best seventy to 100 will be selected for our first excursion. I suggest it should be somewhere near. This will cut costs down and be easier to organise. We can go further afield if we are successful in our first trip. I have been thinking that Greece could be ideal. They have some large casinos there, with around thirty to forty roulette tables in the biggest ones, enough for us to hit many tables at once and busy enough so that we will go undiscovered. We will have to register to join, but that will be OK, with our new passports that we have talked about. We can attack in the middle of the afternoon or evening at the weekend, when it is getting busy, and it will give us enough time to get in and out and back to the airport for the late flight to Italy. You all know my brother, Ernesto, who used to work in the casino and went to America. I have a feeling he may be able to help us too, but I will tell you more once I talk to him. We shall send two or three people to the casino in advance, who will report on entry procedures, identify emergency exits, and maybe they will find something else which can help us. We will start the training immediately after the town hall meeting that I am going to call in a couple of days and as soon as I can get some equipment in. The training will be vigorous. It will take a long time. We have to make sure every participant reaches a high and consistent skill level. It may take years. I, my brother, and friends will be in charge of that, if nobody objects? Good,' he said when there was no response. 'The excitement you feel now may lessen and your confidence may diminish as time passes, but keep your faith. This thing can be done and it will be done, for it is not for your benefit, nor mine, but for the town as a whole. It is not greed, but need—always keep that in mind.' Capone was impressed by his spontaneous final comments. He contacted his brother the next day and found him more than willing to get involved in the training, and within a few more days, Ernesto had organised another ten past-posters, many from Tolo or surrounding towns, who were also keen on the idea.

Back in the present, the mayor reflected with satisfaction on the success of the initial operation. He realised that the second attempt would be more problematic. What would the casinos have learnt about them? What measures would they implement to prevent it happening again? Certainly, the attacks hinged on anonymity. If one of them was caught, the whole stack of cards could fall. He was constantly thinking along those lines. He had thought of going to Singapore next—with their two huge casinos and the third just completed, but he had started to go off the idea. He knew how well Asians organised everything and felt their casinos would be harder to crack than most places. Capone was increasingly moving his target to South Africa. From his casino connections, he knew that Durban was hosting the next ICSA conference. He knew that most of the top Surveillance guys from the South African casinos would be there. He had seen the numerous Internet comments and press articles about the 'Blitzkrieg' scam and was sure top meetings would be held in an attempt to come up with preventive measures.

Capone figured that—just as he had seen the scam as being almost impossible to stop—the casinos would have come to the same conclusion and would be meeting at the top level to try and figure something out. What better place than at the conference, where all the top executives were already going to? And he thought, 'What better time to hit a casino than when they were understaffed and the top guys were absent?' His brother Ernesto had also been to South Africa and had mentioned that in most of the casinos, there was no entrance registration and that the roulettes were busy at most times. 'Sounds good,' thought the mayor, having just about made his mind up.

The money from the Greece raid had totalled around €920,000 and had been divided among the towns 2,300 adults, after the expenses of around €50,000 had been deducted. It came to around €400 for each person. It was hardly life-changing, but the people were very grateful and the scam participants made no demands for an extra share. They felt proud, like returning soldiers, and received many free meals and small gifts from the local business owners. So all was well and there was a contented atmosphere around the town. Everyone knew not to say a word about what they were doing, and he reiterated it on a daily basis as he met the people in the town.

However, Marco realised that if they were going to get enough money to open a decent hotel, reopen the bottling plant, or even reopen the casino, as some had talked about, much more would be needed, which would mean a longer stay in their target destination, or riskier cheat moves, or further targets? All three strategies had their own inherent risks, and much deliberation would be needed before a final plan could be established and done before any team set off for Durban. The problem, Marco knew, was that every hour, a table score was done by the pit boss. If the team stayed for two hours, the pit would be completely aware of how much money was going out and be more attentive. This, to him, would make further cheating dangerous, even though he had faith that his team would not be caught. He went on the side of caution, deciding that the attack would remain only one hour, at most. The town had decided that after expenses, half of any money collected would go to the townsfolk and the other half put towards their investment plan. If it all went well, one or two more strikes and they would be able to stop.

It was finally agreed that the large 'International' casino in Durban would be the target. It had forty-five roulette tables, which were obviously very popular, judging by the owning company's posted profits. There would be a quick attack and then a late-night flight back to Milan.

The casino was only a kilometre away from where the ICSA conference was being held at the Marine Parade Centre. 'That would be a lovely irony,' thought the mayor. Right under the noses of the top casino guys in the world—who would be discussing the Greek scam—while a few minutes away, another casino was getting mauled.

The conference started in a week—time to get the organising team out again. He was glad the discussions were over, and things were finally moving. He felt such excitement and already felt sad that one day it would have to end—there was no way they could go undiscovered forever. Eventually, a mistake would be made. 'Need, not greed,' he reminded himself. Think of the future. A nice hotel with a small casino was his favoured investment plan, but being a fair man, he would go with the wishes of the townsfolk. He also had a strong desire to go on one of the raids himself. Why not the next one? He truly wanted to see his team in action. How they kept their cool? How they decided to make their move at a particular time? They had all told him. It felt like being on a football team or even in the army. The friendship and close bonding of the team was unbreakable.

# Chapter 7

Morris had woken and for a few seconds thought he was still in Greece, until he felt the warm limb of Linda's leg wrapped around his own thigh. He made no attempt to wake up Linda for the moment. Instead, he watched her breathing peacefully, her long black hair reaching to her bare breasts. He had lived with her for more than a year, and in that time, they had never had a single argument. She had a very quiet temperament ('Until you get into bed,' he smiled.) and always seemed to understand his point of view. He felt that they had definitely been headed for marriage, even though they were both in their early twenties at the time. But he knew that at that age, he was not ready to settle down in one place. He had finished his training in Edinburgh and wanted to see a bit of the world, and when a casino job was offered to him in Sun City, he asked her to go with him. It was good money, he had told her, for South Africa, at any rate. There were not many well-paid jobs in Lochinver, and none would have provided sufficient savings for a house. She understood this, but had too many family ties to feel comfortable leaving, and she had felt Africa may not have been an ideal place to be left alone when he was out working, especially as he would have to be doing his share of night shifts. They had decided that he would go, work hard for a couple of years maximum, and then he would come back and they'd marry and get a house, etc.—all the usual dreams that were made when in love.

So he had gone to Sun City, with his pal Cain from the Edinburgh training school. Morris had spent two years in Sun City but had not returned to Lochinver. By the age of twenty-five, he was assistant casino manager in a casino in Poland, earning 25,000 pounds a year, with his housing paid for. His bar job in Lochinver had paid him a third of that, without a housing allowance. He started to feel he could not come back to that. He wanted to be, not wealthy, but in a position hopefully that he did not have to worry about money for the rest of his life. Ten years, he thought, even imagining that he could retire before forty. But he could not expect Linda to wait for him for that long in the prime of her life, just seeing him once or twice a year when he could get away for a quick holiday. He made the decision that he should split up with her, even though she had made no indication that her interest in him was waning. He hoped that she would still be there for him one day but loved her so much that he also hoped that she would meet a great man who would look after her and give her the kids that she longed for.

After two years in Poland, Cain had offered him 40,000 a year as the general manager in a new casino in the Bahamas—with the proviso that he trained in Surveillance while he was there. Cain was pushing him fast and he appreciated the faith being placed in him. He had phoned Linda, explaining to her that he was going to the Bahamas. Again, he asked her to come with him, but her mother had taken ill and she said she could not leave. He said that it was unfair that she should be stuck in the house looking after her mum and no partner to relax with and suggested that maybe it would be better 'for now' if she forgot about him.

She said no, but six months later, she phoned him and said that she had met someone and said it was time for him to forget about her. He almost felt relief when she hung up, though he could not figure out why. He had sometimes thought of that call as the defining moment of his life.

The Bahamas contract had only lasted just over a year, as the authorities were keen to reduce the number of expats working there and to promote the local population, which both Cain and Morris thought was fair enough. Morris had received some excellent surveillance training out there by the director, Gary Morrison, a fellow Scot. Cain had heard about the ex-Soviet Union opening up, and after a trip and some meetings in Russia, he said to Morris, 'Get packed. We are going to Moscow tomorrow—to make our millions!'

'Sounds good to me!' replied Morris. Moscow—would you believe it! And so, the adventure continued, but just then, looking at Linda's closed eyes, her long slim legs, and her open lips, he felt he should never have gone. How could he have left such a girl? He moved towards her, wanting only a kiss.

'What took you so long?' she said, suddenly opening her eyes. 'I could feel you staring at me for the last ten minutes. How could you resist me that long?' Her eyes were alight and she was smiling the most beautiful smile. She pulled back the covers to reveal Morris's limp appendage. 'Feeling a bit tired, are we?' she said, as if addressing a child. Morris looked down and laughed. Suddenly, he reached down and pulled the dead organ from its resting place on his thigh. He used his thumb and forefinger and spoke through closed lips, ventriloquist style, while moving the head of his old pal up and down, 'Feeling tired? I'm bloody knackered!'

'Poor soul,' Linda said, warming to the theme, 'maybe I can help you feel better?'

She brought her legs over Morris's, and her breasts swung from side to side as she did so. Morris took his hand away, but Linda's words had remarkably done the trick and he found he was ready again.

'Can't believe it!' he said. 'Come here, you beautiful woman.'

All in all, he had made love to her four times in about twelve hours.

'I didn't know I had it in me,' he sighed when they had finished, his hair matted with sweat.

'I didn't know you had that much in you,' she replied with an arched eyebrow.

'Fancy a walk up to Suilven?' he asked.

'That would be perfect,' she said.

Morris phoned Cain, apologising for being a little later than he had intended.

There was genuine warmth in Cain's voice as he replied, 'For once in your life, I didn't expect you to be punctual. You know how often you talked about Linda over the years?'

'I guess I did go on a bit,' Morris said. 'I was thinking this morning that I should have never have left her. I didn't treat her well, running away like that.'

'Nonsense, you had to do that. Never underestimate the power of adventure and looking to improve yourself. It's an instinct.'

Morris laughed. 'You are probably right, John . . . Look, can you pick us up in half an hour? I'll just get to the shops and pick up some supplies.'

'No need, all done. What do you think I've been doing while you have been in love's embrace? See you in a bit, at Linda's gate. Half an hour. We'll park the car at Inverkirkaig and walk up from there, your preferred route, if I recall?'

Morris had no need to confirm the fact.

Cain duly picked them up, and in less than an hour after the call, they parked the car at Inverkirkaig and walked the short distance to the bridge over the river which separated Ross—shire and Sutherland. Opening the gate next to it, they started the walk towards Suilven. The sun was out and a slight breeze was keeping the midges at bay. Cain walked up the path, keeping slightly ahead of them, stopping occasionally to turn round and look at the view of Kirkaig Bay as it retreated further and further back. They diverted slightly and walked down to the Kirkaig falls, whose roar broke the silence and could be heard long after their visit. When the path started to turn left towards the imposing shape of Suilven, they rested a while and had some rolls and tea. Morris thought of the Famous Five—he was in a blissful state. Only the day before, he had woken up with a monster of a hangover and in deep depression—it seemed weeks ago just then. He remembered that they were sitting on some of the oldest rocks in the world, Lewisian Gneiss. The rock beneath them was something like 1,000,000,000,000 days old. Suilven rested on those rocks and was composed of layer upon layer of Torridonian sandstone—maybe half a billion years younger. Suilven had remained looking out to sea all those years he had been away and Linda had stayed. It was his time, he thought. He had had enough travelling; what better place in the world to settle down? 'Would she be interested?' he thought. His heart started to beat quickly, and he felt a hot flush covering his body. Linda noticed and asked what was wrong. Not now—soon, he promised to himself.

They reached Loch Fionn at the base of Suilven and did a bit of fishing as they talked and sipped their drinks. Morris had caught a char once and been told it was a rare catch of a species left behind when the ice caps had retreated from Scotland thousands of years before. Before this, all of Scotland had been covered in ice a mile thick, which meant that even Suilven, sitting as it did now, would have been submerged.

Back they meandered towards their car at Inverkirkaig. The breeze had almost gone, and Cain stopped and said to the others, 'This is why I love Lochinver. Don't say a word for a second—don't move. Just look.' They all looked around the landscape. As magnificent as it was, the really impressive thing was the silence. They could see a dozen miles in all directions—but not the faintest of sounds could be heard. Quite an incredible experience! 'The sound of silence . . .' Cain said after a minute or two.

They drove back and had a cold beer at the Culag. Cain said he had to go, as he was expecting some calls regarding the meeting in Durban. Morris and Linda left a few minutes later and walked slowly towards her home.

'Do you remember that girl . . . What was her name . . . the one that used to throw men out of her caravan if they had failed to please her?' Morris said.

Linda laughed. 'What made you think of that? Maggie Munro, or the Terminator, the Black Widow, Mons Mag . . . she had many a nickname!'

'Mons Mag. Don't remember that one. Did she really physically throw guys out her place?'

'Yep. One lad broke his collarbone. She would get awful drunk and target some poor boy at the pub. They'd be desperate to lose their virginity, and it almost became a right of passage to go with her. The blokes used to bet on who would be the first one to satisfy her.'

'Where did she live?'

'She had a wee caravan just past the bridge. Nobody lived nearby, and if they did, they would have fled with the noise she used to make! Like an unknown, wild, Highland animal.'

'Why did she throw them out?'

'She had some sort of thing that if the lads didn't satisfy her, they were using her and being rude and disrespectful! And she would just suddenly lose her temper and shove them out the door, with a kick as well sometimes.'

'Is she still around?'

'Eventually, her supply chain dried up, not enough young virgins for her. She went down to London, I heard. Probably found lots of guys into that down there.'

'Crazy Lochinver,' Morris shook his head.

'Just as daft as any place, but because it's wee, everyone hears all the stories that would be missed in a big city.'

Morris paused for second and made sure he caught Linda's eye. 'You know, I really feel that I'm sort of home now. I've been running around the world like a madman, but whenever I come here, I just feel at peace. Shit, I feel I've wasted my life—apart from having two great kids.'

'Nonsense,' Linda said. 'You know how many people would swap their lives for the one you had? So many here said they wished they had done something when they were young, but had missed the boat. You're lucky, Sam.'

'I know, I know. But I was always restless, ended up drinking too much a lot of the time. Always liked the job, though, I must admit.'

'What will happen about that now?'

'I don't know, Linda. I think I've had about enough of it. I really think I want to live here.' He slowed down and came to a stop and turned towards her.

'Linda. It is so great seeing you again. You look as gorgeous as the first time I saw you—really. And you are so nice and . . .'

'Sam. You know that when I heard you were coming, I felt great. I don't go to the pub often, but thought you and John would be there. When I saw you standing there, I just felt so good inside.'

'Me too,' said Morris. 'When I caught sight of you, it was, I don't know—as if everything before had been sort of surreal and you were the only real thing that had ever existed. Sorry—a bit dramatic there!' he blurted out.

'I knew you would come back some day,' Linda smiled, grabbing his arm.

'I was scared to try and contact you. I guess I thought you would be married or hate me or something. Look, Linda . . . I want to be with you. I love you . . . I could buy a nice house here and get a wee job . . . no pressure or anything. We could live together. I would be so happy.' He could feel his vocal chords trembling. He was looking her straight in the eye. She pulled him towards her, not answering—the movement being answer enough.

The next morning after breakfast, Morris phoned Cain and arranged to meet at the latter's house. When he got there, Cain took him through to his office and made some coffee.

'Right, no arguments. I'd already booked the flights for Thursday morning, Inverness to London and on to Durban. We get there late at night, but Ged will pick us up, and he's booked us in the Beverly Hills at Umhlanga, Kerzner's old place— Don't worry, my treat,' he smiled. 'Return flight on Monday. Don't want to keep you away from here too long, do I? You look very happy, Sam. Anything to tell me?'

'Yes. Linda and I are going to settle down here. I plan to get a house and maybe get a job to keep the old brain ticking over. I feel great. I've told her that I will be away for a few days and she can start to look around for a place. She fancies moving out of her own place. She says she wants to make a clean break. If she can sell it, she'll put some of the money towards our new place.'

'Great news,' replied Cain. 'I'll have my best pal for a neighbour—and a happy one, at that. Look, I know old George wants to sell his house up on the hill, lovely views and handy for the town. He'll give you a good price. I think he wants to go cruising and has no relatives left. He still has a wee place in Badnaban, which he can live in when he returns.'

'How much do you think he would want?'

'Less than a hundred, and it has three bedrooms—as I said, a great place.'

'I'll tell Linda, and maybe when we are away, Magda can arrange with George for her to see it?'

'OK, I'll sort that out this afternoon. Sam Morris retiring—never thought I'd see the day—must be true love, my boy.'

'I think it is just that, John. So about five days away. Hopefully, I can make some contribution to catching these guys. Maybe someone will come up with a bit of information that can lead us to them and I can settle down here in peace. You will let us know any information that you get, John?'

'I'll do my best. But sometimes—you know these big meetings—we can be sworn to secrecy, and I wouldn't want to be the one that breaks the promise. They might put on a pleasant enough front, but some of them are real bastards. They didn't get where they are by being nice. A couple of them have connections that you wouldn't like to know about . . .'

'I've heard a few such rumours,' replied Morris. 'These guys won't be pleased at all. Not by the scam, but by the potential of future ones and the probable cost to the industry in preventive measures. We really have to find a way to stop them. I can't see them stopping either. I'm sure they are on a beach somewhere, living it up and planning the next one.'

'Where would they go next?' Cain queried.

'Possibly anywhere! Interesting that—presuming they are actually Italians— that they went so close to home the first time. Maybe they will do the same the next time, which could suggest Switzerland. I'm not sure, though. Switzerland is well documented as being tight on the tables. They haven't held back surveillance investment, and the tables by law are all one table, one inspector, rather than Greece's one inspector for every four, which as I've told you is bloody madness.'

'I know, I know, but the company wanted to cut costs, and I couldn't swing the vote.'

'Anyway,' continued Morris, 'for that reason, if they have done their research, and it looks like they are well organised enough to have done so, I doubt it will be Switzerland. Also, needs to be a big casino. It wasn't a coincidence that the first one they hit had more roulette tables than any other casino in Europe. I think it will be outside Europe. The next really big casinos are in Asia and some in Africa. Another three massive places have opened in Singapore in the last year and another two are planned.'

'Maybe we'll bump into them in Durban,' suggested Cain.

'I wouldn't rule it out entirely,' Morris pondered. 'Durban, I think, has one or two big places, but the largest casinos are in J'burg and Cape Town, so I'd guess there. Singapore or Macau are the Asian possibilities. There's also a new place in Cambodia in the capital that's massive. The Asian places have mostly Punto tables, but again, they are so bloody big that even the so-called 'few' roulette tables they have far outweigh the number of roulette tables found almost anywhere in the world. Maybe even Goa in India. They will probably be looking for somewhere that's not too tight, security-wise, or is just starting up. In fact, Goa could be a real possibility. It could be happening now. Must admit, this is the most exciting scam I have ever been involved in, just sods law that we were the first ones to get hit. Glad they only stayed an hour. Can you imagine the possible damage if they had stayed? That again suggests they are well organised. Wonder who the leader is? Clever bloke, that's for sure. It is going to be very interesting preparing the scam profile, and some of the feedback should be interesting. I'm looking forward to going and then getting back here as well.'

'I think you managed to stop thinking about Linda for about two minutes there,' smiled Cain. 'Dinner at the Culag tonight?' he suggested.

'Sounds great, but my treat,' insisted Morris. 'Get Magda to come as well. I'm sure she and Linda will have a lot to talk about. John,' he said as he stood up, 'I'm feeling very happy now—just a couple of days ago, I was feeling rock-bottom. As you always told me . . . things change, things change . . .'

# Chapter 8

Back in Italy, everything had been arranged. The new passports had arrived and another meeting in the old casino had been called to outline the next raid. Marco Capone stood up to loud applause, which he soaked in for a few seconds before addressing the crowd.

'Thank you all . . . thank you. Well, it feels like only yesterday when I was speaking to you before—when we were getting ready to launch our first mission. As you know, it was a great success. We kept to our plan and reaped our rewards—with not a single incident being noticed by the poor Greeks.' The crowd applauded again. 'As you know, every family received their fair share of the prize, but as you also know, that few hundred is not enough to save our little town. We have done the calculations, and we feel it is necessary to strike again and then again. If all goes well, we can open a new business after these two more trips. Maybe we can even re-open our own little casino, but no cheats will be allowed!' He glanced towards and smiled at his brother and colleagues. Again, applause and cheering rang around the casino. 'Our scouts went to Africa a few days ago, and after their report, it is confirmed that we will be paying a visit to sunny Durban. The casino which we will visit is very big, and on Saturday nights, they have a big lottery, so it will be very busy and so perfect for us. Ladies and gentlemen, from the report I have read, the casino security is not strong, and so we are going to extend our visit by another hour. This brings some danger, but I'm sure we all have faith in our special team. Regarding this team, it has been decided that those who missed out on the first trip will have their chance in Durban. They deserve it too, as they have been practicing like crazy. Let's hope they are as successful as our first heroes. If all goes well again, both teams will be used for our last collection. Again, I must say to you all, you must not say a word about our plans to anyone, not a relative in Milan or a cousin in America. The whole future of our town depends on this. I must tell you too that some of the casino owners are not very nice people, and our team's lives could possibly be in danger if they are caught. So please, please, keep quiet.' He raised a finger to his lips in emphasis. 'Right, the new passports have arrived. Again, we are Italian and proud of it. For those going, please go to the tables and get your details sorted out. The flight is from Milan in the morning on Friday, so we will travel down on Thursday and stay the night at a hotel, don't worry, a cheap one. Please wish us luck. Remember to keep quiet and pray that we come home well and on our way to achieving our dream. On this trip, I have decided to go myself, not as one of the team, but to organise and hopefully to enjoy. My flight has been paid for by myself, of course.'

The crowd affected disapproval of this, then erupted in magnanimous applause as he walked from the stage. He spent the remainder of the evening having dinner with the young new team and discussing tactics and possibilities.

In Lochinver, about the same time, Morris, Cain, and their partners were enjoying a seafood meal next to the window overlooking Enard Bay as a fishing boat chugged homeward through still waters, the gulls swirling around the vessel . . .

Early on Friday morning, Linda drove Morris and Cain through to Inverness's little airport and the flight to Heathrow was uneventful. They talked almost exclusively of the coming conference, as it was near. Cain made a last check at head office to see if any information had been gained which might lead to identifying the cheat team members. Nothing had been gleaned. He passed this on to Morris as they sat having a coffee in Heathrow, waiting for the flight.

'Not one of them seems to have a history—bloody weird!' replied Morris. 'Watching the footage, I didn't recognise any of them myself, and I've got a pretty good blacklist memory. It did strike me how young they were, but they were so good. It must be a new team and that, to me, means they were all probably trained in the same place and by the same person or persons. But where and by whom? Given that they are Italian—and it's likely but not definite—how do we find this place and then what do we do?'

'We can decide that once they are found,' commented Cain grimly, 'but we need some indicator for sure. There must be a clue somewhere.'

'At least all the casinos in the group have the photos and identifications now,' Morris confirmed. 'That should give them a heads-up, but the problem remains when they all enter at the same time again. It's too much for any Surveillance department to handle all at once. This is the basic problem all the casinos face. There's no way they are all going to hire dozens of extra staff just in case the team hit them, especially in these times, and they can't just shut down the casino if they do manage to recognise someone . . .'

'True,' said Cain, 'but at least a few of them can be caught before they get away and that should lead to information on who they are and where they came from, so hopefully, if there is another Blitzkrieg, we can at least start to take some preventive action . . .'

'Should be—perhaps—I don't know,' said Morris on a train of thought on his own. 'Remember, they are well organised. They may have something up their sleeve.

Maybe there is another bunch of guys or they will have new names, even new faces, plastic surgery, who knows? Anything is possible!'

'Can't see seventy guys getting plastic surgery just to hit one casino,' said Cain, shaking his head.

'Nor can I,' said Morris. 'I'm just giving an extreme example and emphasising that nothing at all should be ruled out. On the other hand, with the amount of money potentially involved . . . Let's get to the damn conference and try and sort this mess out before we go mad. Kidonas, our technical guy, has got some good footage to show the guys at the conference. They will be amazed when they see how adroit the scam team is. He was preparing the "highlights" when I left.'

'You will have a full and captive audience, that's for sure,' Cain remarked.

'Perhaps someone will pick up on something, recognise a face maybe,' Morris offered.

'I think, since you sent pictures all over the world, that would have happened by now, but you never know.'

Their British Airways flight was called and they made their way to the gate.

The team from Tolo had stayed the night in Milan at a cheap hotel near the airport and had enjoyed a meal while discussing tactics and potential shortfalls.

'Right, we have many advantages in this casino compared to Greece,' declared Capone, 'and so we do not need so many "distractions". That is why the girls are not with us this time. We are going to try for a two-hour attack, because the scouts have seen that on the night of the lottery, the hourly estimate is not done. The pit bosses postpone it, as they are too busy. Also, very important and similar to Greece, they have four cash-out points, and they do not ask any questions when the amount is less than 5,000 rand. So make sure the runners cash out at different points and the sums are small. This way, we should avoid any suspicion from the cash desk staff as to where the money came from. Then we get out, just before the hourly score is started. So in at 19.50, just after the dealyed score is done, and out at 21.35, just before the count is started and after the nine o'clock lottery.

'There are three roulette pits, a total of forty-five tables, so we have a good selection of tables to choose from. Remember, third dozen, third column only, but if it's clear and you can manage it, number twenty-four as well, no higher up the table! You know to only make the move if you are sure the staff are not concentrating and will not see it. If one of you are spotted, try the innocent "don't know the rules" routine, but if they call the cameras to check, just get out. Don't bother cashing in. We can sort that out later. Make the signal to our guy at the entrance and leave. Go to the taxi rank round the corner from the casino. I'll show you it before we start. And get to the airport and wait. The rest of us will be along as soon as we can. Again, don't try and be the hero as the guy who cheated most. Wait for the right moment— it's vital. If you don't get a single opportunity, don't panic. Play a bit and find another table where you will have a better chance. No drink at all until we are safely on the flight home, with our pockets bulging! OK, any questions?'

There were a few daft questions, such as a request to stay a few more days and enjoy the Durban beach and pretty women.

'Great idea,' said Capone with mock sarcasm. 'Let's hang around while the Surveillance guys review the footage and see seventy of us sitting on the beach with our white skins and talking Italian. Where did I get this guy?' Capone laughed, knowing the question had been asked half-jokingly.

The conversation drifted to a close. They went off to bed and by 09.00 the next morning were on their way to Durban. They used their own passports for the flight. Getting into a casino with a false passport was one thing, but they were unwilling to risk it at a high-security airport check-in.

In fact, Cain and Morris and the Italian team arrived only a couple of hours apart at Durban International Airport. Kidonas had flown there the day before. The Italians took the bus into town, and Cain and Morris were picked up by Ged Sheeran—their old friend from their time spent in Africa. They had not seen each other in twenty years but recognition was immediate. Ged had put on only a few pounds but remained fit-looking, and his short black hair only had the faintest hint of grey at the fringes.

They embraced warmly and Ged drove slowly towards town, just as the Italians were unpacking and preparing for dinner.

'Bloody hell!' exclaimed Cain. 'It's looking an awful lot different from before.'

'Well, it has been a while,' remarked Ged. 'We can't have the luxury of having places we fondly remember stay as they were . . . but you'll find some of the old haunts still going. Tonight we can have dinner at the Curry Tavern, if you want?'

'Is that still open?' said Morris in surprise. 'We had some good nights there. That would be great! What time?'

'One in the morning too soon? Give you a bit of time to relax and we can grab a couple of beers at Father's Mustache—that's still open too.'

'Looks like they kept our favourite places open just for us. A bit of nostalgia never hurt anyone,' smiled Cain.

They continued the journey enjoying several bouts of laughter. The memories came flooding back.

'Ged, you remember that night at Sun City when they let us dress up in fancy costumes for New Year? They did it for a couple of years, although we all thought that it would be cancelled after the first one. It was such a disaster. Everyone got wrecked!'

'A disaster? It was a great success. The customers loved it apparently. It was a one-off experience getting dealt to by King Kong, while the Grim Reaper was inspecting and Dracula was walking around the pit doing scores!' said Sheeran laughing.

Morris's thoughts turned to those early utterly mad casino days . . .

He and Cain had been in their early twenties then—their first job abroad. At its peak in the 1980s, Sun City had been incredibly successful, casinos in South Africa being illegal. So Sol Kerzner, who actually came from Durban, where they were driving towards, had seen his opportunity and opened a casino in one of the newly created 'homelands'—Bophuthatswana.

It had developed rapidly and he had made it an attraction, not just for gamblers, but he had built a golf course, artificial lake, and great restaurants and hotels. The cinemas even played old American porn movies, which would be packed every night with men and women seeing something that was also unavailable to them in South Africa. It was like a speakeasy for the Afrikaners, and the resort soon became known as 'Sin City'.

There being no trained South African casino staff, Kerzner had decided to recruit from the United Kingdom—so soon, hundreds of young people were flying out from London, Liverpool, Manchester, Dundee, and Edinburgh—glad to escape the lack of opportunities afforded to them in Britain in the early 1980s. Cain, Ged, and Morris had been on the same flight out in 1984.

Accommodation had been pretty basic, and initially, two people shared a small prison-style room, with a tiny, predominantly green-coloured kitchen and similarly sized bathroom. But for many, this was an improvement on their British accommodation. Morris, for example, had come from a cold bedsit which had cost 30 per cent of his take-home pay. He had to share a bathroom with six other tenants. This collection of young croupiers' average age was early twenties, but many of the pit bosses and managers were in their fifties and sixties, although they seemed to act just as daft as the less-experienced staff.

There was an air of living life to the full at that time. Morris's friend, Allan Platt, had called it 'the quickening' from the phrase in the movie Highlander. Take a risk, come to Africa, and try and make something of yourself, and if you couldn't, it was still better than the United Kingdom.

Morris had quickly noticed that there was this common purpose among the staff—work and play hard. Just after he had arrived, he heard that about forty staff had done a parachute jump after a couple of days' training. Marty Block, the casino manager, was not particularly pleased when about a dozen of them failed to come in to work that night due to broken bones, dislocations, etc. But it had been a 'great laugh' apparently.

Even more bizarre was the group of croupiers who decided to ride ostriches at the local farm to see who could go the fastest.

'Damn things can go pretty fast!' one of the guys ruminated to Morris later in the bar, holding his drink in his left hand, as his right hung limply in a sling.

Eventually, a memo was sent reminding staff of the necessity that they turn up for work in a fit and proper state and refrain from excessive 'activities'. Things calmed down a little after that. 'My kind of place,' thought Morris at the time. Although people stopped jumping out of airplanes and riding ostriches—keeping their limbs firmly on terra firma—wild drinking remained a popular activity in the staff pub and Raffles Bar or parties in someone's tiny flat.

One of the main reasons for such excess was that drink was far more affordable than in the United Kingdom, and also dealers found that due to the good tips they were receiving at the tables, they were on a comparative salary to high middle-class earners, like a junior doctor. The staff pub was run on a non-profit basis, and even at the Raffles Bar, with attached disco, prices were reasonable and discounted.

The staff didn't hesitate to take advantage of such good fortune. Raffles Bar was adjacent to the gaming pits, and staff would simply finish their shift and walk up the three steps to the bar and start drinking while their colleagues continued dealing, looking up in thirsty anticipation of the end of their shift. Sundays were totally mad. If you were starting days off, you finished at six in the evening. Many (most, it seemed to Morris) would not go home even to change clothes and simply go straight to the bar. The manager on duty was normally kind enough to have a case of beer behind the bar for those going on to days off. On Sundays, the casino would start to become quieter around midnight, so, as the tables closed, a dealer would be told to 'see the man', the words they longed for. In nearly all cases, this meant that you would be told by the senior pit boss that your shift had finished.

So, just as the initial group of drinkers were slowing down slightly and even perhaps thinking of going home or for something to eat, the next wave of drinkers would hit Raffles and the atmosphere would regain its tempo. The bar would be packed with staff until six in the morning, when one could walk home as the sun came up, a perfect way to start days off. And then it would be back in the pub at lunchtime for a review of the previous night's events and a cold beer, 'just for medicinal purposes, you understand,' one guy always used to say. This was the same guy who when asked how he was when he had a few drinks, adopted an American drawl and said, 'Carpe diem good boy!'

Ged, Cain, and Morris had become firm friends there and enjoyed their time while getting some great casino experience in what was certainly one of the busiest casinos outside America. They were there too, when some of the cup scam guys got out of prison. A couple of them briefly retuned to Sun City to pick up some things, and Morris was shocked to see how they looked. Withdrawn and silent, they had succumbed to greed and had paid the price. Morris just couldn't understand at that time how greed could lead people to make daft, irrational decisions. The thing Morris always thought about is that once you had stolen or been involved in collusion, the deed was done and could never be undone. Someone could find out and either sack you, blackmail you, or worse. How could cheating be worth it in the end? Obviously, other people thought differently, and he supposed he should be grateful, as the fact that there were always cheats around had supplied him with a job and a chance to see the world. Sun City had been a tiny enclave in a vast continent, but he had learnt much from it.

Morris, Cain, and Sheeran arrived at the hotel just before midnight, and Sheeran set off for the restaurant to have a beer while he waited for the other two to join him.

Capone et al had decided to split up. He felt a bit uneasy about such a large group of people eating out in the same place. Someone could get excited and slip up, say something that would arouse suspicion. Far better to stay in small groups and keep a lid on things. Capone arranged to meet up with everyone at breakfast and headed off to meet Lorenzo, an old casino friend from Italy for a drink and some pasta.

He had met his friend on a casino training course in Milan, and they had stayed in contact even when the Tolo casino had closed. He often kept Capone up to date with casino news—the stuff that could not be found by trawling the Internet. Lorenzo was in town for the conference, and Capone hoped to learn a few things and to see if there were any rumours of their scam in Greece. Lorenzo was as unaware as everyone else of the identity of the culprits.

They met at the restaurant entrance and found a table. After exchanging pleasantries and small talk, they soon got round to the topic of casinos and work.

'How's things in Milan then, Lorenzo? Heard the casino is down a bit?'

'A lot,' replied Lorenzo, raising his hands, showing a wide gap between the two. 'Minus 52 per cent on three years ago. We've had to sack staff and lower the salaries of the rest. Things are bad. We have had a big increase in cheats as well.'

'Italian guys?' asked Capone.

'Mostly, but we also had some Russians with a device for predicting jackpots on slot machines. Took quite a lot from us before we received information from ICSA and managed to get rid of them. Big group apparently hitting casinos all round the world.'

'Yes, I read something in the papers about a big team of international cheats, but I thought they hadn't been caught,' said Capone.

Lorenzo shook his head as he chewed some pizza.

'No . . . no. You are thinking about the Blitzkrieg scammers.'

'The what?' Capone replied with a quizzical look. He hadn't heard the phrase before.

'Blitzkrieg—you know—the German word for "lightning attack", or something like that. There is this group of they think Italians—well, they had Italian passports—about seventy of them, in groups of three to four, all entering the casino and hitting different roulette tables at the same time. They got away with a million, and not one was identified or caught!'

'Impossible,' replied Capone, thinking that he liked the Blitzkrieg description. 'Casinos have efficient surveillance systems these days and have the big blacklist to identify cheats.'

'No, no,' Lorenzo continued. 'These guys were new. That's what is driving all the casinos mad. Hundreds of e-mails were exchanged—probably every casino in the world was asked if they could help identify even one of the cheats. Nothing—not a single one. Believe me, the casinos are scared. This is something new to them. Apparently, they are not set up to handle this Blitzkrieg-style scam. Too many people at once. There is a huge meeting about it all in the conference. The poor general manager is going to make a presentation and show some footage of the moves. Big, big interest in it all—I can tell you.'

Capone tried to look nonchalant. 'Fascinating stuff. Must admit it would be fantastic to see the footage. Make sure you tell me about it!'

'Don't need to, just come yourself.'

'I can't. You know I don't work in the industry any more,' Capone replied, feeling he had got himself into a situation he didn't want to be in. 'They wouldn't let me in.'

'Nonsense,' said Lorenzo. 'Just turn up and introduce yourself at the Reception. You will have to pay, since you don't have an invitation, but you'll get in, no problem.'

Capone was thinking furiously. Would it be risky for him to go? Probably not, since it was obvious that no one had a clue about any of the team. He could also learn a lot about what people knew about them, and seeing the footage would be not only a real treat, but would give an insight into how the moves looked from a Surveillance viewpoint. He quickly decided that the benefits outweighed the risk.

'OK, then. That would be great! Thanks a lot. Can I meet up with you before you go? When are you going?'

'First thing in the morning. I want to make sure I get a ticket for the scam demonstration.'

They finished their meal and Capone made his excuses as he arranged to meet Lorenzo at eight in the morning for a quick coffee before the conference.

'Well, that was unexpected,' he thought to himself as he walked to his next meeting to see the scam scouts that had been there for a week preparing their 'security report' for the mayor to analyse in more detail than they had done over the phone.

The three 'scouts', who were brothers, Mario, Giuseppe, and Marcus Amari, were waiting for him in a quiet corner of the bar that they had arranged to meet in. They talked immediately of the job at hand. Marcus, who was in charge of the small team, did most of the talking. He was tall and confident-looking. They had been the same scouts that had visited Greece, and Capone had been impressed enough with the accuracy of their reports to bring them to South Africa as well. They had examined the casino in Greece for several days before the main team arrived. They had played enough to assuage suspicion, and there was no reason at all that any connection would have been made between them and the main team.

'Mr. Mayor . . . things are looking perfect . . . in fact, I could hardly imagine a better casino to hit than this one.' Marcus's Greek report had been excellent, including a casino map, exit, and cash desk points, number of gaming staff, and estimated Surveillance staff. He had analysed the potential risk and numbers of team players that could be distributed around the roulette tables. He had also noted the busiest times. It had been Marcus, in fact, who had suggested the added distraction of including attractive girls as part of the scam. Capone relied on him and trusted his African report would be as succinct as his previous one.

'First—and a lot of what I say is just confirmation of what I've told you on the phone—one inspector for four tables—same as Greece—amazing, isn't it? The inspectors are supposed to track the players, and most of the time, their heads are buried in paperwork. Most of them look up at the winning number instinctively just after the ball has dropped, and that's fine for us. The move will have been done a fraction before. By the time they move their eyes to the layout, the team's hands are well away from the winning number. Secondly, the games are very busy all through the week, and tomorrow's lottery will ensure the place is packed. The tables will be full, and we have seen a lot of call bets being thrown in as the ball is spinning—'

'Great,' interrupted Capone, 'keeps the dealer occupied right up until the ball drops. Could the crowds present a problem for our teams getting a position at the table?'

'Should be OK. The main thing we need is the distracter at the top of the table, leaning over the wheel and placing confusing bets as the ball is about to drop. There are plenty of roulette tables to chose from, forty-five—not many players stand there. Most like to sit.'

'All right then. We'll presume that we're OK there.' Capone nodded and made some notes.

'So the inspectors and dealers are kept busy. We located the Surveillance Room, or at least the door leading to the office and kept an eye on those coming out. On the evening shift at the time we are going in, there was a maximum of four staff—one normally on a break. We saw one suited guy going in and out, so we can presume that he is the shift supervisor or manager, so a small Surveillance team. Cash Desk is fine too. They take hardly any interest on how much people are cashing out, don't even ask what table they got in from. There are four cash-out points . . .'

'Amazing . . . good, good,' commented Capone. 'But we'll make numerous small cash-outs, just in case, and with the runners using different windows. I'll be in a position at the bar if it is deemed better to slip the cash-outs to me.'

'Security is strong, this being South Africa. It looks to me that the whole emphasis of the casino is to protect against armed robberies, which you know are rife at casinos in South Africa. The officers are around Reception and the Cash points— not around the tables.'

'Very, very good. Compared to Greece, where we needed all the extra distractions, this should be easy, but you never know, of course.'

'Cash Desk will also change the rands to dollars,' Marcus added.

'Good,' said Capone. 'You think of everything.'

'I try my best to,' said Marcus with a smile.

'Right, we are basically set for tomorrow evening. I am going to the casino conference in the morning, which will hopefully tell me if we will be able to continue operations once we have finished with Durban. Mind you, I would like to be at the conference when the news filters through that the casino next door has been stung for a couple of million!'

They laughed together—they could hardly admit to each other that this was the most exciting and dangerous thing that they had all ever done in their lives. But it could be seen in their eyes and the rapid manner in which they were conversing.

'Let's hope we can get some sleep tonight,' said Capone, and all the other three could do was laugh in acknowledgement of their mutual nerves. 'Come on. Let's get back to the hotel. It's going to be some day tomorrow.'

# Chapter 9

The day of the conference and scam attack started for Morris and Cain just after seven. They had enjoyed a couple of hours with Ged at the restaurant, which hadn't changed a bit. Some of the waiters were still there from all those years before and even remembered Cain and Morris, and they had talked about Durban, Rangers, Arsenal, and Queen Victoria oddly enough. 'No Churchill—thank god,' Morris thought. They had a nightcap in Father's Moustache bar, but that had changed and there was a different, younger crowd there now. Cain and Morris had headed back to the hotel just before three in the morning and both slept immediately—it had been a long day.

Morris was suited up by 07.15. Checking himself in the mirror, he was a little nervous, as it had been a while since he had done a presentation, but he was also looking forward to meeting many of the executives that would be at the conference. He had missed the last two ICSA meetings. They were both informative and good fun, as the pressurised Surveillance directors and managers relaxed away from their bosses. This time, of course, it would be different. The big guys were in town. The billionaire owners from Vegas, Macau, and Singapore—four men, all self-made, tough guys: an American, a British guy, a South African, and a Chinese Malaysian. Between them, they made something like 40 per cent of the total worldwide casino profits. 'Not the type to compromise,' mused Morris as he adjusted his tie for the third or fourth time.

'Would they come to his presentation? Highly likely,' he thought. They would be as interested as anyone on finding out details about the scam attack. Morris pondered on what their solution to the problem might be. Cain had suggested half-seriously that they would glibly drop a bomb on Italy if they thought that it would solve the problem. He was quite looking forward to at least seeing them, Morris admitted to himself. Not too often you get four billionaires in the same room.

Morris bought some Biltong for his son, met Cain at 07.30, and they decided on a coffee and then a walk along Marine Parade to the conference centre. They were OK for time. The conference started at 08.00 and Morris's speech was scheduled for 10.30.

'Well, here we go,' said Cain. 'What will today bring?—Some good news, I hope. Good luck with the speech. I hope to make it, but I have been asked to talk to the big guys at some time. Don't know if it will be before, during, or after your thing.'

'You haven't met any of them before or you didn't mention it?'

'A bit awkward, this,' said Cain. 'I actually know them quite well, but I'm not supposed to talk about it. Let's just say I'm often used to represent the owners of our company, who of course are not in the same league as them, but still big enough that they want to know what we are up to. All I can say, Sam, is that these guys are incredibly strong-willed. Mostly, they are calm enough and can charm the pants off you when they want. They are also rumoured to have all the necessary connections, contacts, and resources to maintain their grip on the casino market share. And I mean "all" the resources.'

'Like what?' said Morris.

'That's it—that's all I can say!' Cain had raised his hands involuntarily. 'The times I have met them, whenever the conversation goes out of mainstream casino talk, they repeat the phrase, "This is our little conversation."—meaning that no one can say a word of it to anyone else—including their own directors. That is why when anything is done, it can never be traced to them, or if it ever happened, they know it would be one of the circle, which I am allowed to be on the periphery of, sometimes. Anyway, I've told you plenty enough. Let's get to the centre. Good luck with your talk. You'll be fine. You're at your best when you have to be at you're best.'

As they approached the conference centre, they could already see several people heading towards the entrance. It was a lovely morning, with a deep blue sky and just a hint of a breeze. The sunlight glinted off the large glass doors through which the guests were entering. It was 08.10, and after entering, Cain saw someone he knew and parted from Morris, with a smile and a reassuring nod. Morris smiled back and headed for the registration booth. He saw Kidonas was already there picking up his pass and various information leaflets and event vouchers.

'Hello, Stratos,' he called giving his technician a friendly slap on the back. 'Glad you're here. I need all the help I can get!'

'Ah, you'll be fine, thanks to my brilliant footage presentation! It will blow then away, I can tell you.'

'You're right. I'm sure a lot of the Surveillance guys will be a bit smug at how we failed to see so many cheat moves. I think they are in for a bit of a shock.'

'I've watched it so many times now,' replied Kidonas. 'With only one or two exceptions, these guys are all brilliant past-posters. There must have been an even bigger selection group to get so many that were so good.'

'That had crossed my mind as well. Scary. Want a coffee before we go to the presentation room? It's the "Swan Room" on the second floor?'

'Yeah. I'll just get my equipment from the car. We can set everything up, have a test, and then relax a bit. We'll have a coffee then. I've heard the big owners are in town—Do you think they will come to our little show?'

'I'd be surprised if they didn't, or at least one of them, to see for themselves and report to the others.'

Morris went out with Kidonas to his rented car and helped him in with his equipment. Then they headed towards the escalator. It was 08.30.

Cain had, in fact, arranged to meet the man he had seen upon entering. He was one of the big bosses top advisors and the only one trusted by all four. Mr Andrews was of medium height and build, blond hair, with a slightly large and crooked nose. 'Mr Cain, how nice to see you again. Magda fine?'

'She is indeed,' replied Cain. 'How you doing, Anthony—the guys treating you OK?'

'They're OK, definitely a bit nervous about this scam thing though, between you and me. Worried that with the size of their casinos, they could get hit for tens of millions, or even more if it's not stopped.'

Always say 'between you and me', Cain remembered—giving the feeling of trust without really saying too much. Clever that.

'Well, that's why we are here,' Cain commented. 'Hopefully, we'll sort something out. Are we meeting up today?'

'Would eight be OK for you?' asked Andrews, knowing that it would have to be. 'Early drinks in the royal suite of the Plaza?'

'Fine. Looking forward to it.'

'Any further news on the scam team?' enquired Andrews hopefully.

'At the moment, no, but you never know, perhaps by the end of the day . . . after all, that's what these conferences are supposed to be about—gaining new information and contacts.'

'OK.' Andrews replied, his face showing a little disappointment that he could not rush off to his masters with some helpful information. 'Right, I'll see you at the lobby of the Plaza at ten to eight, if not before. Have a good conference.'

'Will any of the group be coming?' asked Cain, but Andrews had already turned his back, heading towards the exit.

'Smarmy git,' thought Cain as he headed towards the main conference floor, intending to stroll around and maybe meet up with a few old cronies before heading up to the Swan Room. He noticed Morris and Kidonas gliding up the escalator, equipment in hand. He had a sudden urge for a cold beer, despite the early hour. He too was feeling a bit tense—getting a bit old for all this travelling and meetings. He thought of Lochinver and longed to be home.

At 07.45, Capone got out of bed, or rather sat on the side of the bed, with his feet planted on the floor.

'Today's the day, my friend. Don't screw up—everything must be right,' he found him telling himself. 'It's OK. It's OK . . . I'm ready,' he announced to the room. He stood up and stretched. Despite just getting out of bed, he found that his mind was racing at an extraordinary level. He had found that when his brain was in what he called fifth gear, he could think at amazing speeds and all his senses were at their peak. It was a sort of natural high. He had often got this feeling when he had been in charge of the casino, when he had had to be in control as numerous things were happening at the same time. When like that, he felt very confident in his own abilities.

He showered and headed down to meet the team for breakfast. Most of them were already there. He could feel the tension and excitement. They congregated in the corner of the breakfast room where no other guests were sitting. Capone brought out his thick file, and they went through the individual scam teams once again, the tactics, and the contingency plans if something did happen to go wrong. It had all been done before, but Capone felt another reminder would concentrate the minds and help alleviate the electric tension amongst the group.

Capone sat with them until 09.15, then announced he was going to meet a contact. He had told no one bar the scouts that he was going to the conference. He felt it better to keep it to himself for the moment; better they concentrated on the job at hand.

Capone reminded them to be back at the hotel by 04.30 in the afternoon. The casino lottery draw was scheduled for nine in the evening and the crowds would start to enter from about six onwards. They had a good part of the day to relax if possible, get some presents for the trip home, look like tourists. Capone reminded them to pack their bags before they went to the casino and be prepared to leave at a moment's notice if needed.

By 10.00, after returning his file to his room's safe, he had met up with Lorenzo and they entered the centre together. He had hoped to register with an assumed name—something non-Italian—but Lorenzo was with him when he went to the desk, so he had used his real name. When he was issued with his badge, he discreetly pushed it slightly under his shirt. They asked if there were seats available for the big morning event, which was the scam presentation, and were told the Swan Room seated five hundred persons, so it was not anticipated that they would have a problem finding a seat, but if they were worried, they should go there as soon as possible. It was just after 10.00, and looking around, Capone saw that the place was filling up very quickly.

'Let's get up there right now,' Lorenzo said. 'I bet all these people are here for the same reason.'

As they approached the Swan Room, Capone could see it was already nearly full, with barely fifty seats remaining. He almost felt proud that his decisions and actions had caused all this reaction. 'Keep calm,' he reminded himself.

Entering the room, he could see two people at the podium, adjusting wires and moving papers around. He knew which one was Morris, of course, although he had never met him. At the Earls Court Casino Conference, he had quietly enquired who the GM was of the Greek casino that they intended to hit. Morris had been pointed out to him discreetly, and he had then arranged for him to be approached and 'warned' of his brother's intended visit. The diversion was his own idea, and he felt it had been a pretty smart move—proved correct by the success of the operation.

He and Lorenzo got a seat and settled themselves into their chairs, just a few minutes before the talk was due to start.

'Should be interesting,' Lorenzo said with some excitement in his voice.

'Should be,' echoed Capone, staring straight ahead.

Just then, there was a sort of collective turning of shoulders towards the Swan Room entrance. Capone found himself following the collective gaze and immediately recognised the group that was entering. The big owners. 'Jesus Christ!' he thought and he felt a small flutter in his chest. Four men had entered, with at least a dozen people in their entourage, including Andrews. The men had a definite aura about them. The group moved to a specially assigned group of chairs. They settled down, and after a bit of murmuring, the room went quiet as Morris approached the podium.

'Good morning, all,' he started. 'Thanks for coming so early. This presentation was, of course, scheduled for later in the week, but there was such demand for it to be held early—and I know many of you have come a long way specifically for this meeting—that it was changed to this morning's time.

'Well, I have to say, being in charge of the casino that was hit made me think twice before appearing here, but having swallowed my pride, here I am—and I hope we can shed some light on this team, which can lead to their identification and hopefully prosecution at some later date.

'As you all know, the hit on our casino in Greece has been widely referred to as "The Blitzkrieg Scam". Although a bit sensational, it does aptly describe the operation. The whole concept of the scam was to be in and out very quickly, so that the casino would have no time to prevent it, or to be able to organise a response. In this sense, I have to admit they were very successful. In addition, the group initiated one or two distractions—diverting attention from the roulette cheats working the tables. We are sure well-known international cheat Ernesto Capone—who will be very familiar to many of you—was introduced to deflect attention from the main team. He was using the name of Wiseman—for the first time apparently—at our place. As well as all this, at exactly the same time, our casino was in the middle of ending another local scam—in fact, I was doing the interviews as the money was pouring off the tables. In that sense, the scam team had a lucky break, but overall, their organisation and skill was quite breathtaking, hard as it is for me to concede.'

Leaning forward in his seat, Capone, who couldn't help but feel sorry for Morris, who seemed a decent enough guy, felt a surge of pride at the last comments. He wondered what they would all do if he stood up and confessed. He had stolen a quick glance at Lorenzo when his brother's name was mentioned. He hadn't flinched, seeing nothing suspicious in a shared surname. He had no idea that he was Marco's brother.

'Now to the details,' Morris continued. 'I know many of you here do not have a Surveillance background, so I'll be as non-technical as I can. At the end, I hope we can discuss the scam and—any questions, I'll answer then.

'The group mostly registered the night before the hit. They registered as Italians, but with false passports which were of a good enough standard to not arouse suspicion. They presented themselves as a group of Italian tourists, rather than gambling types, and acted as such—drinking, walking around the casino, and playing only a little. Being Italians, with of course the reputation that they have, all the names were checked on the blacklist, and most of them were watched, which of course is what they anticipated and expected. I quote from the Surveillance log dated that night: "Large group of mostly young Italians entered. All names checked. Watched. OK—hanging around, not playing. Left by 23.30. No need to watch again."

'So that was it. By registering the night before they made their move, they knew that if they were going to be observed, they would be on that night and dismissed as a threat. Clever, and to me, it suggests a knowledge of casino and Surveillance procedures for checking out new members.' Capone was about to nod but caught himself in time.

'So there we have a small possible lead in our attempts at identification, if you want to note it down. Possible casino/insider knowledge.' Many in the audience scribbled on their note sheets.

'So on the day of the hit, the Italians entered again en masse. All Surveillance's resources were directed towards the Greek guy, Markopoylos, and Capone, who entered at the same time, which was something we had not anticipated, to be honest. This led us to initially think that somehow Markopoylos was part of the distraction, but we have since discounted that and as I said, it was just bad luck. So the young scam team was more or less free to go about their business. Oh yes! And some girls had been brought along just to divert attention from the tables further. So, let's see what they were up to!'

He indicated to Kidonas to get the prepared discs ready to play.

'Although the monitors are quite big, those near the back are going to have trouble seeing the footage clearly, so please feel free to come forward, as I know most of you want to see how good this group is. Bigger screens would lose clarity, and we want you to see it in the best possible way,' urged Morris.

A few people got up, at first hesitantly, and then there was almost a scramble to get a prime spot in front of one of the eight monitors arranged around the room. The atmosphere was livening up as Kidonas started to show the footage.

'Most of the footage is from the table cameras. Obviously, since we weren't watching them, there was no zooming in. We'll play the cheat moves on several tables firstly at normal speed and then in slow motion. Believe me, it's a worrying sight. OK, let's go'. He picked up his notepad and said, 'Footage No. 1. Team 3 on AR 5, winning number 27. Three hundred euro chips and five yellow colour chips placed on the wining split 27/30. OK, Stratos—go.'

There was a collective lurch towards the screens as the footage began. Six people could be seen at the table, which was busy with lots of chips on the layout. The dealer had just spun the ball. One of the customers could be seen placing a few hundred euro chips on the layout. Morris pointed out that he was one of the team. At the bottom of the table, another Italian was playing with yellow chips and was stretching up the table, placing bets on the first dozen. 'The past-poster.' Morris pointed out, 'Keep an eye on him—if you can.' The last member of the team was identified by Morris. He was leaning over the wheel towards the dealer, giving him chips to place on the number as well as call bets announced in a muffled voice, which the dealer was obviously straining to understand. This cheat member was the main distracter and was doing such a god job that the dealer was paying nearly all his attention to him. The ball was about to drop. The distracter gave over yet another call bet. 'Too late!' the dealer yelled as the ball dropped and passed the last chips he had given back to him— stretching over the table in the process. The man at the bottom of the table stood up slightly as the ball dropped. He had placed some yellow chips next to the dealer during the spin, but the dealer had been too preoccupied with the distracter to notice them. He now reached over with one hand to take the chips back, and the other hand could very briefly be seen near number 27. Next thing, the number was being cleared by the dealer and on the split of 27/30, five yellow chips lay on top of two hundred euro chips. A few comments such as 'Bloody hell!' and 'Shit!' could be heard, but it was also obvious that many of the spectators had not noticed the cheat move.

'Let's have a look in slow motion,' Morris said reassuringly.

'Yes, please,' someone replied in honest admission that he had failed to see any cheat move.

Even in slow motion, the past posting could not be seen, largely due to the fact that the past poster's and the distracter's arms covered the table camera's coverage of the number as the ball dropped.

'We need to see this with a rover,' stated Morris.

Kidonas next showed a rover, or general purpose camera, which had a part view of the table where the scam was taking place. A very sudden movement could be seen by the past poster. There was no sound of the ball dropping to prove that the chips had been added after the ball dropped, but experienced observers noted the unnatural haste in which the chips had been placed and the hand removed.

Morris noted the excitement that the footage was generating. When he had worked in Surveillance, cheat moves were always the first thing office visitors wanted to see.

The rest of the footage was shown. Nearly all of the moves were practically identical in the timing and methods. Altogether, he showed half a dozen incidents, and he could sense the disappointment when the review was finished. He glanced over at the bigwigs' table. They had not a trace of admiration on their faces—only pure worry was evident. One of them was shaking his head and appeared to be swearing under his breath.

'OK, everyone—quite a show, as you'll probably admit. The legally important thing is that, in a court of law, we could not prove that the bets were actually placed after the ball was dropped. Right. I'm sure there will be some questions—fire away.'

As he had expected, several hands were raised. He saw the big bosses move towards the platform, still in discussion.

'Colin Hunter,' one guy said as Morris indicated to him to ask the first question. 'Gaming manager at Holloway Casino, Blackpool, in England. Thanks. Well, I have to say, I find that footage worrying. I would like to know what you think is the background of this team and how they were not known before. How could they be so good if they had apparently never been in a casino before? Are you sure they are not well-known cheats in disguise or something?'

'Good questions and ones that we have tried to answer since the incidents happened,' Morris replied. 'You have to remember that the photos of this team have been sent to maybe 30 per cent of the casinos in the world and a 100 per cent of the big ones. Not a single person had been recognised as a casino cheat, a suspicious person—nothing at all. If they had been known, even if they had been disguised, someone in the casino world would have picked up on them. Believe me, I know these Surveillance guys—they would all have been desperate to identify even one of the team. It would have been a real feather in their cap. So they were definitely new to cheating in casinos. Most of the casinos are still trawling through their membership to see if they had even ever visited their casino—let alone do something suspicious. But having said that, it is obvious that they knew about casinos, and of course, they were very aware of roulette tables, dealers' and inspectors' habits and camera coverage. I would suggest they actually have an intimate knowledge of casinos, even though at the moment, it appears that they have never been in one. A bit of a paradox, I agree. It could well be that someone had got hold of a few roulette wheels and recruited young men to learn how to cheat. It's possible this trainer may well be an ex-cheat himself, knowing that they would be recognised at once if they went into nearly any casino in the world. This cheat trainer, through his previous experiences, would have developed at least a working knowledge of casino operations and the best moments to cheat, etc.'

Capone was listening intently. 'Close—but not quite,' he thought.

Another man raised his hand and stood.

'Sean Hand—World Casino Networks.'

'Go ahead,' gestured Morris. 'Nice to see you again, Sean.'

'Likewise,' replied Hand, who continued.

'Do you agree that the team will try again somewhere? Aren't casinos now ready for them and posted with photos and modus operandi? Could it be a one-off Blitzkrieg sort of thing?' he asked, sitting down.

Morris was nodding even before Hand had finished talking.

'That's the big question. With all the commotion this has caused, which has even reached the newspapers, the team must be only too aware that every casino is on the lookout for them—with the team's faces drilled into every operator all over the world and Reception phoning Surveillance whenever an Italian enters. The team is quick, but they do need some time and, of course, can't make their move every single spin. So, you have to figure that they would be caught within, I'd say, fifteen minutes of entering the casino—so it's a great risk. I'd like to say no to another attack, but something tells me that they are not going to rest on their laurels.'

'You'd be right there,' thought Capone. 'In a few hours, you will have confirmation.' Again, he suppressed a smile.

'It's a clever team and they may come up with something else,' continued Morris. 'Possibly entering in disguise with different names . . . any ideas from you guys would be useful.'

'I agree with you,' said Hand. 'They've tasted success and they will want another shot—although you lost a lot—it's not retirement amounts for sixty to seventy people. They may well try entering with aliases of different nationals—Maltese, Swiss, something like that?'

'I think most of the casinos are ready for any suspicious mass entries of any nationals,' said Morris in reply. 'Any more questions?' he asked as he could see the number of hands raised were down to one or two.

A tall man stood up, adjusting his tie as he did so.

'Stuart Hughes from Megaworld in Cambodia. In your introduction, you mentioned this likely distraction that the team had—the Capone cheat. Now, as is he is known—have you tried to establish the scam team through any connection with him? Possibly, he trained them—or you could check out his cheat associates for any possible clues?'

'Yeah, we hoped that could lead us to a way to identify the cheats. If Capone had come back the next day, we were ready to haul him in the office and even use some heavy treatment on him, but he and his pals checked out of the hotel about an hour after the scam team had left, confirming to us, if there was any doubt, that they were all connected. We used all our resources and all the feedback we got through communications with other casinos to try and find any link at all. Addresses, known movements, telephone numbers, dates of birth, identity numbers, and facial comparisons—you name it, we tried, believe me. Not a damn thing, and we haven't heard from Capone or his associates since. There was a gap in his cheating history, and there does remain the possibility that he trained the cheat team—but where, when, etc., we don't know. Certainly, the techniques used by the team had a strong similarity to the moves that he is capable of. Could be that he knew that his quickness of hand was fading and he has trained people and he gets a percentage? I think that is a strong possibility. All the casinos are, of course, on major alert, and if he appears anywhere, Surveillance will interview him until he gives us something. There will be no quietly letting him walk out any casino till we know something—that's for sure!'

There were a few grim looks on the faces of the onlookers. The casinos had decided to get tough, if necessary, many were assuming. Morris spared a quick glance at the big bosses. They were looking at him directly, silently, right in the eye. Just as he turned his gaze back to his audience, he noticed one of them lean over and whisper something into the ear of another, who nodded once quickly. Morris felt a slight uneasiness and was glad to focus again on his audience.

'Anyone with any more questions or suggestions? It's not far off lunchtime and we can have a more informal chat in the Neptune Restaurant, and if there is anything anyone wants to say to me privately, you know you will remain anonymous—even though we will use any information given if necessary.'

A few people shifted in their seats, and it was clear that, for then, the audience was satisfied. The four big owners had already got up from their chairs and were moving towards the exit.

About 200 of the crowd headed towards the Neptune Restaurant for the free buffet being supplied by John Huxley. The rest of the crowd headed back to the main conference floor to see new products, meet old colleagues, and arrange social events for after the conference's first day, which ended at 6 p.m. A lot of business got done at casino conferences. And a lot of boozing too.

Morris felt it had gone well, although nothing really new had been garnished. Perhaps, as the rest of the day went on and discussions continued, something would come up. He saw Cain approaching.

'Nice one, Sam,' he said. 'You're good at these things, if you put your mind to it.'

'Thanks, John. Mind you, I'm glad it's over. I seemed to be getting the eyeball from the big fellows over in the corner. Maybe they think I'm in on it too.'

'Wouldn't surprise me,' replied Cain. 'Not the most trusting of types. Despite their different routes to the top, there are a lot of similarities in their character, believe me. Tough, clever, networking types—on the go and never rich enough. Anyway, let's get tidied up and get a coffee and see who we can chat to.'

As Morris, Cain, and Kidonas collected their equipment before packing it away and heading towards the restaurant, three of the Italian team were lying on the beach on Marine Parade and enjoying the sun. Paulo Rossini, Frank Zapalate, and Giovanne Nero were life-long friends, had played football together for the town team, and were a natural pick to be one of the teams for the upcoming casino raid. They had been disappointed to be not part of the first Greek team but had believed Capone when he said that there had been no grading of the team, that all had been equal, and if they missed the first, they would all get their chance. They had believed him, even though there was, of course, talk that some sort of graded selection had been made.

'Not long now,' Rossini commented, looking towards the sun hovering over the Indian Ocean. He half-expected to see a shark fin gliding through the still water and had decided against going in for a swim and was mocked by his two friends for doing so. 'We are the only sharks around here,' laughed Rossini. 'Today is the day we get a big chunk of meat.' Rossini stared at the others. 'Yeah . . . and hand it all over to M.r Mayor Capone. "For the sake of the town." Great. Then where will we be? . . . Back to being poor in bloody Tolo!'

'But Mr. Capone has promised the money will be used wisely and we will all benefit,' commented Zapalate.

'I trust him, sure,' replied Rossini, 'but have you ever felt excitement like this? Do you want a dealing job in a little town casino or a job in a bottling factory? This is what I know is right for me. Travel, excitement, the thrill of being caught, and the pride of real achievement. I don't want to go back. And given half the chance, I would stay here or travel around, trying our tricks in casinos around the world.'

The other two were looking at him directly then—no more fooling around in the sun and sea.

'Me too, I have to admit,' said Zapalate, staring at the sand at his feet. 'Maybe we will get the chance one day to get out of Italy and travel together.'

'Maybe, maybe—that's all we think!' Rossini said. 'Don't you see—this is our chance. We are already here! After the raid, we hand over the money and tell Capone we are going our own way. What can he do about it? I'm sure he would understand. He travelled when he was young—he knows the urges of youth.'

'This place is great,' Nero smiled, looking around at all the female sunbathers. 'If this is what the rest of the world is like, I'll stay as well!'

'Well, if we all agree, why give Capone the money?' Rossini said sitting upright. 'We could keep our earnings—it would give us a start. Head down to Cape Town— lay low for a while. I hear it's a great place.'

'Keep the money!' Zapalate said incredulously. 'Capone would kill us.'

'Rubbish—what would he do? Hang around the airport waiting for us to appear and miss the flight when he has a couple of million down his socks? Or we could give him some of the cash saying we weren't able to post as often as hoped and tell him we are staying.'

'He would be too suspicious. He's not daft. You know that,' insisted Nero.

'Well, let's talk about this seriously,' said Rossini. 'What do you really want to do and do you have the balls to do it? We have to decide very quickly. This could be our last chance to get away from that shit town.'

'It's not bad,' Nero said defensively. 'Our parents live there. And what would happen to them if we disappeared? They'd be blackballed.'

'Ah!' Rossini commented after a while. 'I think I have it—and it won't compromise our families. Here's my idea.'

They talked rapidly, and by mid-afternoon, they believed they had it all figured out. They still had about six hours to pass before the casino raid, but it was their escape plan that was now filling their thoughts and making them nervous, not the scam itself. After relaxing over a coffee at a little Italian coffee shop they had found, they made their way back to the hotel, where they tried to sleep for an hour or so, showered, and dressed appropriately for the cheat moves. Rossini would be the past poster, and he wore slightly long shirt sleeves intended to cover his hand movements as he placed the chips after the ball had dropped. He also had his shirt out of his trousers, which would help disguise his hand movement when he reached over the table to place that bet. Since they were unknown, they, as in the first group, spent little time trying to disguise their faces. Marco trimmed his eyebrows quite short and placed some cotton wool along the front of his gum. Looking in the mirror, he was surprised that even this simple modification changed his look quite considerably. Enough, he thought, that if someone he knew was offered a less-than-clear picture of him to identify, there would be quite an element of doubt. 'Not that it would ever come to that,' he told himself. By seven-thirty, they had left their rooms and met at the lift before heading down to the foyer to meet their compatriots. They would make no move towards the casino until Capone told them.

Capone had not lingered long around the restaurant area after Morris's speech. He decided on a few more minutes in the centre itself, just to see if anything interesting caught his eye. It had been very interesting, and he was glad he had come, but he was feeling a little nervous and was starting to become preoccupied with forthcoming events. He bade his farewells to Lorenzo, who said he had an appointment. Capone wanted to meet up with the scouts one more time before they entered the casino. They would go in and have a look at the set-up and see if anything had changed or was different in any way. Perhaps a cash desk would be closed, perhaps more security than expected would be there. Capone found himself rubbing his fingers together nervously as he checked for the umpteenth time that his name badge was not fully visible. As he was doing so and at the edge of the Neptune, he bumped into Cain's shoulder as he walked into the restaurant with Morris.

'Sorry . . . sorry!' he blurted out, realising the apology was slightly overdone. Cain smiled in recognition of the apology, but for no reason, Capone suddenly heard himself say, 'An excellent speech, Mr. Morris,' and then he made to move away rapidly.

'Thank you,' replied Morris. 'Are you in the industry yourself, Mr . . . ?'

'Used to be . . . I'm sorry. I'm really very late, and I have an appointment. Important . . . Lorenzo . . . from Malta.'

Morris handed over his business card, which contained his mobile number. 'If you pick up anything that might help us catch these guys, give us a call please,' he said, as it was hurriedly grabbed by Capone.

Morris and Cain said nothing as the man turned round the corner. Morris stopped for a second.

'Looks a little familiar,' he thought to himself, but he couldn't remember hearing the name of Lorenzo ever before.

He and Cain continued into the restaurant and the incident was soon forgotten as several conference people and old friends approached them for a chat. He was still hoping that something positive would emerge before the day was over.

Capone gulped in a large mouthful of air as he exited the conference hall. 'Idiot!' he chastised himself. 'Why did you speak to him? Was he suspicious?' He calmed down a little as the fresh air relaxed him. 'Why would he be suspicious? I only bumped into his friend. Sort yourself, out—you have a big job today. You can't look nervous in front of the team. They get their confidence from you,' he reminded himself. Nevertheless, he was definitely feeling anxious, which he reasoned was natural enough, since he was about to try and steal around two million dollars and get home safely, avoiding capture and being skinned alive. 'Yes,' he concluded, 'it's impossible to be calm—just be on the ball.' He sat on a bench on the beach for a while, thinking methodically, before heading to meet the scouts for lunch and to hear the last report before the action began.

Back at the conference restaurant, the time was approaching two in the afternoon and Cain and Morris were still chatting to various people, when Cain was interrupted by a tap on the shoulder. He turned slightly to see Mr. Andrews smiling broadly at him. 'Sorry to interrupt. John, I'd like a word, as soon as possible, if you can?'

'Right,' replied Cain and made his apologies to the two casino managers he was talking to and nodded to Morris, who was talking to the Surveillance director who had asked him a question at his presentation earlier, Stuart Hughes.

Andrews ushered Cain to a quiet corner and said quietly, 'The group would like Morris to come with you to the hotel tonight. They want to talk to him personally about the scam. I think they are hoping that he can come up with some preventive recommendations.'

'I think he more or less dismissed that possibility at the talk,' said Cain. 'I can ask him if you like, but he's his own man.'

'Quite,' responded Andrews with a smirk on his face.

'Was this the phoniest man he had ever met?' considered Cain.

'I think it would really be in his best interest to attend,' continued Andrews. 'There is talk of some sort of special team being created to sort all this out, as really you all seem as far away as ever in attempting to identify this group. It's likely that Morris will be asked to head it. Good money, and I do presume he is intent on capturing those that embarrassed him so?'

'Indeed,' Cain said, 'I agree that could interest him, but as I said, he's his own . . .'

'Just make sure he comes. See you just before eight,' stated Andrews firmly and turned on his shiny shoes and marched towards the exit.

'What a pompous twat! Wonder if he ever has any self-doubt? Unlikely.' Cain concluded. He knew the type. He returned to Morris, who had just moved away from Hughes.

'Proposition for you!' he smiled and explained what Andrews had suggested.

Morris listened intently. 'Sounds ideal to me if they offer me a job as head of an investigative team, with the unlimited resources they have at their disposal. I could go anywhere and check anything—it would make our chances of catching them much better. Don't really care how much they pay me—a bonus if we catch them and we get the money back would be reward enough.'

'So you are up for it, then. Sure? We'll go to the Plaza together, then. I think I'll head back to the hotel for a little nap first. How about you, Sam?'

'I've more or less seen everyone that I wanted to, but I'll do the rounds for another hour. See if I can pick something up. I'll catch you at the hotel—say about seven?'

'OK—see you then. Of course, if you get anything, phone me immediately. I'll walk back, I think—last chance to see the old Marine Parade for a while. Kidonas will get the equipment back, OK? He's going back tonight?'

'Yes, at ten,' Morris replied.

After Cain had left, Morris decided an hour more would be more than enough. He admitted to himself he was looking forward to meeting the four casino owners.

It was a large auditorium, with more than fifty companies being represented and several thousand people looking around, trying out new equipment, talking business, or trying to find a job. Several people recognised him and mentioned his earlier speech. There was considerable interest in the scam attack and the possibility of a new one—although most expressed an opinion that they would not get away with it a second time.

He lingered at a stall where a company was selling a new type of face recognition system—something which had not quite taken off in most casinos he knew. He was about to ask the representative a question or two, when a face appeared in front of him.

'Excuse me, sir.'

'Yes,' he replied.

'Mr. Sam Morris, I believe?'

'That's me,' replied Morris, handing another card over automatically. 'How are you?'

'I am fine. It was a very impressive speech you made. Strong. Many thought you would not like to appear, but you made an excellent show.'

'Another Italian,' thought Morris. 'And you are?'

'Nico Lorenzo,' came the firm reply.

'Lorenzo,' repeated Morris shaking his head slightly. 'You are the second Mr. Lorenzo I have met in the last couple of hours, and I can't recall hearing that name before. Did you come with a brother . . . ?'

'Another Italian Lorenzo here in South Africa? Was he a casino guy?' replied Lorenzo, with a look of surprise.

'Suppose so,' shrugged Morris. 'He said he was at my speech. Anyway, what do you do, Mr Lorenzo?'

They continued talking for some minutes before Lorenzo made to head off.

'Must try to find my old friend, can't see him anywhere. He's a mayor of a town, but I think he is here looking for a job, I think, although he's too proud to tell me so. Goodbye, and I hope you catch the bad guys. All of us Italians are not so bad, believe me!'

'I'm sure, I'm sure,' smiled Morris, thinking this Lorenzo was quite a decent chap.

'What does your friend call himself? If I hear his name somewhere, I'll say you are looking for him.'

'Mr. Capone, like the gangster, but that's his name. He is a very nice man. I was surprised he came all the way out here. As I said, he was probably looking for a job and missing the casino crowd after his casino was closed down and he'd be happy to be here . . .'

'Capone again!' Morris did a double take. Another coincidence, it seemed. Maybe there were loads of Capones and Lorenzos in Italy. Maybe they were all cheating bastards.

'Goodbye, Mr Lorenzo,' he said and headed out, coming to the conclusion that he had had enough discussions, offers, and coincidences for one day, and he still had a meeting with the big owners to come. Yes, a few pints in order after that, he concluded decisively. He went to a couple of more stalls but soon tired of the sales pitches and false friendliness and headed out of the casino and back to the hotel for a break. It was just after 3 p.m.

After leaving the scouts, Capone returned to the hotel with renewed confidence. The news had been as much as he could have possibly hoped for. Marcus and the others had been in and around the international casino from about eight in the morning. At eight thirty, they had seen a large group of staff gather at Reception and leave together, presumably towards the casino conference. From their previous visits, they could see the casino manager and Surveillance boss, along with several other suited individuals. The cash desks were operating as before—with four stations open. 'Good,' agreed Capone when told. Numerous smallish cash ins were vital to the success of their operation. Security levels were the same as before—with most personnel being assigned to points of cash vulnerability—none were near the tables. Pit bosses and inspectors were at previous levels—although before lunch, only two pit bosses could be seen, instead of the usual three. Perhaps one had been allowed to go to the conference. After lunch, the casino was filling up nicely, as it was a public holiday—but was not nearly busy enough for the attack to take place earlier than planned. So all was good, and if anything, the casino would be less staffed than normal—particularly at the higher levels.

Capone showered and changed into a loose white shirt and light blue trousers. He packed and deposited his small suitcase at Reception, ready to go. He double-checked that a porter would be there to bring the team's bags to the taxi rank outside the hotel. He paid the entire bill in cash, leaving an acceptable tip.

He joined the team, who were all sitting around tables in the closed lobby bar. He looked at them all in a sweeping glance and was content with what he saw. They looked a little nervous, but that was good—improved reaction time. At least twenty of the team were moving their fingers, as if playing the piano, or cracking their knuckles. He smiled. He reminded them once more of the absolute importance of keeping to the in/out timetable, only making moves when confident of success, the need for the runners to cash in frequently, and the escape strategy if caught. He reminded them to leave all credit cards or anything else that could reveal their real identity at Reception.

He looked around one more time, his heart pumping vigorously in his chest.

'Let's go, let's go. Good luck—see you back here. I'll be in the casino keeping an eye on things, but no one is to approach me. This time tomorrow, we will be back in Tolo and our future will be nearly secure. Do Tolo proud. This will be the greatest day in your lives. Come on!' he said aloud like a football coach. The young scam cheats rose enthusiastically in unison, suitably inspired.

While Cain and Morris were in discussion before taking a taxi to the Plaza Hotel, the scam team mingled with the large crowd at the reception of the International Casino. There were no registrations, only an entry fee of R100, and within twenty minutes, the entire team was in and heading towards the roulette tables, which were already busy. There were twenty-one teams of three individuals and twelve runners to cash in the proceeds of the moves as they were happening. One man was stationed at the exit door. If any of the teams were caught, they would signal this man by raising their hands straight up in a mock yawn and stretch. He in turn would shake his head from side to side as well as sending an alert text message to all the teams. The scam teams, who knew to keep a constant eye on this exit, would then leave immediately, straight out the casino, to the taxi rank, and to the airport. Chips that they were holding would be taken with them and discarded. Because of the constant cash-ins by the runners, hopefully enough money would have already been cashed in and changed to dollars. However, Capone was confident it would not come to that. He entered the casino a few minutes after the last past poster had entered. There being no casino registration, there was very little chance of a good photograph of him being available after the hit—perhaps a grainy long-distance shot from a rover camera. And since he was not directly involved and was for all purposes just another customer from anywhere in the world, he could in no way be directly linked to the team.

Capone sat at the bar and looked around in general. Checking his watch as little as possible, he tried not to direct his gaze at the three roulette pits, all visible from his bar stool, as the teams found positions around the tables. The distracters moved next to the wheel and remained standing. The three scouts, Mario, Giuseppe, and Marcus Amari, were also doubling up as distracters, having completed their initial role. The 'high roller' player sat down in the middle of the table buying in for large value cash chips and some colour, while the past poster positioned himself at the end of the table and bought in for several stacks of colour chips.

Capone watched them all arrange themselves. On a couple of tables, conditions were not suited for any moves—normally they were not busy enough or someone was already standing in the distracter's position. In a few minutes, all were in place, and the first subsequent spin resulted in two successful cheat moves. Capone could not see from his position, but after a few spins, he started to see the runners going to the cash desks. 'So far, so good,' he muttered.

The runners would cash out about R50,000 each time at alternative cash desks. They would then return to the table to be slipped some more cash chips. Several of them were good enough to also act as distracters and would swap places with one of the team for a few spins while the person he replaced would cash out for a while. The teams had been reminded not to take all the high value cash chips from any table. This would mean a fill was needed, and it could raise suspicion among the staff as a fill showed clearly that the table was losing money rapidly. Capone had made his calculations, and the scouts had reported that the float total value was very high—obviously in order to prevent fills—which slowed the games down while they were being processed.

After half an hour, the runners had cashed out the equivalent of about half a million dollars. 'They actually looked quite tired, some of them,' Capone thought almost smiling. He was feeling nervous and worried. In one way, he just wanted to get out, but in another, he wanted to stay in his seat forever.

He glanced at the exit door. Leon was standing there looking intently over his panoramic view of the roulette tables but pretending to look a little impatient, as if waiting for someone. The runners intermittently went to the Foreign Exchange desk with their accumulated takings to change the rand into high value U.S. dollars.

It was time for the hourly count, but as the scouts had seen, it wasn't done, as the tables were too busy and the pit bosses could be seen rapidly moving around their pits doing paperwork, etc. Capone had no doubt that they would have a sense that a lot of money was going out and their pit was doing badly, but until the hourly results were estimated and then collated into a final total, the terrible scale of loss would be unknown.

After an hour, Capone had worked out that somewhere around a million and a half dollars had been pocketed. Not long to go now—he was very satisfied. Anywhere near two million would be great. He just wanted to get away—he was shaking slightly. He started to move out of his chair. The pit bosses would be doing their count soon, and then it would be time to go straight out the door. Another ten minutes passed. The lottery draw was about to take place. That would be a big chance for one final, mass past-posting move. Despite their best intentions, Capone knew that when such lotteries took place, even the staff looked up to see who had won the big prize, which in this case was a Mercedes car—making any moves easier to do. If all went well, a lot could be made on the spins being held at the same time as the draw. Another twenty minutes cheating after the lottery and then it would be time to initiate the exit plan. The team would cash in, change the money to dollars, and leave with the rest of the team and the customers, many of whom would be leaving after the disappointment of not winning the Mercedes.

The scam team members were probably the only people watching the ball drop in the number, including the inspectors, when an old man's ticket was drawn from the lottery box. Cain noticed that the runners were extremely active just after the lottery—the cheat teams must have done well during the distraction.

Another fifteen minutes passed, and just as the teams were starting to leave the tables, he saw two arms being raised above the head from one of the roulette tables, and darting his glance towards the door, he saw the lookout shaking his head quickly and working his mobile phone. He felt the vibration of a message coming in on his mobile at the same time. He could see that it was Rossini and his group who were in danger, as there was a heated discussion at their table.

'Shit, shit!' he said, moving quickly but not suspiciously towards the exit. He saw security moving even quicker towards the table where Rossini, Zapalate, and Nero were already surrounded by guards. He did not even give them a further glance as he left the building; they knew the rules. He headed round the corner towards the hotel.

Fifteen minutes later, the team was in taxis heading for the airport, chattering excitedly. The rest of the team had got out easily enough. Most had managed to cash in and change up the rands before the alert went out, but they had still been holding about 500,000 rands of cash chips that they had had no time to cash out. One of the team, on leaving the casino entrance and with 120,000 in chips on him, saw a poor-looking old man walking along the street. As he passed him, he said, while handing over twelve ten-thousand rand chips, 'Have this, old man, as a present from "The Italians". One thing! Cash it in slowly, a few chips a day, or you'll be going to jail instead of me . . . Ciao!'

# Chapter 10

An hour after the fleet of taxis had left for the airport, Rossini, Zapalate, and Nero slowly passed their hotel. They had no real need to take their bags, as they had 65,000 dollars between them, but they wanted to be absolutely sure that none of the team had hung around waiting for then despite instructions to the contrary. Paulo eventually couldn't stop himself and entered the hotel. He asked the receptionist if he had missed his group going to the airport. She replied that they had, mentioning that she had never seen tourists collecting their cases at such a speed. 'They must have been late for their flight,' she said. 'Are you going to catch them up?' she asked.

'Will try to,' replied Rossini. 'We got held up in town. My friends are outside. I'll take the bags and get a taxi outside. He brought the bags outside and asked the taxi driver to take them to the bus station. There was a bus leaving for Cape Town at 23.45, which they had bought tickets for before meeting up with the team pre-scam. At the bus station, they found a quiet corner and sat quietly nursing their cokes and beer.

They felt tired now that some of the adrenalin was wearing off.

'I don't feel that great,' said Zapalate. 'In fact, I feel a bit sick.'

'Probably stomach acid from the excitement,' suggested Nero. 'A good night's sleep on the bus and you'll be OK.'

'I hope this will all be worth it,' said Zapalate. 'We could be on a plane now with the others. Why did we do it? If I could change now, I would. We are greedy bastards . . . I already miss Tolo.'

'Shut up, both of you,' said the stronger-willed Rossini. 'There is no changing now. What's done is done. We can have a good life for a while, and we can go back to Tolo one day soon, if we want—but why should we? They will have no reason to suspect us. You saw them all leaving the casino when we signalled we had been caught. We can go back at any time, as long as we shut up about it! We'll just say that since we missed the flight, we decided to have a small holiday. Then we phone and say we found good well-paid jobs and have decided to stay. Believe me, after a few weeks of the good life we will be leading, you won't even give Tolo a moment's thought. Imagine: hotels, girls, casinos, and sunshine!'

'Hey! The plan worked perfectly though. Didn't it?' said Zapalate, smiling a bit now. 'Did you see that look on the dealer's face when you called her a fat cow and told her how you had screwed her mother an hour before coming to the casino?'

'She was shocked all right. The inspector went straight to the pit boss and Security was there within a minute, just as we hoped for. So we gave the signal. Once all the others were gone, it was easy enough to apologise profusely, give every one a large tip, and cash out quick and go. Worked fine. As far as the others will know, we got caught cheating and were arrested and detained. Wonder how much they got in total? How much did we give our runners?'

'Plenty—plenty,' said Nero, 'although I kept a little extra back each time. This will go down as one of, if not the greatest, casino raids in history!'

'Shouldn't we get out of the country quick then?' said Zapalate.

'Why?' replied Rossini. 'They don't have a name, probably no good pictures . . . I don't see a problem.'

'Still, if we were found, it could be dangerous,' said Nero.

'So can crossing the road. Calm down. We'll be fine. I fancy another beer. Come on, guys—sixty odd in our pockets and plenty of casinos in Cape Town. In fact, I can't be bothered waiting a couple of hours for the bus. I'm taking a taxi to Cape Town. It can't be more than a couple of hundred kilometres away. I can afford it. Don't worry. I'll pay it from my share!' enthused Rossini.

'Sounds great, and when we get there, the first night is on me!' declared Zapalate, now almost upbeat.

They climbed into the taxi, which was a brand-new Mercedes Sprinter Mini Bus.

'Cape Town, please,' declared Nero, who had also perked up.

The driver tried to remain cool but found he was blinking and there was a brief flutter in his chest. He muttered the words, 'Betal jou bliksem! Then in a clear voice, 'Certainly, sir—are you in a hurry?'

'All the time in the world,' Nero laughed.

The taxi driver, Neels van den Berg, headed out of the bus station. 'Tourists—I'll take the long route,' he thought to himself, calculating how he was going to spend the windfall. He briefly thought of taking them via Namibia but thought that would be a little too much. He decided to get off the N2 Highway and meander down the coast road. 'Thirteen thousand rand coming up,' he thought, preparing himself for the 1,000 kilometer-plus journey.

At the International Casino, there was a palpable silence as they tried to comprehend what had happened. The casino result seemed to have dropped seventeen million rand in two hours. 'Strange?'

'Check the scores again!' said the relief manager, Van Bronkhorst, who was hoping to impress the casino manager while he was away at the conference. It was his big chance for promotion and he did not want to blow it. No, it was just not possible for the tables to drop so much—it was all the roulettes, the black jacks had won. Forty odd roulette tables had each lost an average of a four hundred thousand rand. They had all seemed to lose about the same amount, which was also strange.

People were running around all over the place in frantic activity. He phoned Surveillance.

'Did you see how much went out?' said the Surveillance supervisor before Van Bronkhorst could say anything.

'Did you see anything?' pleaded Van Bronkhorst to the Surveillance supervisor.

'Really big roulette games,' replied Smuts. 'R5,000 chips all over nearly all the roulettes. Biggest action I have ever seen in my life. Looked like foreigners too. Must be a wealthy tour group.'

'Well, they're fucking a lot wealthier now!' shouted Van Bronkhorst in exasperation. 'We dropped seventeen million rand in two hours. Check every roulette table for every spin for the last two hours. Call in people on days off, holiday, anything. And I tell you, if something has happened, you are going down the shit hole with me.'

And that would be exactly where they ended up.

At eleven, Van Bronkhorst reached for the phone to make the most reluctant call he had ever made in his life. He knew the owner of the casino, Mr. Harrison, was in town from the United States. He had never even been there before. It was a large casino, but small fry to him, compared to his places in Vegas, Macau, and Singapore. He was going to be really impressed with tonight's result, when he found out. For a moment, Van Bronkhorst hoped that a couple of million dollars would not be missed by Arron Harrison. The thought didn't last long, being replaced by a more sinister possibility. He realised with a start that he himself would come under suspicion, and he started to worry about staying alive—keeping his job seemed suddenly irrelevant, and when he remembered that at the beginning of the night he had been hoping that soon he would be promoted, he let out a hysterical laugh, which, he realised, sounded just like the mad police chief in the Pink Panther films.

'Apt,' he thought. 'I'm already nearly mad.' He wanted to cry as he phoned the casino manager's mobile.

'That's what I like—punctuality,' smiled Andrews as Cain and Morris presented themselves at the Plaza. 'Enjoy the conference, did we?' He didn't wait for an answer but continued, 'Right—the big boys are already upstairs. We'd better get up there.' He immediately turned and headed towards the private lift that would take them to the Royal Suite. They ascended quietly, not saying a further word.

They reached their level, which Morris presumed was the top floor. The lift opened and in front of them was a huge glass window displaying a breathtaking view of the lights of Durban and the Indian ocean beyond.

They walked down a corridor reaching another door, which Andrews ushered them through. The room they entered was breathtaking by any standard. It was at least forty metres from the door to the long glass window, similar to the one they had seen on leaving the lift. Morris figured it must have stretched around the entire circumference of the floor. In the far corner, he could see a long bar, invitingly shaded by soft colours from overhead lights. The carpet was a thick dark blue, and leather sofas were placed around the room. Morris could see that four others were already at the bar, looking far more relaxed than Morris had seen them at the conference. As they approached, one of the four, Steve Kruger, moved towards them. Medium height with broad shoulders, he was immaculately dressed.

'Hello, John. Andrews persuaded you to bring your colleague then,' he said, looking closely at Morris and offering his hand. 'Hello, Mr. Morris. Glad you could come to listen to our offer. But first, have a drink. We don't meet up that often, and it's good to have a break from the public gaze. Nice room here, I'm sure you'll agree?'

'Very nice indeed,' Morris replied, pleased that the group were making him feel at ease.

Kruger introduced them to the others—all of whom seemed in an amiable mood. Arron Harrison stood out, as he parted his hair like Adolf Hitler.

'Somebody should have a word,' thought Morris.

'Right, couple of drinks, a bit of food, and then down to business—OK by you two?' Kruger offered.

Morris listened to the conversation, which was friendly, but a lot of it was about things that he did not have much knowledge of, such as hedge funds, takeovers, and various names of people and companies he was unaware of. For these guys, knowing what the other players were up to was paramount, he guessed.

'A good speech today,' one of the others, Stanley Ling (or Mr. Vegas as he was often called), mentioned suddenly and then resumed his conversation about a new casino he was planning to open in Macau. He was Chinese Malaysian but looked more Japanese to Morris: tall, thin, and imposing.

'It's got 2,500 rooms, expected occupancy 89 per cent, 45 tables and 6,000 slot machines. Investment of 3.5 billion paid off in two years—after that, a nice little earner, thank you very much,' and the others nodded in impressed agreement.

'Asia is just a gold mine,' said Kruger. 'Can it last, though? The new Chinese government is making some sounds about higher taxes, etc.'

'They'll be OK in the end. The taxes they receive already are billions—they don't want to jeopardise that, but they have to utter occasional platitudes, as if they disapprove in some way of Macau. Doesn't quite fit in with the communist ideal—corrupt as it has become,' commented the fourth member of the circle, Jim Pullman, often referred to as 'JP'. He was short, fat, and with a large squashed nose and tiny beady eyes.

Morris and Cain talked with them a little but mostly between themselves, until after they had eaten and Kruger ushered them towards a large table with about a dozen chairs around it. Morris noticed that despite several drinks being consumed by the group, they suddenly appeared to become more serious and the joviality disappeared completely by the time they had taken their seats.

'Right then,' Kruger stated clearly. 'Mr Morris—I'll call you Sam from now on, if that's OK with you. You probably wondered why we asked you to come here and talk with us to try and find a solution to this problem we have. We all know that the sum taken from your casino was of little consequence in the general scheme of things, but . . .' He picked up a file which was on the table in front of him and slapped it against his hand. 'This is a report we received three days ago from the top Surveillance guy we have, who in fact works for us all—Alistair Campbell. I'll let you read it, of course, but the gist of it is that we should all take the possibility that the team will strike again as a given, rather than as likely or a maybe. He believes the chances are above 90 per cent—based really on the knowledge that the methods they are using of quick in-out ventures will in all likelihood continue to be successful.

'As you know, all of us in the group here, we own some of the biggest casinos in the world, and frankly, we are very concerned that the team may target one of our places next. We are as ready as we can be, but we are nervous. We want to find this team and eliminate them, so to speak. A million for a small casino like yours could equate to tens of millions in one of ours.'

Morris nodded slightly, never having heard the casino in Greece being called a small operation.

'Sam, we were very impressed by your talk today and also by the fact that you did not run away but came here to face the potential embarrassment head on. Cain has told us that you are determined to find out who hit your place and get the bastards. We like that—and that's why we want you to join up with Campbell, lock your heads together, and solve our problem. Quickly. He's in Singapore organising surveillance for the new casinos, and you'll fly out in the morning and meet up with him.

'Our casinos there have all the latest information and technical staff that can help you in any way you need. We'll pay you 10,000 dollars a week and a bonus of 250,000 if you and Campbell give us information that will enable us to eliminate the threat to our casinos—how that transpires will be up to us. The bonus should help you concentrate on the job at hand. OK? It goes without saying that your expenses are paid and a private jet will be at your disposal, if needed to get some place in a hurry. It's reserved for you for tomorrow morning.'

Morris was trying to remain calm but was already thinking of telling Linda and his kids that he had just picked up a quarter of a million bonus—if he could find the Blitzkreigers.

'Agreed—thanks very much for giving me the chance. I hope very much I will not let you down. Campbell is one of the most respected Surveillance guys in the world. I've met him a couple of times—Cain too,' he glanced at Cain, who was nodding.

Kruger continued, 'Excellent, then. Andrews has everything ready. Keep in contact with us via Cain. If, or I'll say once, you have identified and isolated the team or as many of them as you can, do not make any further moves. We will take it from there.'

Morris felt that this sounded a bit ominous, but he only gave it brief consideration, and before he knew it, he had thanked everyone, told Cain that he would meet up with him later, and headed back to the hotel. His flight was at 10.30 in the morning. Before packing, he phoned his kids and then Linda. After packing, he had a shower and headed down to the bar, where he had arranged to meet Cain for a nightcap or two at about eleven. He was feeling pretty good.

Cain discussed casino business with the four and was just about to head off, when Andrews came busting through the door. Cain could see that he was bursting to tell some bad news. 'Did it make him feel important or something—the sad bastard?' he thought.

'You won't believe—another hit, here at the International, about two hours ago. Two million gone—dollars, not rand! Same modus operandi—it's them, for sure!'

The group outwardly remained calm, exchanging quick glances amongst themselves, before Kruger spoke.

'Right, this really shows we were right to be worried. Shit . . . that's one of your casinos, isn't it, Arron?'

'Fucking right, it is!' came the furious reply. 'I'm gonna kill the bastards. Two million. How the . . . ?!'

He reached for his phone and walked over to the bar to get a drink. His friendly demeanour had been entirely replaced. His eyes were bulging with absolute hatred.

Andrews continued, 'The casino manager is at the casino gathering all the facts, but it seems that the attack style was the same as in Greece, but for a longer period. No one recognised any of the team, despite all their photos being everywhere—not one of them was picked up on. The whole management was at the post-conference get-together at the time having dinner at the precise time, I believe.' Cain could see Andrews almost smiling as he said the last words. He had to get that last little bit in, ensuring the loss of jobs, no doubt satisfying his perverse morality.

Harrison was shouting down the phone in a high and threatening tone. 'What's his name and where is he? Find him and tell him to phone me within ten minutes, or he's a piece of dead fucking meat! No one robs me, do you understand? No one!' he roared, saliva dripping from his gums.

Cain thought for a second of that vile temper he had seen in so many of the top guys—was it the strain of the job or something they already had in their character that helped them rise through the ranks? It was absent from him, he concluded, and he was glad it was, looking at the twisted figure of Harrison.

The tantrum seemed to do the trick, as after five minutes, Harrison's phone rang, and he moved over to the window to concentrate. He listened a little but mostly barked commands and requests. He returned to the group.

'Yes—same style as Greece, but they are sure it's a different group. They have looked at the thieves, and there are no matches with the Greek mob. What the shit do we have going on here? Two different groups with the same style. Is there a goddamned training school for roulette cheats somewhere turning out seventy-odd bastards every time? What's next? Another group somewhere else—maybe tomorrow?'

The rest of the group stood silent, looking at each other.

'This is really bad news for us,' commented Pullman in extreme understatement.

Cain interrupted them, 'I think Morris should postpone his trip. He should get a look at the footage and any photos that they have put together.' He nodded briefly to Kruger, 'OK?'

Kruger, lost in thought, eventually nodded and the others soon agreed. Cain could see who the main man was. Cain phoned Morris, simply telling him that things had changed and to wait for him in the bar. Kruger called over Andrews, telling him to contact Campbell in Singapore and to contact the general manager of the International to get up to date. He also told Andrews to cancel Morris's flight.

Cain stayed with the others as they discussed strategy and again contemplated what they could do. A second group really was a worry. If there had been only one team, they would eventually have been recognised somewhere, and that would have been the end of it. But a second group and maybe further teams out there . . .

After some more calls, Harrison asked Pullman if he could have 'a word'. They moved to the bar and talked quietly amongst themselves.

'JP, this has to be solved. The audio situation in Singapore alone calls for it. Too dangerous by far, get my drift?' he was looking at Pullman intently, making sure the unspoken suggestion was understood.

It was. They had just decided to wipe out forever more than a hundred people, if that's what it would take to halt the Blitzkrieg Scam team.

# Chapter 11

Capone sat looking out of the plane's window into the pitch dark and thought and thought. He just wanted to be back in Tolo. Amazing how at times the little town could hold so much attraction.

After the high of the operation, he was feeling absolutely exhausted, and as he peered around the plane, he could see that nearly all of the team was fast asleep. It had gone brilliantly well of course—apart from the end. He cocked his head to the side in contemplation.

'What the hell had happened at the end?' The last spin and they were caught. What would happen to them? If they were as good as the rest of the team in hiding the past post, there would be no definite proof against them. But the fact that they were caught suggests that something had been noticed. The last bloody spin. Would they confess and give the game away? He thought not. There was no way they could be connected to the rest of the team, and most of the time, they would be interviewed and released and maybe their money confiscated. Capone had often wondered about why casinos were so light-handed with cheats. Very few cheats ever went to jail or even faced prosecution. Most of the time, they were simply taken out and barred. He supposed casinos wanted to present a non-nasty image—he wasn't sure.

The worst scenario he could contemplate was that the boys would be threatened with serious action unless they gave the names of the rest of the team. He was sure they were not that naïve, and in case, even if names were mentioned, none of the Durban scam team would be on the next hit. So what would happen? It's not as if they were going to come to Tolo and demand their money back . . .

Yes, he fully expected to hear from the boys in a day or two. There would probably even be a message for them when they got home, saying they were fine and would be home soon. He hoped they would keep any money they had and not blow it on a good time before they left.

'No, no, good boys. Fine young men,' he concluded, satisfied that his fears were unfounded.

His thoughts eventually turned to finances and the future. Two million minus the table buy-ins and the expenses, which he kept a meticulous track of. One and a half million dollars clear. It was enough to get the casino running again or open the bottling factory, if that was what the town decreed, and to give the remainder to the people of Tolo. 'One more would really establish us,' he thought, realising he was loathe to give up on the casino raids. He thought of the possible location. Singapore? It was a long way to go and a long way to escape from, but he had heard some information that made the new casinos there particularly attractive to past posters. He admitted to himself that part of his thinking to carry on was not based on rational economic terms, but came from his desire to feel that excitement again. He had never experienced anything like it in his life.

On the road outside Durban, Paulo had been initially a bit annoyed, when after four hours in the taxi and when he had asked how much further to go, Van den Berg had stated glibly, 'About 900 kilometres, sir.'

Paulo looked at the meter and extrapolated what the final fare would be. 'Wow—shit!' he thought. But realising there wasn't much else he could do, he started to laugh.

'Not as if we can't afford it!' he found himself saying out loud. He brought out the wad of money from various pockets and counted it again, away from the gaze of the driver.

The other two had fallen asleep, but he was too worried to nod off with 60,000 dollars on him, even in a taxi.

Eventually, the others woke, and once they had their bearings turned to Paulo.

'Not there yet?' said Nero.

'Eh . . . it's a bit further than I thought—by several hundred kilometres. It's OK—I'll pay from my share . . .'

'Don't be crazy,' Nero said happily. 'We are a team—the Three Musketeers—we rise and fall together!'

After another three hours or so, they agreed that they needed something to eat.

'Where's the nearest casino?' Paulo asked the taxi driver with a wry look. The others darted glances at him.

'Port Elizabeth. I think they have two casinos there,' came the reply. 'We will be there in about an hour, and that will nearly be halfway through our journey.'

'OK—we'll go there. We would like to go in the casino for a meal and a drink. I have an extra two thousand for you if you can wait another hour or so?'

'Fine,' replied Van den Berg. 'Where you guys from anyway? Italy—Milan?'

'Have you heard of Tolo?' said Zapalate, smiling. 'It's quite famous, you know.'

'No,' replied the driver with a shrug.

It was, in fact, an hour and fifteen minutes when they pulled into the parking space of the Reef Casino in Port Elizabeth. All three were already moving their fingers and massaging their palms. They were ready for another hit.

'There's a small chance that we will have to leave very quickly,' Rossini casually mentioned to the driver. 'Will you be parked here and ready to go if necessary?'

'I will,' came the reply, accompanied by a worried look.

By the time Cain walked into the bar, Morris had had a few beers already. He was feeling pretty good. The money on offer only added to his desire to nail the team. Working with Campbell was something he looked forward to as well. Seeing Cain look so serious made him a bit apprehensive.

'Let me get a drink first,' announced Cain, raising his hands in a postponing gesture. He returned a moment later with two beers and two malts. 'You're going to need this,' he said, making eye contact with Morris.

'What the hell has happened now?' said Morris.

'They, or I should say not they, have hit again, and guess where? Right here in Durban—at the International, just round the corner from the bleeding conference centre where we were all discussing the possibility of another hit. You couldn't make it up!'

'Wait—wait! You said "they or not"? Was it the same group . . . ?'

'No, no—not the same group. From what they have seen so far, none of the faces match the Greek cheats, but the same style—another Blitzkrieg—in and out—although this time, they stayed longer.'

'That's interesting in itself. A different group—shit! That changes a lot of things,' Morris added.

'Look, it has been arranged for you to go to the casino in the morning and look at what happened—look at the footage, that sort of thing, and see what you can come up with. You can fly to Singapore when you are ready. The ante has suddenly been upped, so to speak. Arron is the owner of the International, and he hit the roof when he found out. The general manager and Surveillance director—both of whom were enjoying a meal at a top restaurant after going to the conference, despite the fact that their casino was very busy with a lottery, anyway, they were both fired an hour ago.

'If the group were worried before, they are shitting themselves. The thing is they feel helpless, and they are not used to feeling that way. I don't even want to think of what they will consider to stop this team or teams. Sam, just make sure you are not around once they are located. It could get nasty.'

'They're not going to kill them or something? Stealing from a casino is one thing—killing someone for doing it is an entirely different matter. What, kill a hundred odd people? No way.'

'Look, I'm just saying be careful. I'm sure it will all be fixed peacefully enough in the end.' Cain took a large gulp of beer followed by a sip of whisky. 'OK—you go to the casino first thing in the morning,' he said. 'Maybe tomorrow, you will have found something and be on the way to retirement.'

'Boy that would be great,' replied Morris. 'I'm dying to see both the kids and Linda as soon as possible. That's another incentive for me to wrap things up. Was the team the same size as the last one?' he asked.

'They think so, judging by the number of tables that took a massive hit. We'll see in the morning. Can I get some food here?'

'The barman told me the steak sandwich was good. Will I get a couple of these?' Morris said, already standing up.

'Great then, bed for me. Get another drink while you're up there,' Cain added.

'I'll buy you a good malt. It isn't every day someone helps organise me a job that pays 10,000 a week. You know, I'm looking forward to going to the casino and seeing all the stuff. I can imagine the remaining staff are feeling as low as I was—it certainly affects you personally. I'm sure they will have been working through the night to collate all the information. Hopefully a report is prepared . . . Looks like this lot will just fade away like the last group. God, I'd love to know where they are based. A school of cheats—it would actually be a good idea. But if you are only going to be used once . . . ?'

'We can't say that for sure,' suggested Cain. 'We have had two different teams so far—but if there is another attempt . . .'

'There will be—it gets into their veins,' interrupted Morris. 'It might be another new team or a mix of the two. Can't imagine there is a non-stop supply of new teams—it has to stop somewhere. All we have to do is locate where they are coming from, and we should be able to stop it from there. It must be one location—can't be a sort of franchise of cheat schools opening up all over Italy or wherever! It's one group somewhere, with a common goal. If it is the case that each team is only being used once, then they are working towards something. That sort of skill takes hundreds of hours' work—nobody would learn that just to apply it once.'

'If they are working towards something,' said Cain, 'then they might suddenly stop. Maybe Durban was the last one?'

'As I said, it is very hard to stop once you have a taste for it,' Morris said. 'The group would need tremendous discipline throughout to suddenly stop. Either that or the goal they are looking to achieve is worth more than the thrill of the scam. I really think we are looking for some very special person behind all this—one who can keep the team tight and under control and be able to call a halt to it when we get too close or when they have got what they want.'

'This is interesting, Sam,' said Cain. 'I can see you are getting somewhere. Just be careful, as I said. It is a strange case. I don't feel so good about it. Arron's face scared me—really. Such hatred . . .'

The sandwiches arrived and were as good as the barman had said. They both started to get tired as soon as they had finished, and the last talk was of arrangements for the next day as they headed to their rooms.

Rossini and his pals were having a laugh. The Reef Casino was tiny compared to the International, but it was fairly busy and enough people were hovering around the roulette tables to give them a chance to make their move. They had had some food first and a couple of beers and had got talking to some girls at the bar.

'We might have to get the taxi driver to wait a bit longer,' said Zapalate with a smile.

However, the lure of the tables eventually overpowered even the appeal of the girls, and after giving them some money to 'treat' themselves, they started walking casually around the casino. They had no scout reports to help them; they had no clue about security or surveillance or cash-out procedures. That had all been done by Capone and the Amari brothers. Rossini, though, felt a strong desire to show that they could achieve success without the back-up of Capone. He was convinced that their technique would overcome any threat of getting caught. They had glibly discussed how much they would 'win' and had settled for the equivalent of 5,000 dollars—ten or so moves with the Reef's limits. 'Should take us about an hour, and then we'll be on the way to Cape Town with a bit more spending power,' said Nero, stretching his fingers. Soon, they identified a suitable table. They bought in for high value cash chips and positioned themselves in their respective positions, ready to begin. They started to feel the excitement they had felt in Durban.

The third spin hit number 30, which was ideal, and the chips slid on to the split of 30/33 with no one batting an eyelid. When the payout of fifty-one black chips was announced, the dealer prepared the payout and then waited for a check from the inspector, who stared at the bet and nodded his head in agreement.

The casino manager, Don Roberts, passed him by a few minutes later when doing the hourly result checks. By that time, the team had scored for a second time.

'Anything happening?' asked Roberts, a small, portly man with long hair tied in a ponytail at the back: not your normal casino executive by any means. He had had a long and frustrating career and was miffed to have ended up at the Reef, which he considered a backwater.

'A bit has gone out on AR 3. New guys in have been pretty lucky. Some of their bets are coming in a bit late. The dealer seems to be a bit confused by their call bets. Don't think they are South African at all . . . European, Italian most likely.' Roberts immediately raised his gaze from the clipboard that he had been writing on. What he saw made him immediately nervous. One guy was reaching up the table to place his bets. 'Why not get the dealer to place them?' Another player was stretching all the way from the wheel to the layout to give a call bet to the dealer. 'Unnatural,' Roberts thought and alarm bells started ringing. He moved quietly back to the pit podium and called Surveillance, requesting a complete review of all the play since these new players had come in and live observation of the game in progress.

'Get a rover camera behind the guy at the bottom of the table, if you can. Send one of the guys down as well to hang around behind the guy at the bottom of the table, but make sure they don't block the camera's view—if they are cheating, I want to be certain that the chips are going on after the ball has dropped. I don't want us to be hit like Durban was today. I am not losing two million dollars to some bastard Italians. Get security to stand by the door and to block all exits at a moment's notice. And look for others. I hear these guys hunt in packs.'

He was feeling excited—as he had done in the good old days, forty years ago. He was sixty years old and looked it, but he knew what he was doing, and one thing he knew was when some bastard was trying to steal from 'his' casino.

'Bastards!' he snarled, temper rising. Don Roberts had never been known for having a balanced perspective on things. For him, something was good or something was bad. Simple really. He knew in his bones that these guys were scumbags. One look had been enough.

He kept his distance but watched the table discreetly from the podium. He saw a Surveillance operator come out of the door near the cash desk and move slowly around the casino towards the roulette table. After another spin, Roberts was absolutely sure what they were doing—the distractions, the body language. He felt pleased that he was about to get a cheat team, when the guys in Durban had been hit for two hours without it being noticed. There's never a substitute for experience. He smiled to himself, in his mind rewarding himself with several large vodka and oranges once the police had been called and the scumbags had been dealt with. He could see that no more money had gone out, and the team were just waiting for the next number in the third dozen to hit. The Surveillance girl was standing right behind Rossini with a Pepsi in hand and looking innocent enough. Roberts called Du Plessis, the security manager; tough guy, had been in Angola many years ago. They met up every day for after-work drinks.

'Ready? Do you know the guys we are going to pull?' Roberts said.

'Yes, on Table 3. Police have been called and are on their way. Shall we just hand them over or shall we talk to them first?'

'Oh, I want to talk to them myself. I fancy doing the scare tactics with this lot. If they are Italian, definitely. I've been dying to do it for years.'

'OK, it's the dungeon then,' Du Plessis replied in reference to the security office.

Roberts watched the table—the ball was about to land. The distracter was calling to the dealer, 'One five neighbours by one five,' which made no sense to the dealer, who stood looking at the chips in front of her in utter confusion.

At the bottom of the table, he saw Rossini stretching up the table with his left hand across his body and his right hand hidden from view. The ball landed in number 33. Immediately after a very quick look in the wheel, the dealer placed the dolly on the number. Roberts had seen Rossini's right hand jerk back unnaturally quickly just before but did not see any chips being past posted. 'Shit—good team!' he had to admit. He looked behind Rossini at the Surveillance operator, who was raising her eyebrows looking directly at him and nodding vigorously.

'Gotcha!' he said. He left the pit, collected security, and gave them instructions on who to grab and where to go. They moved behind the team and Roberts said to Rossini, 'Excuse me, sir . . .'

Rossini turned briefly in surprise, and then on seeing the security presence, he tried to move past Roberts.

'Sorry, sir. Would you come with us?' Du Plessis said, and all three were grasped around the arm and marched off to the security office.

The escort attracted some attention on the floor—at least for a few seconds as the other customers raised their heads. But on realising it wouldn't affect them, they returned their attention to the tables.

The security office was pretty small. Most of the security guys left, and Roberts, Du Plessis, and one other security guard stood as the three Italians were ordered to sit down. Phil Smith, the Surveillance boss, came into the room.

'OK, here we go,' thought Roberts. He wasn't in the mood for a quiet approach. He was feeling great.

In the corner of the room was a baseball bat, which he kept as a visual threat to those brought to the dungeon. He picked it up casually and placed it on the table. He looked at the three in an attempt to identify the weakest. Rossini still looked relatively calm, but Nero was looking at the bat intently and then he jerked his head towards Roberts in obvious fear.

Then Roberts picked up the phone and pretended to call Surveillance. 'Is that Surveillance?' he said slowly. 'I'm in the security office. Can you turn the cameras off and the audio?' he said, looking directly at Nero, whose eyes widened further. 'I always knew I was a sadistic bastard,' thought Roberts. In his mind, he had been rehearsing this for years. Then he asked for the main lights to be turned off. Du Plessis obliged, and all that was left was a little light coming from the office table lamp. Roberts was transformed into a shadow.

Nero had never been so scared in his life. He was thinking of his mother and friends in Tolo. 'Why had he stayed in South Africa?' He determined that if he could get out of this, he would get back to Italy as soon as he could—whatever the others said.

Roberts picked up the bat and walked around the room for a few minutes saying nothing. Then suddenly, he smashed the bat on to the table just a few inches from Nero's hand. He jumped up and felt something give in his groin region. He already wanted to tell them anything they wanted to know. He wondered if they knew about Durban.

Suddenly, he felt a hand grip his knee and a whisper, 'Shut up. It will be OK.' The voice was that of Rossini. 'I'll do the talking only. Shut up!'

'What was that, you cheating bastard?!' roared Roberts. 'I'll speak. You shut up, OK? Where are you from?'

'No understand,' replied Rossini.

'Italy?' replied Roberts. 'Italiano—yes? Speako the Italiano? Inter Milan, Ethiopia, Mossolini, Mafiaso?'

Rossini only shrugged, remaining calm.

Roberts turned to Zapalate, who was looking straight at the wall. He picked up the bat and hit it on the table again, but it did not seem to scare the three as much as he had hoped for.

'OK, Jan, empty their pockets,' he told the security guard. There was about 22,000 rand in chips from the Reef as well as one or two from another casino and a few euro coins. There were also numerous straps of dollars. And when they were placed on the table, the fear seemed to return—even in Rossini's eyes.

'What do we have here, then? Listen, Mussolini,' Roberts said softly, trying to look as terrifying as possible. 'Tell us who you are, where you are from, or we take all the money—understando?'

Rossini considered the situation. 'Yes, I do understand a small English,' he replied, 'but that is our money. You can't take it.'

'Yes I can. What are you going to do about it? This is South Africa. We can do just about what we want here. You are from Italy—yes?'

'Yes,' Rossini said.

'What are you doing here? Come all the way to this small casino to cheat? Why?'

'We were not cheating. The dealer just let us place late bets and some of them won.'

'Ha! Fucking ha!' snorted Roberts. 'Do you think I'm stupido?! You cheat—like all spaghetti men. I will take your money now,' and he reached for the cash.

'OK, OK,' said Rossini, desperately thinking how he could get out of this. 'Look, we are businessmen on our way to Cape Town. We are looking to open a restaurant there. The money is for our cousin to buy a little place. Please we need that money. We did try to cheat, as we need a bit more, but we were just leaving when you came . . . We are sorry . . . Please don't call the police or anything. We will give all the money back and even a few thousand as a tip to your men as a thank you.'

'Typical Italians,' replied Roberts. 'Corrupt bastards. I thought you just said you were short of money and were trying to get a little more, but now you want to give us some extra cash. No way, amigo!' He realised his language was getting a bit extreme, but he had been waiting years to do this—it was the first time he had been able to act out his fantasy and he couldn't control himself. 'See if the police are here. If I could, I would stick this baseball bat up your arsehole,' he announced loudly.

Du Plessis left the room with the Surveillance manager, who was grinning after Roberts's muscle-man performance.

Rossini realised the game was up. They were going to be held in a police cell, probably charged, and then spend years in an African cell. No, they had to get out of this. The taxi was outside. If only they could get out. He was inwardly praying to God.

Roberts continued his rant against cheats and Italians. 'No spaghetti bolognaso where you're going!' he smirked. 'Only big black sausages—understand?!' He made a sexual gesture with a maniac look on his face.

Rossini looked at the office door and then noticed that the door to the safe was slightly ajar. He could see what appeared to be the handle of a gun. Then his mind went into overdrive. All they had to do was get out of that office, and they would be

OK. Without thinking further, he leapt to the safe, swung open the door, and grabbed what was indeed a gun. He had never even held one in his life before.

'OK. Stop! Stop!' he shouted, waving the gun wildly. 'Leave us alone. We are not criminals, and we are not going with any police—no way!' He pointed the gun at Roberts and the security guard alternatively. 'Just let us go, please!'

Roberts was stunned and remained motionless. He had had a gun held to his head once before, and it had been a terrifying experience and had a lasting affect on him. The same feeling as before crept over him: the knowledge that in a second, you could be dead—your whole life finished in an instant. He continued to look at the gun but spoke quietly to the security officer.

'Jan, don't do anything. Just let them go!'

But it was too late and Jan sprang towards Rossini, who jumped back in horror and pulled the trigger involuntary. The bullet hit Jan in the side of the stomach, and he collapsed on the floor clutching it and making gurgling noises. The noise of the shot exploded around the small room, and Roberts found he had dived under the table. After the shot, Rossini threw the gun to the floor. He and the others grabbed their belongings from the table, pulled open the door, and rushed through the casino. The casino exit was just a few yards away. They saw another security officer, who hadn't heard the gunshot due to the sound of the casino, but who started to move towards them on seeing their hasty departure.

Suddenly they were outside. About sixty metres away, they saw several security officers talking at a side entrance while they waited for the police to arrive. They were talking calmly and had obviously not heard the shot.

'Walk slowly and calmly,' Rossini hissed, and the others tried to slow down as best they could. Thirty metres behind, they saw two security officers run out from Reception. They saw the Italians and brought their guns out, but then hesitated and changed direction and ran towards Du Plessis, still waiting at the car park for the police, who were as usual taking a long time to respond to the call.

Rossini, Zapalate, and Nero reached their taxi and were grateful to see the driver awake and reading a paper.

'Let's go, Driver—let's go!' shouted Rossini as they clambered into the cab.

'Did you have a good time?' asked Van den Berg nervously as he slipped into gear and headed back on to the main road.

Nero was crying uncontrollably.

'Must have lost,' Van den Berg thought with a shrug.

Rossini leant over and spoke to the taxi driver, 'Change of plans. We need to get back to Italy quick—how do we do that?'

'I take it you don't want me to drive you there?' Van den Berg joked. 'We are nearer Cape Town than Durban now,' he replied. 'You can get a flight from there, but of course, I don't know when there are flights to Italy.'

'It's OK. We'll go anywhere. If the rest of the population is anything like that madman, we'll fly to Afghanistan. We got in some trouble back there. Can you drive a bit faster? Extra money for you. Straight to the airport. Is there a way to go that the police might not suspect?'

'I'll look on the map,' the driver replied.

Both he and the others suddenly became aware of a mechanical roar from behind their car. Looking round, they couldn't believe what they saw.

Roberts was no more than fifty metres behind. He was driving an old Harley Davidson motorbike. He had a maniacal look on his face—free from fear. His hair was blowing in the wind, adding to the fearsome image. He was still dressed in his suit, his tie flapping behind his shoulder.

'This guy is fucking nuts!' thought Rossini.

'What did we do to deserve him?' Zapalate cried out.

'We ran out on the team . . .' said Nero.

Looking back, they saw Roberts reach for something tucked down his trousers.

'Oh, Jesus, it's a fucking gun!' Nero sobbed. Now he was shaking and twitching as the mad biker drew closer.

'Faster, faster—we'll pay you what you want. Get away from that bastard!' Rossini shouted.

Van den Berg needed no incentive. He too was having fearful thoughts as he forced his foot down on the accelerator.

'What a bloody day! Started with a great fare to Cape Town, and now I am surrounded by crying Italians and a madman on a motorbike.' He almost saw some humour in it all.

They sped up, but if anything, Roberts seemed to be getting slightly closer. He brought out a gun from his pants and almost swerved off the road as his right hand was removed from the handlebar, but he brought the bike under control, aimed, and fired. In the taxi, they heard the bang, but nothing hit the cab.

Rossini wished he hadn't dropped the gun like a hot potato in the casino office. They were helpless unless they could speed away. He saw they were approaching a corner and realised that the taxi driver, in fear, was going way too fast to handle the turn. Roberts was drawing closer, only about ten metres behind them, and was raising the gun again. He was going to hit something this time, Rossini was sure.

Van den Berg tried to hold the corner, but the car started to skid across to the other side—a rock face suddenly lurched towards them! They were going to hit it at full speed. It seemed to hit them like a meteor, such was the sudden rush. They didn't really even have time to have a last thought, as further rocks fell from the rock face, crumpling the car like a soda tin. Roberts came wildly round the corner, still holding the gun in one hand. Seeing the wreckage, he threw the gun on the road and tried to regain control of the bike, but the bike overturned and skidded along the floor, throwing Roberts on to the road at 80 kmph. He bounced twice before landing up a few metres from the wrecked car. Even though he didn't realise it and believe it at that moment, he would survive.

The others were mangled together in one mass of blood and body parts. The taxi driver's head lay on the road like a lost football. A few moments later, the first car to be at the scene was the police car, on its leisurely way to check out the disturbance at the casino. They called an ambulance, which responded much quicker than they had done to their call. The quick response was to save Roberts's life. He was transferred to Port Elizabeth Hospital, where he would recover over the next few weeks as he was drawn into the Blitzkrieg Scam investigation. The mass of Italian bodies and the South African taxi driver were sent to the Port Elizabeth morgue, and the Italian embassy was contacted with the names of the dead that were stated on their false passports.

# Chapter 12

Morris was at the International Casino at 08.30. He waited in the casino coffee shop after telling Reception that he had arrived. A few moments later, Jeff Wrethman, the new Surveillance manager, joined him. A tall man with a thick beard, he looked tired. Without waiting, he spoke, 'Sorry for my appearance—I probably look a wreck. It's been some twelve hours or so.'

'I'm sure,' emphasised Morris. 'I've been there myself.'

'Of course—you were the guy in Greece,' came the reply.

'Welcome to the Blitzkrieg Victims' Club. Any final figures yet? Too early for a report, I guess?'

'Actually, it's nearly done, just got to tidy it up a bit,' replied Wrethman.

'Give us what you have, and I'll see the footage later at your convenience.'

'Whenever you want. You can do whatever you want, when you want. That's the message from Harrison.'

'What's he like?' asked Morris. 'I just met him briefly yesterday . . .'

'Don't know—never met the guy, although he owns the place!'

'Rich bastard—one of the big group of owners. Shouldn't say that—I'm working for him now!'

'To find who hit us?' asked Wrethman.

'Yes, and the one in Greece, if it was the same mob—which we think it is. The idea is to stop it happening again. There is a lot at stake.'

'Let's hope we can. Right, we believe the final amount taken from the tables was 1.9 million dollars after an incredible 400 or so past post attempts. They were picking up nearly 5,000 dollars each time, and each team was past posting about eight times per hour, some more than others, but pretty consistent per group. Not one was picked up on—can you believe it? Must admit, I feel ashamed, even though I was on days off.'

'Don't—or try not to,' Morris said. 'I felt the same. Look, I know how good they are. I'm sure your footage will confirm it. What else?'

'Judging by the table results and after seeing most of the footage, we think there were twenty-one teams of three cheats. They also had people going up and down to the various cash desks, and some would change with the cheats at the table. We will definitely be changing our cash-out procedures after this and a few other things,' Wrethman said.

'I'm sure,' Morris replied. He took out his pad and noted down pertinent points.

'We had a strange case. Right at the end—when most of the team were already leaving in fact,' Wrethman mentioned.

'What was that?' enquired Morris.

'Well, one of the tables which got slaughtered had three guys playing there who fitted the cheating pattern. Out of the blue, one of them started insulting the dealer. Security took them away. Then they were all apologetic—gave a large tip and left. If we had known at that time—we could have maybe caught a team for you.'

'Why did they start insulting the dealer? That would only bring attention to themselves. That doesn't make sense at all. When we go upstairs, I think I'll look at that footage first, if you don't mind,' said Morris keenly.

'No problem. What else to add? Well, as you probably know, we have no registration here. People can walk off the street and play.'

Morris confirmed he was aware.

'So, no names for you, I'm afraid. You'll see from the footage that they look European, Mediterranean types. Well tanned, most of them, and some look quite similar to others—possible cousins, maybe brothers. Anyway, as normal, the report will be sent, a disc prepared, and any decent photos we can muster up will be emailed around the world. That's about all I can offer you at the moment,' Wrethman concluded.

'OK—that's great. Some more possibilities there. Let's go and look at this footage. Could I see the one where they insulted the dealer first? Very strange that . . .'

They moved through a few corridors and climbed up a couple of levels before they reached the Surveillance office. On entering, Morris immediately saw the panicked activity that was taking place. He had expected it, and it duly reminded him of the pain he had felt a couple of weeks ago.

'Come into my new office,' Wrethman gestured. 'It's less frantic, and we can watch the footage there. Right. Let me go through the report to find that incident . . . right . . . here it is. "AR 43. 21:20. Customer rude to dealer".' He entered the time and date on the digital playback. 'OK, here we go. Pull up a chair.'

Morris did so and started to watch. He was bemused by what he saw, but he felt it was important nevertheless.

'The dealer said nothing. Why the hell is he drawing attention to the team when he is cheating at the table?' he said, shaking his head. 'This was just the time that they were all leaving—right?'

'Yep.'

'So, was he trying to get the whole team caught? No one approaches them or tries to help them get out of their apparent predicament. That could have been pre-arranged though. Any shit and you are in it for yourself.'

Then he saw Rossini's hand being raised suddenly. Morris leant forward intently.

'That's a signal—definite!'

'Definitely looks fake to me,' agreed Wrethman.

'So, next question: Why did he make a signal just after causing a commotion at the table?'

'Another distraction?' offered Wrethman.

'Possible, but it wasn't needed. They were already on their way out, and it was obvious that they had not been detected. The answer is there somewhere, but I can't get it—shit! I'll maybe look at that again later,' he said. 'OK, let's see some of the cheat footage.' As it was played, he was immediately struck by something. 'It's like watching the stuff in Greece all over again. The moves are almost identical and the skill level just as high. The positioning—it reminds me of the old cheat teams, but done quicker than the likes of Starcey or Capone.' Capone again. Capone . . .

'Where the hell did this team train? One thing I think I can say I'm pretty sure of now. It's all one group and they have all trained together somewhere. Can't say how big the final group will prove to be, but Greece was Team Number 1, and this looks like the second team. So far, I haven't recognized a single one of this team as being the same as the Greek mob. I believe they are Italian and that our old friend Capone is connected in some way—probably trained them. Bloody strange case, all right . . .'

By lunchtime, he had watched most of the footage, and by then, he wasn't learning anything more.

'So they used runners to cash in constantly. They must have known that the cashiers wouldn't ask any questions when they did so. They seemed to know when the place would be busiest—with the lottery draw. Safe to conclude that they had scouted the place beforehand. Same as in Greece. They knew what they were doing. They constantly cash in, so that if they are rumbled, they can at least escape with cash rather than holding chips, which they might or might not be able to cash in afterwards. Skillful, well trained, and organised, I'd admire them if I didn't hate cheats so much,' Morris said.

A supervisor knocked on the door and handed Wrethman what Morris guessed was the final report and a disc with all the footage.

Wrethman opened it up before handing it to Morris.

'Final loss to the company, 1.6 million dollars. What they stole minus their buy-ins. Bad . . . bad. Anyway, that's your copy and footage. You can sign for it on the way out.'

'It's bad, but it's the potential the big guys are worried about. It's like a team of bank robbers who have figured out how to rob a bank and the bank owners have no idea how to stop it, save closing the banks, which they obviously do not want to do. I'm sure the big guys would be happy enough to settle for a couple of million loss if they knew that there would be no more Blitzkriegs. Mind you, I'm not so sure about Harrison. My boss, Cain, told me that when he heard about this place getting hit, he took it very seriously and way too personally.'

'I must admit I feel I would kill them if I had a chance right now,' Wrethman said ruefully.

'That's because they made your casino look bad and your job could have been lost—natural enough feeling for a day or two. I felt the same. But Cain said Harrison looked totally nuts. Between me and you all this, by the way, that's why I was asking if you knew him.'

'Think I'll keep my head down if he ever does deem to visit our place,' Wrethman concluded, raising his substantial eyebrows slightly.

'OK, then, Mr. Wrethman, pleasure meeting you. Looks like I may be off to Singapore later today. Looking forward to seeing it again—an amazing place. Biggest casinos in the world. Started of with nearly all punto tables, but now there are more than 100 roulette tables in each of the five casinos.' He turned his head and looked at Wrethman. 'Would they dare . . . ?'

The South African police soon established that the passports found in the hand luggage of the three dead men were fake. They had contacted the relevant authorities in Italy and the names had drawn a blank. They had guessed that they were possibly dealing with a mafia group, until word came through via the injured Roberts that the 'Italian bastards' had been involved in cheating and a shoot-out at a casino in Port Elizabeth. They had also found a chip from the International Casino in Durban, suggesting that they had been there possibly recently. One of the officers thought of contacting the International to see if they had been involved in any criminal activities there. When he phoned, the casino had not been very helpful at first, until it was mentioned that the dead bodies were more than likely Italians.

Eventually, the officer was put through to Wrethman, who confirmed that the casino had been subject to an Italian cheat team, without giving out further details for the moment. Wrethman felt that the chances of these Italians being part of the Blitzkrieg group were remote, to say the least, but still was disappointed to learn that the passports found were fake. He was not able to help with the names, as they had none, and asked the officer if he could send photocopies of the fake passports and he would see if he could match up the dead bodies with the cheats. He told the officer that if he did discover any names of the cheats, he would be the first to know.

The officer said he would transfer the images via email within a few hours as he had other stuff to attend to and thanked Wrethman for his cooperation.

'How did they die?' asked Wrethman.

'Taxi crash on their way to Cape Town, judging by the texts the taxi driver had sent to his wife.'

'Poor guys,' muttered Wrethman.

'Don't be too sorry for them,' came the officer's rather harsh reply. 'They shot a security guard in the casino at Port Elizabeth—He's in critical condition. The casino manager is hurt too. He was chasing them, but he's going to be fine.'

'A shoot-out at a casino—What, were they robbing the place?' said Wrethman, getting more interested by the second.

'No. Roberts, the injured manager, said they had been caught cheating and had been taken into the security office. That's where the shooting took place. One of the Italians grabbed a gun from the safe—stupid that—and the brave security guy jumped him. Must have thought it was his duty or something. Daft bastard.'

'Bloody hell!' said Wrethman. 'Dramatic stuff,' even though he had been in South Africa for long enough to know how often that sort of thing happened in casinos in the country.

After the call had finished, Wrethman thought for a few moments and then picked up the phone to contact Harrison, who had asked him to keep him informed of any developments. There was no answer. Unsure what to do and knowing that Morris could be on his way to Singapore at any moment, he found the business card that Morris had given him and phoned him instead.

Morris was lying in his hotel room on the bed studying the notes that he had laid out on front of him. He answered the phone.

'Sam Morris?'

'Yes.'

'Hello there. It's Mr. Wrethman—we met this morning.'

'Of course. How's it going?'

'Well, as a matter of fact, it could be going well. I just got some interesting news. Three Italians were killed in Port Elizabeth yesterday. They had a chip from our casino, and they had been caught cheating on roulette at a casino in the town.'

'They weren't killed for cheating?' said Morris incredulously.

'No, no, they escaped after shooting a guard and then were killed when their taxi crashed. The police are going to send me photocopies of their passports. The officer told me the passports were fake, but I reckon it is probably one group of the Blitzkrieg team, but can't think what they would be doing in Port Elizabeth. I would have thought they would have all returned to their base country by now. Too risky to hang around.'

'I can—running away. I'm sure you'll find that the photos in the passports match the three guys who attracted attention to themselves by insulting the dealer. Look, thanks, Jeff. I've got your card. Will you be there for the rest of the day? I've got to make some calls quickly.' On hearing an affirmative response, Morris ended the call and immediately called Cain.

'Where are you?' he asked.

'In my room,' Cain replied.

'Stay there. I'll be there in a minute.'

A moment later, he entered Cain's room.

'OK, we are getting somewhere,' Morris announced.

'Aha!' replied Cain, interested and sitting upright from his bed. 'What've you got?'

Morris filled him in with all the latest developments. He was sure that the guys now lying dead in Port Elizabeth had been trying to separate themselves from the team, presumably to keep some or all of the money that they had stolen from the International. He had racked his brains, but it was the only explanation that sat with all the facts. This was backed up by the knowledge that rather than being back in or on their way to Italy, they had been found elsewhere in South Africa. They had obviously decided on solo careers. 'Greed again,' he thought. He came across it every day. Never underestimate the power of greed as motivation. He was sure when he checked that they would be the only cheat team that was in that casino in Port Elizabeth.

'So it looks like we have located part of the team, but since they were dead, it doesn't look like being a great help,' Cain commented. 'But you never know. We might get something. Maybe fingerprints or DNA analysis can lead to us finding their real identity.'

Morris and Cain decided that a talk with Roberts could be helpful, at the very least to discover how they had been caught. Since he was still due to go to Singapore, Morris asked Cain if he would mind going down, saying with a smile, 'You can use my private jet if you like. I'll drop you off on my way to Singapore.'

'I'll try and get Harrison on the phone and arrange it,' said Cain.

'You could be there and back in a few hours. Maybe you'll get to see some of the footage too. When are you flying home?'

'Tomorrow night. Is going to Singapore so urgent?'

'Yes, I need to meet up with Campbell and find out how they can help us with all the high-tech stuff they have out there. Also, if you think about it, if they are going to hit again, Singapore or Macau would be near the top of the list. Apparently, they are mobbed with tens of thousands of people per day, and the hundreds of tables are jam-packed with customers—perfect for our guys. Singapore's three new places will have relatively inexperienced staff too, especially the one that's just opened. It wouldn't surprise me if they had some people out there right now casing the joint.'

# Chapter 13

Morris was right in his half-joking presumption, although the timing was a day or two off. The team were back in Tolo, and Capone's thoughts were already turning to the next possible hit. Europe had been done and now Africa, and although there was no particular reason why they could not have visited another African casino, or indeed another European venue, thoughts had been turning towards Asia, and Singapore in particular. Macau he had dismissed quickly. It was a town that really had only casinos. He didn't feel the team could arrive and mingle without drawing attention to themselves, false passports or not. Singapore, from what he had read and seen on the Internet, was a cosmopolitan town with millions of people passing through every year. Lorenzo had also told him something he found very interesting and made the country even more attractive as a target. Lorenzo said he had been told by an Italian Surveillance director that the newest casino in Singapore, the Seven Winds, had no audio feedback on the roulette tables. There was a rumour that this was done to cut costs when the budget for building the casinos had been exceeded. Capone knew that being able to hear live and playback audio was an absolute necessity when confirming roulette cheat moves. Most surveillance roulette cameras around the world zoomed in fairly close to the roulette tables, so they could cover as much as possible to help them see the chips placed on the table. By doing so, normally at least half the roulette wheel would not be in the default camera position—normally termed 'Shot 1'. And because of this, when viewing a roulette table, sometimes the ball would drop in the half of the wheel not covered by the camera. In such cases, having the back-up audio system, where one could hear the ball actually dropping, making the identifiable metallic sound as the ball bounced around the number rims—was vital for Surveillance departments.

In Singapore and especially as news had filtered through of the Blitzkrieg attacks, the Surveillance heads of the new place had been panicking. They had good well-paid jobs there, and they could see all that disappearing if their casinos got whacked under their watch. They had had several meetings with the General Manager and even pleaded with the owners when they occasionally bumped into one of them, but the situation had still not been resolved. Two of the four big owners,

Pullman and Harrison, had put most of their money into the Seven Winds and were well aware of the danger and of the expense of fitting the audio systems—estimated at twenty million in costs and lost income. The two million lost in Durban was fairly small in comparison. They wanted these cheats caught badly. Without their threat, they could get by with an occasional scam costing a few thousand dollars. Lorenzo had heard these comments at the conference and passed it on to Capone. Singapore was looking good for a visit, and as soon as possible, before they figured this audio problem out. Capone had discussed the target with his brother, but because of the relative recent openings of the casinos there, he admitted that he had never tried his hand there.

'A word of warning though, if you are caught, you will be going to jail for a long time. The authorities in Singapore don't mess about. Capital punishment still exists, and there are tough laws for all sorts of things, from spitting gum on the floor to crossing the road in the wrong place. But I see the attractions of it, as you say. No audio would really help the team. Get the scouts out quickly to this new place, and see what they can come up with. Hard to believe, but the sources of your information sound genuine enough,' Ernesto said.

'So you think it's risky but too good an opportunity to miss?' asked the mayor.

'You could really hit them. Also, the dealers will all be Asian, and with most, a few years' experience—should be easy pickings. Surveillance could be another matter. They could have some of the world's best guys out there. You'll have to be careful in that regard.'

'We will. Don't worry about that. Look, I'll call a town meeting. This should be our last, but wouldn't it be great to just go on . . . !'

Ernesto Capone laughed. 'I always told you, you should come over to the other side. You were too honest, staying as a casino manager while I was away having a great time all around the world. Admit it—the excitement is fantastic.'

Marco could only nod in agreement.

'But in the end, I have to do what is best for the town, and we would get caught eventually. We have enough now to open the casino again or the bottling plant, and we'll discuss that at the meeting. Another hit would set us up with a nice retirement fund for the town and to help us if the business we do decide to open has a bad period.'

'I agree,' replied Ernesto. 'But one more only. What will I do though—when we stop?'

'You're a born cheat—you'll never stop,' said the mayor with a smile. 'If you do, come back and live here in Tolo. Be the casino manager if we reopen, but no stealing, right?!'

'Sounds good to me. It would be nice to work on the other side, trying to catch the cheats. It takes one to know one, as they say!'

'Right, sounds like the future is getting nicely mapped out now. You get the teams brushed up on their skills. They are itching to go, and they want to try and get beyond the two-million mark,' the mayor said.

'That will depend on what the scouts report—how busy the place is, the table minimums, how long we can operate, etc., but I imagine that such an amount would be possible,' said Ernesto.

'Time for a coffee for me,' Marco said, heading for the door. He stopped suddenly. 'No word from Paulo and the others yet? I thought even if they had been arrested, they would have been able to at least phone home.'

'No, nothing at all,' replied his brother.

'Their parents are getting worried now. They are coming to my office every day,' said Marco. 'I'm worried they have tied them in with the rest of the team and are trying to get information from them. They, like everyone, were instructed to deny everything—admit to putting on a few late bets and that's it. There is absolutely no way they can specifically associate them with us. They should be OK. Still angry that they got caught. I thought they were right up there as one of our top teams. Guess it was bound to happen one day . . .'

'What if they did talk and mentioned Tolo? A little visit to our town would soon confirm that the teams are all from here,' Ernesto said.

'In the end, I can't guarantee it, but would they ask "Which town do you come from?"?—Don't think so. They would ask who their associates were, not which town they lived in. Can't see anybody figuring that we all come from the same town—country maybe. If any questions were ever asked, everyone knows what to say. On this date, Nic was working in the bakery as usual, and Tony was serving drinks at the café as he does every day. That photograph does look a little like him, but I assure you he was here on that day! What can they do in the end?'

'Kill us all!' Ernesto exclaimed. 'Remember Argentina? Lupi was murdered after he was caught.'

'Ba!' said Marco. 'Kill us all. Where would that get them—criminal charges, jail. Their casinos would be closed down. They could apply a bit of heat, but contrary to what people believe, they don't go around killing people. Lupi was a one-off. It was more likely he was mugged than killed by the owners.'

'Then maybe they could get us arrested,' Ernesto insisted.

'Possibly they could try. Do they have exact evidence? I saw the footage in Durban, remember? You know the bets went on late, but you can't prove it. The move is always blocked out by hands, arms, and the like. Would be very hard to get us on that. No, they would need hard evidence—confessions, etc. Anyway, enough! I can't see how they will pinpoint the town. Come with me for a coffee and relax, man. Trust me, everything is going to be fine. Singapore, then retirement, here we come . . .'

In South Africa, Cain had got through to Harrison and arranged first to see Roberts at the hospital and then to go to see the footage of the cheat moves and the team's capture. It was decided that Cain would be dropped of in Port Elizabeth, and Morris would head on to Singapore. Morris had suggested staying with Cain, but Harrison insisted they wanted him in Singapore as soon as possible. He was bemused at the absolute urgency but agreed and, in any case, trusted Cain to glean the relevant information. They said their thanks to the hotel staff, left a decent tip, and headed off to the airport.

On reaching Port Elizabeth, Cain wished Morris luck and unusually shook his hand.

'We're getting there, Sam—I can feel it. I'll phone you as soon as I'm done here. Should be roughly the time you arrive in Singapore. What's the hotel you are staying in?'

Morris looked down at his file, which he had been given at Durban.

'The Mandarin—supposed to be top notch. Doubt I'll be spending much time there though. Got work to do, old chap.'

'Try and relax a bit too. I hear there are some varied forms of entertainment out there, if you know what I mean.'

'Aye, the famous Boggie Street, if it still exists. I'll be keeping well away from there. Might have a few beers with the Surveillance guys, looking forward to that. Good top American guys, honest and hard working.'

'Right. I'm off. See you, mate,' and with that, Cain headed down the steps.

Soon the private plane was arcing into the night sky, Singapore bound. Morris looked out of the window for a while and then found himself nodding off.

Cain went straight to the hospital and, after a few directions, located Roberts, who was lying in bed watching Liverpool against Manchester United in a private ward.

'Mr. Roberts,' he said, approaching the bed. He did not offer his hand, since both of Roberts's arms were obviously broken.

'You'll be the guy who's come to talk with me. My boss said to tell you all you need to know. I've already talked to the police, but what do you want to know?'

'First things first. How are you doing? You look in a bit of a bad way.'

'I'll be OK. If the casino docks me for being sick, I won't be!'

'I'm sure you'll be OK,' said Cain smiling. 'Can you just tell me what happened? By the way, good work! I believe it was you who first noticed them? Do you know these guys are part of a large team going around the world and you were the first to catch them? Well done . . .'

'Think I'll get thanks for it? Story of my life,' Roberts said sourly.

'A bit pissed off, this guy,' thought Cain. Mind you, he would need a temper to get on a bike with a gun and chase a taxi.

'Right, I was suspicious from the start,' began Roberts. 'Body language and the fact that they appeared Mediterranean. They were just a little too smug, and we don't actually get too may tourists in our place. Anyway, we watched them and caught them soon after. Got good footage from a rover, by the way, which I haven't seen yet, of course, but I was told you are going to look at it later?'

'Right after this, I will,' confirmed Cain.

'Well, we caught the guys and took them in the office. Next is a bit embarrassing. I got a bit excited and tried to play the strong guy. Also, I have issues with Italians—one of them ran off with my wife.'

'Bastards!' Cain said, shaking his head in agreed disapproval.

'Bloody right,' continued Roberts, sensing the genuine sympathy in Cain's voice. 'Anyway, we had called the police, more as a scare tactic, really. Doubt the casino would have gone to the trouble of prosecuting them for the amount they had taken by the time they were caught. So, they got spooked, and one of the guys grabbed a gun from the gun safe in the security office and started waving it about. He looked as scared as everyone else . . .'

'What were you doing keeping guns in the security safe?' said Cain.

'Are you serious?' replied Roberts with a snort. 'Each night, more than twenty guns are handed in by the customers before they come in. We keep them in the safe and give them back when they leave. Because so many come in and out, we leave the safe open. Maybe we won't in future. Anyway, this terrified young Italian bastard was waving the gun about, and before I could stop him, Jan, the security guy, jumped for him—must have thought it was his duty—or maybe he didn't like Italians either. Anyway, he got bloody shot. Then, they grabbed their stuff from the table and ran out.

'Then?' said Cain, utterly engrossed in the story, although he had already been updated on most of what had transpired.

'I just lost it totally,' Roberts continued. 'You see, I was in a robbery before and had a gun placed to my head. I thought that was it . . . Anyway, after a few seconds of shaking, I just thought no bastard is going to do that to me. I took a gun from the safe, called Security to attend to Jan, and ran into the car park and started chasing them in my bike. I just saw them get in a taxi. I was ready to kill them all. Jesus, I wasn't even thinking of anything else. Don't know, it seemed a chance to escape this shitty life here in this shitty backwater. Anyway, as I said, I was totally gone. I fired a shot, missed the taxi completely, and I think I must have hit some rocks. The taxi smashed into the rocks, and then a huge rockfall happened. I fell off the bike and luckily landed in some soft ground. The police thankfully came and got an ambulance for me. That's about it. I feel sorry for the driver. The police told me he was a genuine taxi driver, not one of the bastard cheats or anything.'

'Exciting stuff—bloody hell! Look, did they say anything at all about where they had come from, who their friends were, when you interviewed them? Did you hear any names mentioned?'

'Can't think of anything. They were scared all right, especially one of the young ones, when I started waving the baseball bat around.'

'Baseball bat?'

'To scare them, of course. I'd seen it in a film about Al Capone, where he was in a meeting and suddenly produced this bat and smashed it into a guy's head, who had been ripping him off. Bloody great! I wasn't going to hit the bastards, just wanted to scare them like hell. It's not a nice feeling to be that scared. I wanted to let them know what it is like.'

'This guy's in a bad way,' thought Cain with some sadness. 'Seen too much . . . too much bad stuff.'

'OK, then . . . I'll let you rest,' he said. 'You're from Liverpool, right?'

'Yeah and we're losing one–nil,' Roberts replied, looking at the television.

'Would you fancy coming home to the United Kingdom? Could get you a good job. Pit boss or higher at a nice, quiet casino I partly own—decent money—get to see Liverpool live!'

Roberts's eyes opened wide. 'My god, could you do that? Could you and would you really do that for me?'

Cain was amazed to see that tears were in Roberts's eyes. He could only hazard a guess at the things this guy had gone through.

'Fucking right, man—you're a hero, man! You deserve it. Get yourself fit and give me a call.' He left a card by the bedside. 'And don't worry. I never go back on a promise.'

Just at that moment, Liverpool equalised. Roberts roared in delight and tried to raise himself from his bed. He hadn't been so happy in twenty years.

As he left the ward and headed to the car that would take him to the casino, Cain became contemplative. He had gone in there expecting either a macho type or a madman—but Roberts had been neither, just a bloke whose whole life came to focus on a single moment and had acted as he saw fit.

By the time he had entered the Surveillance office of the Reef Casino, he had regained his focus. The office was alive with activity. He met the security boss, Du Plessis, and then the Surveillance manager, Smith, who said, 'Mr. Cain, very pleased to meet you. Well, it's all kicking off here. We are getting calls and e-mails from all over the world. The photos we sent of the cheats we got from the cameras were pretty good—good enough anyway for them to be recognised in Durban, and once that happened, we have been inundated with information requests.

'The owner of this place, Mr. Smuts, tells me that he has been contacted by the big guys themselves and made it clear that we should cooperate with you fully, and I'm more than glad if we can help. Just got a call from a guy in Singapore who is very interested in the whole case—seems to know a lot too. Told me to give you one of the footage discs personally. Anyway, do you want to see the moves? Old Roberts caught them nearly straight away. Good bloke. I told the owners they shouldn't get rid of him. Went a bit daft after that robbery, but you can't beat experience.'

'That's right,' agreed Cain. 'I've just met him at the hospital. He'll be fine. I guess you know the Blitzkrieg group thing. We have been trying to locate and stop the bastards, so anything can help. OK, you have no names. At all?'

'Right. Update there. One of our team had the good idea of going up to the bar and asking the girls if any of them had heard any names. We traced their movements since they entered, and they headed for the bar first, had quite a few beers actually.'

'Interesting,' thought Cain, concluding this seemed to back up Morris's theory of a renegade group. Not professional—drinking before the moves, never done normally.

'One of the girls said she thought she heard the name Paul or something similar, but that's all. We listened to the audio at the table where they were playing, but they never referred to each other by name. No audio in the Security office, of course.'

120

'Paul, well, that could be something. Did the police say if one of the passports had that as a first name?' Cain asked.

'No,' said Smith. 'So a good chance he slipped up and that is or was his real name.'

'Good, I agree,' said Cain. 'Mind you, a lot of Pauls around.'

Cain couldn't resist and asked to see the Security office footage first. It was both exciting and scary to watch.

'Wow,' he said after. 'Dramatic stuff. How's the security guy?'

'He'll be OK apparently. Bullet in the side of the stomach—he should be out of hospital in a week,' Smith said.

Cain made no comment on Robert's behaviour, but he could see by the look on Smith's face that he had expected him to do so. Cain imagined for a moment some Italians walking into a quiet casino in Liverpool and being assailed by a bat-waving madman who he had just given a job too. He quickly pushed it out his mind. He then watched the footage of the cheat moves.

As in Greece and Durban, the table cameras could not establish a definite past-post attempt, but when the table footage was shown in unison with the rover camera from behind the table, it was clear that the bet had been placed after the ball had dropped.

'Good—excellent stuff. That would be enough to convict at least the past poster at the table—shame he's dead . . .'

'The one doing the actual past posting is the guy who was called Paul, according to the waitress who heard the name. She had a look at the footage this morning,' Smith said.

'That's good too. I'm sure we'll get the rest of the group in the end, but it's taking a while. But we can now link a definite and proven cheat move with these three who were in Durban at the same time as the rest of the cheat team. In many people's eyes—although I'm not sure about the legal guys—that's sufficient proof to act on them,' Cain surmised.

'What will they do? From what I gather, there must be about 200 cheats involved,' Byrne asked.

'Not quite as many as that, we think, but well over 100. We'll try and get the money back, maybe try and prosecute, but the main thing is to make sure they never do it again. They have to be given a very serious warning. Let's put it that way.'

'So the rest of the team are probably back in Italy and will eventually turn up somewhere else?' Smith suggested.

'That seems likely at the moment, unless we track them down first,' Cain replied.

They discussed the scam team a little longer, had a brief social discussion, and then headed for a local hotel to get a beer and some dinner. It had been quite a day or two for Cain. He felt he just needed a good sleep to get back to his usual self. In the morning, he thought he would go the police station and see if they could update him with any more information. He had two beers, a large malt, a steak, and then headed to his room.

He woke just after 07.00 and had breakfast and then headed to the police station. He was not sure if they would cooperate, and indeed, it took one or two verifying calls before they did so.

'Mr. Cain, come in,' said the chief officer at the station, opening a file, once he was satisfied that he could discuss details of the case with Cain. 'What can I do for you? The three dead bodies have still not been identified. You know the passports were fake—although of good quality—definitely fake. We have, of course, informed the Italian embassy, who have taken custody of them until they can be identified. At the moment, we do not know for sure that they are Italian, but we found a couple of receipts in their pockets for Italian bars, etc., and this seemed to satisfy the embassy.'

'Could I have a look?' said Cain, pretending to be calm.

'Only photocopies here. Originals are with the embassy. Photocopier needs a bit of ink . . .' The officer handed over the papers.

'Damn it! They are a bit smudged,' said Cain, squirming at the paper, although he consoled himself with the knowledge that, if necessary, he could get hold of the originals.

'Cigarettes from Milan Airport,' he brought out a pad and started making notes as he managed to decipher one of the receipts. There were another two or three from various shops at the airport, but a few more from a supermarket somewhere else, which definitely did not look like Milan. It was too smudged.

'I'll have to contact the embassy.' He tried to make photocopies of the photocopies, but it was useless. The police wouldn't let him take them even for a few moments to find a good copier elsewhere in the town.

'All the rest of the stuff is with the embassy now. Quite a bit of money, one or two cash chips from Durban, which you know about. Their suitcases, of course . . .' continued the officer.

'Anything in them?'

'Just clothes and a few souvenir gifts. No address book, if that's what you were hoping for. No credit cards or any potential source of real identity found anywhere— bad luck!'

'So just the chance of a receipt that might not be from the airport.' It was something maybe. Anything might help. 'Do you think the taxi driver knew them in any way?'

'No, for sure. They just got into his taxi at Durban Bus Station, and they were headed for Cape Town.'

'Bus station?' echoed Cain. 'Strange. How did you know they were going to Cape Town anyway? Did he call in to the controller?'

'Call in? No, he was an independent. He didn't need to inform anyone of his fares. No, the Italians mentioned in the security office that they were headed there according to the Security boss at the Reef.'

'That's not proof. They could have been lying and probably were,' said Cain, frustrated.

'Ah! But the driver sent a text to his wife when he was waiting outside the casino. Here, have a look. His mobile has not been collected yet.' He handed the phone to Cain, who saw there were two or three messages sent to his wife at approximately the same time: 'Of to C.T. cu asap. By for boy somthng'.

The second message read: 'Give D a XX'.

There was a message to a friend arranging a booze-up when he got back to Durban. He was just going to hand it back when he saw the final message that Neels Van den Berg would ever send. 'Whr z Tolo?'

Cain calmed himself, asked to see the receipts again, and studied the one that had interested him as nonchalantly as he could. Now that he had a hint, it seemed clear. 'Lidl Supermarket—Tolo'.

Cain thanked the captain as he walked out of the station trying to appear as calm as possible.

'Oh yes, yes, yes!' he said. He had heard of Tolo too. He had reached for his mobile as he walked out of the station, but put it back in his pocket. 'Think before you leap,' he said to himself.

Tolo, the town of the poussettisti. It was all making some sense now. Looked like old timers had passed their trade to the next generation. Fed up with being recognised and barred in nearly every casino they walked into, they were introducing new, young, and unknown faces, but with new tactics too. Cain figured that they must have some sort of cheat training school, and they would get a cut of the profits. He shook his head in bemusement. 'Would this cheat training school still be open? How would they locate it, and how should they approach it?' He was thinking hard as he packed and headed to the airport to wait for his plane home. He had helped locate the source, and he believed his part in the investigation was more or less complete. He had resisted the urge to phone anyone, though. He knew once he did, things would happen quickly, and he wanted to make sure things were done properly. For one thing, he did not trust Arron. The mad look he had seen on his face made Roberts's Security office tantrum look mild in comparison. He determined that he would call only Morris and trust him not to mention it to anyone for the moment. Then he started to think of maybe having a look at Tolo himself. The more he thought about it, the more it appealed to him.

# Chapter 14

Morris was picked up at the airport in a sleek Mercedes, with Campbell waiting in the back seat with a file and a pile of papers. They knew each other, but Morris could see that he was showing signs of strain and looked exhausted. He looked at Morris and said, after the briefest of welcomes, 'What's the latest? Any more on that Port Elizabeth raid?' His thick grey hair made him look considerably older than he was. He had looked a lot younger when Morris had last met him a few years ago.

'Well . . . don't know what your guys have told you . . . but I think we are slowly getting somewhere. We are 90 per cent sure that three of the team involved in the Durban International hit were killed in a crash after hitting the Reef casino in Port Elizabeth—where they were actually caught cheating before escaping.'

'Identities—useless anyway?'

'Yeah, just their passport names, which will be false. My friend Cain has travelled down to meet the guy who caught them, look at the footage, and also hopefully get some information from the police. I expect he'll contact me soon. But what we have is that we think there is some sort of training school going on in Italy somewhere, which if it proves to be the case, would be great, since, if we find the location, we would have a good chance of getting the whole team, or a good few of them anyway.'

'Yes, that's good,' agreed Campbell. 'The money isn't that important. The bosses are just worried about the chance of another hit, and they are particularly concerned that they might pay a visit here.'

'What about the two million, from the International and of course Cain's Greek casino?'

'Of course, if we can get it all back, well and good, but it's not a major concern. Look, they just don't want them hitting another casino and especially here in Singapore.'

'You said that a second ago. Why? What's up?'

'Maybe you know, and if you don't, don't go around spreading the news—OK?'

'What?' urged Morris.

Campbell looked uncomfortable, but eventually said, 'Harrison's and Pullman's casino here does not have audio coverage on the roulette tables.' He said it slowly, looking directly at Morris.

Morris was staring at him closely, the implications spinning around his head as the fact sunk in.

'Shit! And I didn't know . . . I see the worry. Past posters on tables with no audio, very dangerous indeed. So what are they going to do? Put audio in or . . . ?'

'Too expensive—or rather the disruption caused would result in a loss of income estimated at twenty to thirty million,' Campbell replied tersely. 'We are getting tens of thousands of people every day through our doors, and they are losing millions. To get all the cables in and all the other work, connecting it up with surveillance would take a week. They are trying to find a solution, but . . .'

'The Italians wouldn't necessarily know about the lack of audio though, would they?' offered Morris.

'Agreed, not necessarily. But imagine you were Pullman or Harrison. Would you feel comfortable knowing that an efficient cheat team may have found out that there is no audio? You'd be shitting yourself.'

'Yes, I see. What a situation! So you want these guys out of the way pronto?' Morris said, nodding.

'I have to tell you it could get nasty. These guys are ruthless and have plenty of connections.'

Morris again failed to see the implications of ignoring these remarks, which would come back so clearly to him later.

'Well, as I said, we are homing in. If Cain hasn't come up with something, it might delay us, but I'm sure we will get there fairly soon.'

'You might be wondering why you have been called all the way out here?' Campbell asked.

'The thought had crossed my mind?' replied Morris. 'You have some high-tech stuff that might help, I hear.'

'I've got a pass for you for the Surveillance office. I say Surveillance office, but it's so intertwined with the Singapore police that we have access to so much more. It's like getting the answers to questions you never thought Surveillance had access to: flight lists, hotel bookings, criminal lists, DNA records, full rap sheets, and the like. You'll be amazed. A customer comes in, and ten minutes after registering, we have absolutely everything on him. It's a brilliant surveillance concept—makes our job a lot easier too. We have a great record of catching the bad guys.'

'Yes . . . yes. I can see that would be great. Can we use these databases to try and track down the team?'

'That is why you are here,' Campbell said. 'We want you to go through all the details of the two incidents, enter all the data and any requests that you would normally be able to obtain via the police, and we'll see what we can come up with. So tomorrow, spend as long as you want thinking of the questions you would like to ask, and whenever you are ready, I'll arrange access to the police computers. I have to get back to the office. The driver will drop you off at the hotel. If you want to go out, there is a bar round the corner on the left as you go out called the Singapore Sling—good band there, 'Tanya' or something? Lots of girls there and a few who aren't. Just watch out for large Adam's apples and gravelly voices . . .' He smiled for the first time.

'Thanks for the warning!' Morris laughed, a bit shocked.

He was dropped of at the Mandarin, receiving Campbell's business card as he opened the car door. Before he closed it, he leant down and said, 'You look a bit done in yourself. How about a pint in an hour at that bar you described? After the flight, don't think I'm at my best for thinking. Get a couple of beers, some dinner, and bed . . .'

'Don't trust yourself, eh!' said Campbell. He looked at his watch. 'Bugger it. It's been all work for the last few days. A couple only, mind you, and I'm not talking girls . . .'

'OK, see you there,' replied Morris. He had noticed a visible easing of the strain on Campbell as he had been able to talk about his problems with another person.

The Mandarin was a top class hotel. 'Immaculate' was the word that most came to mind as he walked towards Reception. As he approached, the receptionist looked up, quickly down, and then raised her head smiling.

'Mr. Morris, welcome to the Mandarin and Singapore!'

'What a smile!' thought Morris. He thought of asking how she had known his name, but let it go. He checked in and got the lift to the twelfth floor, declining the porter's offer, since he had little luggage.

'Lovely,' he said, scanning the room as he entered. One of life's pleasures, a beautiful hotel room when you are exhausted. He placed his luggage on the bed and had a quick shower. He then sat on the bed in his bathrobe and brought out his files and paperwork. Despite what he had said to Campbell, he wanted to get some more ideas and to come up with some things to discuss in the bar later.

He had all the fake names of the Greek hit, but that was already known and would have been checked out. Any trace on Italian identity forgers? Could they check flight lists into Greece and South Africa on the days leading up to the hits? For all he knew, that too might have been done, but he would ask again. What else? Despite his fatigue, he felt his mind start to move up through the gears. He was thinking well now, all the possible questions and connections falling into place. He stopped for a few minutes, staring directly at the wall in front of him, and then he started to scribble furiously, and when he looked up at the clock on the wall, it was already the time he had arranged to meet Campbell. He phoned him and found Campbell was also running a few minutes late. They arranged to meet in a further ten minutes.

Morris got dressed. He wore a light shirt—he had felt the humidity earlier—and got directions for the bar from the same receptionist, finding it easily enough. Outside, there were at least a hundred women. All looked slim and attractive. Several approached him, making their intentions obvious. He wondered how they could be so open in a country with so many restrictions as Singapore. 'Brings a lot of tourists in,' he concluded, entering the bar and finding a seat in the corner.

The band was playing. The singer looked particularly gaunt but had a strong voice, and the other two members of the band were happy to let him be the centre of attention. He had been lucky to find a seat, as the place was nearly full. All the women inside were seated and all had a large beer in front of them, which they sipped very occasionally. Several of the girls tried to catch his eye, but none approached. 'Different rules inside,' he concluded.

Campbell entered and Morris waved him over and then went to the bar to get a couple of beers.

'Some place,' he mentioned to Campbell. 'Your local, is it?' he said with a quizzical glance.

'Never been here before,' Campbell replied with a hint of sarcasm. 'What do you think of her?' he said pointing to a tall, slim woman with long hair reaching down to her navel.

'Very pretty,' Morris replied. 'They all are.'

'She's a bloke actually. Amazing! Don't get drunk and make a mistake of a lifetime.'

'You're kidding! I thought some bloke dressed up would stand out a mile. Jesus!'

'Mostly you find them down Boggie Street, but some of the higher class ones come here. He's a regular. Otherwise, I wouldn't have guessed either. Sometimes you see him being approached by a bloke who has been egged on by his mates, who you can see sniggering in the corner as their pal tries to get laid. They often let them go as well, relishing the conversation the next day with the "victim".'

'You'd never live it down,' laughed Morris.

They talked for a while and then Morris straightened up and reached into his shirt pocket and produced the list of questions he wanted answered. Campbell brought out a pair of dark-framed glasses and examined them closely.

He nodded. 'Very good. You're sharp all right. Did you really do this in the last couple of hours? Some of these we have gone through already. What's this one here, "a list of all casinos in Italy", "a list of casinos for sale," "a list of closed casinos"? What's all this about?'

'Well, I figured that, OK, there's obviously some sort of school in operation. Right. So where would they all be trained? If you were teaching or training one or two people, a room would do, but 100—200 and maybe more. You would need plenty of tables, and where better to find lots of tables than in a casino? Either in an empty one or to have access to an open one after hours or pre-opening. The first possibility sounds a lot more likely to be the case.'

'Yes, yes,' said Campbell, nodding vigorously. 'Totally logical, once you say it, but it hadn't crossed any of our minds. We'll run this through tomorrow, contact the Italian gaming authority, if necessary, but we can probably find it on the Internet.'

'World Casino Directory has a list of all the casinos in the world, but don't think they list closed casinos,' Morris said, shaking his head slightly.

'No, the Singapore regulatory authority are on the ball. We'll have a list by lunchtime. You could be on to something there. Time for another?'

'Wouldn't mind some food at some stage,' Morris replied. 'Any place you recommend?'

'Newton Circus, five minutes away. Fantastic and you can get a meal for the price of a beer here. One more and we'll get a cab.'

'Sure, sounds good.'

They finished their second beer while discussing the rest of the list supplied by Morris. The girls and 'girls' had given up on them—they could see they were not available for a 'long time' session, let alone a 'short time' one.

Newton Circus was a roundabout, the centre of which was filled with food stalls at night-time serving any sort of Asian food you could think of. They settled for a fish starter and chicken and rice to follow. They sat outside, Morris's thin shirt soaked through by the humidity and the heat coming from the ovens and grills. They ended up having another couple of beers as they discussed the case. They were both looking forward to meeting the Singapore police and hopefully getting some useful data from the computer searches.

Morris suddenly started feeling very tired and breathed out slowly. 'Wow, catching up with me, I'm afraid. I slept a little on the plane, but still . . .'

'I'll drop you off,' replied Campbell. 'Seven OK in the morning? That's what time I head in to work. Can you be outside the hotel at that time?'

'Yeah, that's fine. Right—better get some sleep,' he announced firmly, getting to his feet. Ten minutes later, he was back in his room and asleep in another five.

When he awoke at six, he felt pretty good, showered, and made a coffee, before heading down to the foyer just before seven. He had only been waiting for a couple of minutes when Campbell's car appeared.

'Morning. Feeling OK?' he said as Morris climbed in.

'Great. Was out like a light. Right, I'm looking forward to today. Should be interesting and hopefully we will get something out of it.'

Morris was impressed when they pulled up to the Seven Winds Casino, which was at the base of a huge hotel.

'Two thousand rooms,' Campbell said before Morris could ask the question. 'The hotel and casino were built in record time, although well over budget. It really is a fantastic place. We are all proud to work here. That's another reason that we don't want anything to happen that would embarrass us and the company.'

'Are you stationed here permanently?' asked Morris.

'Well, yes and no. Because of all the high technical equipment, being director of security, it makes sense that I'm here a lot of the time, but I do go around the other casinos to give them a check-out. But lately, I've been here more often than not.'

Campbell showed him the Surveillance Room, which was impressive enough, but when they entered the office marked 'Singapore Regulatory Control and Compliance', he was stunned by its size and manpower. It looked like there was enough staff to check out every single customer that came into the casino. It was not like a Surveillance room, with its stations and monitors—much more akin to a police station and far more people moving around rather than stuck to their seats.

'Who came up with this idea'? Morris asked in amazement.

'The government has been very closely involved in the whole hotel and casino project since the go-ahead was given to open casinos here. They established the Regulatory Authority, which sort of watches us to make sure we do everything by the book and pay the right amount of tax, treat the customers well, and protect them when necessary, and punish them also, if they do anything illegal.'

'Yeah, we had government supervision in Greece, but it was minor compared to this,' Morris replied.

'The Singaporeans are extremely efficient in nearly everything they do,' Campbell continued. 'Some of the sentences the courts have dished out for cheats or internal thefts have been very harsh indeed, and any incident leads to a prosecution— no walking out of the casino after a confession. Most of the better-known cheats came to realise that pretty quick, but we have had a lot of internal theft and collusion, which has surprised me, I must admit.'

'That will probably slow down once the Singaporeans realise they can't get away with it either,' Morris said.

'It has calmed down a bit in the last year, true. Let's find George Foong and get these questions answered.'

After asking a few people, they located Mr. Foong, the head of the authority, walking towards his office. He was thin and wiry and, with the way he had styled his hair along with the glasses he wore and his sideburns, looked like a sort of Asian version of Elvis.

'You must be Sam Morris,' he smiled, offering his hand. 'Donald told me about you. Do you have some questions for me and my staff to answer for you?'

They sat down in Foong's office and went through the questions, deciding on which ones were of the highest priority. Morris was keen to find out all he could about a possible casino being used by the team, convinced that he was on to something. After an hour or so, Foong had a priority list and stood up.

'Right. I'll need three hours max, OK?'

'That would be great,' Morris said. 'Thanks.'

Campbell turned to him.

'Come. I'll show you around the casino a bit, and then we can get some breakfast. There's a great place! Would you believe it's called "Warren's Buffet"! I think the owner was having a dig there!'

Morris was suitably impressed with the casino, not just the size, but by the way the tables and pits were set up, the amenities, and the friendly staff he encountered.

He met some of the Surveillance guys and went up to the top floor where the restaurant was with amazing expansive views over Singapore Harbour, which Campbell mentioned was one of the busiest in the world.

They had a leisurely breakfast and chatted about old colleagues and days gone by. Morris had expected to have received a call from Cain by then and thought of phoning him, but remembered the time difference. He would wait another few hours, when he could also update him on the news he got from the offices below.

At eleven thirty, Campbell took a call on his mobile and stood up.

'OK, let's go. They are ready!'

Morris felt keen anticipation as they descended the floors in the escalator.

'Come on,' he said to himself, 'give me something good!'

Foong met them and led them back into his office.

'OK, ready,' he said. 'It's all in these printouts. Here, separated by category: "Hotels," "Roulette cheats," "Casino Cheat Lists with known history", "Flight lists", etc.'

On the table was a mountain of information.

'OK, George, thanks again,' Campbell said, rolling up his sleeve and looking at Morris. 'Let's get to work. Better get some more coffee in.'

# Chapter 15

Back in London, Cain had still to phone anyone. He had been thinking what to do throughout the flight and had more or less made up his mind to visit Tolo, not that he wanted to be a hero, but rather out of a persistent worry that the whole thing was going the wrong way.

The big call was whether to immediately phone Morris, who was after all in charge of tracking down the team and supposed to be keeping in close contact with the owners. He figured too, that Morris would phone him before long, wondering what he had picked up from Port Elizabeth. He did not want to fob him off, and eventually decided he would tell Morris about Tolo, but would ask him to keep it quiet until they could meet up. He figured Morris would be back within a couple more days, at most.

Instead of catching a flight to Inverness, he booked in at one of the better Heathrow Airports, had a bath, and went to bed.

The first file Morris looked for and opened was the one titled 'Italian Casinos' and in brackets, 'Closed—Not Currently in Operation'. There were about fifteen named casinos on the list, and Morris started to go through them until one name caught his eye.

'Tolo!' he exclaimed. 'Never knew there was a casino there!'

Campbell looked up. 'Me neither,' he laughed, 'a casino in a town famous for cheats—no wonder it closed down!'

Morris was interested. He could see straight away that this casino could be the location he was looking for. He asked Campbell if Foong could get more information on the defunct casino.

'No problem. Do you think that could be the place?'

'I think it could well be.'

Campbell phoned Foong and arranged for the necessary information to be collated. Less than ten minutes later, they had another file to check, simply marked 'Grand Casino Tolo'. Morris opened the file eagerly and read quickly.

'The Grand Casino opened in 1947, two years after the war, in an attempt to aid the recovery of the town after considerable damage after World War II. The town attracted Italians coming to visit Tolo's Spa and considerable visitors from Switzerland, where casinos were illegal. Switzerland was less than an hour away from the town. The company that built the casino sold it in 1960 to the Santini family, who modernised it and increased the number of tables and opening hours. The casino was successful—publishing average yearly profits between 1961 and 2002 of about two million dollars—and became the town's second biggest employer after the Pepsi Cola bottling plant, which opened in 1964. However, the opening of casinos in Switzerland in 2003 had an immediate impact on visitation numbers and the expansion of the casinos in the main cities of Italy, and the effects of the recession proved to be a devastating blow from which the casino could not recover, and after posting a loss of three million dollars in 2009, the owners closed it.

The report continued. 'Only a few months later, the bottling plant was closed, creating further devastation for the local economy. Unemployment was listed as 32 per cent in 2011, and 56 per cent among young people. Local mayor, Marco Capone, was re-elected in 2011 with a clear mandate to try and re-develop the economy.'

Morris sat up on reading the name, his fist clenched tightly.

'Population 30,452 at the last census, down from 35,000 ten years earlier. Tolo has also received some notoriety in the casino industry for being the birthplace of several famed casino roulette cheats, commonly called "poussettisti" in Italy. Many were arrested in 2006 in a nation-wide sweep and received sentences of an average of four years' imprisonment. It is believed many of them previously worked in the aforementioned casino, before deciding to become involved in past posting roulette.'

Morris nodded. This was fascinating stuff. The jigsaw was nearly done.

'Think we've got it!' he said, handing over the file to Campbell. 'Capone as mayor?' He wondered if it could possible be the same 'calm' Capone as the international cheat. The file said many had gone to prison. Capone, an international cheat, was elected mayor? Odder things had happened.

The next check was on the mayor's background, and again Foong was called by Campbell. This time, the response was longer in coming but equally impressive in quality. There was a full family history, and Morris soon let out an exclamation.

'Marco Capone is the brother of Ernesto! Bloody hell! One a cheat and one an ex-casino manager and mayor. Right, so it was probably all arranged. Let's see. The young dealers who had become unemployed started to train as cheats? Very likely— at least some of them. It would take a couple of years for them to learn to become as good as they are. That fits with the time frame of the casino's closure perfectly.

'Probably after jail, the old poussettistis didn't fancy another stint and turned their hands to training the town's unemployed young men and probably some of their own sons. Makes sense too, and the fact that they were getting on a bit, maybe losing some of their speed? Then they come across this idea to storm casinos all at once—very clever that. Safety and strength in numbers. Think I've just earned myself a nice bonus. Tolo's the training centre!'

'Good work! You deserve it too,' said Campbell smiling. 'Looks like you're going to get the bastards that ripped you off, and all of us can breathe more easily. Right, how do we confirm all this and get it sorted—and quick, just in case we are the next target?'

'That's what we have to consider now,' Morris agreed. 'Let's not be hasty, though. Think it through.' In his mind, though, he was already set to make a call to Cain at the first opportunity, and bugger it if he woke him up wherever he was.

He turned back to Campbell. 'Let's get a list of all the poussettistis we can find with a connection to Tolo. If we are right, I'll bet we'll find in our flight lists their sons, and if we do, we can get the names of the others travelling with them.'

'I thought they had fake passports?'

'For the Greek casino registration, yes, but no way you could get more than 100 people getting through airport Customs with fake passports. No. They'll have used their real passports to travel, then kept them safe in the hotel and issued the team with fake ones for general use or in case they were caught in the casino. Anyway, let's get that checked, knowing that we know a lot of these past posters like to pass on their skill to their sons. We should be able to match up a few names. Then we should get a list of everyone in the team—if we can connect it with incoming flights to Athens and Durban.'

Foong was called again and instructed to enter the data to look for a match between names of the old Italian past posters, and especially ones with a connection to Tolo, and flight lists into Greece and Durban around the time of the attacks. If a match was made, to then print out all the names of those flying in that particular flight.

An hour later, they had what they wanted. Morris slapped Campbell on the back.

'Bingo! Four matches with old poussettisiti, and we now have the real names of all those who were flying—including Mr. Ernesto Capone—the cheat, on one flight to Greece and his brother Marco on the flight to Durban. If we want, we can get the real names of the dead guys by checking who was missing from the return flight compared to the incoming. Could you handle that and get it to the relevant authorities in South Africa at some stage?'

Campbell simply nodded.

'Right, we have the names. I'll bet all the rest of the kids will be ex-dealers from the closed casino or those sacked at the bottling plant. All good news then,' he said, standing up and stretching. 'We have the probable location and the names—not bad for a day's work. I think I might be heading back to the bar again tonight. In fact, I wouldn't mind going there now. Beer tastes better when you feel you deserve it. Thanks, Donnie. You, the casino, and George have been a huge help. I think your casino will be safe now. I would think within a day or two, this whole case will be wrapped up.'

He looked at his watch—it was time to call Cain.

'I'd better update Harrison with the news,' Campbell replied. 'He'll be happy too. Wonder what he will have in store for the bad guys? In fact, Sam, looks like you're work is almost done. The bosses will probably arrange the closing of this particular scam by themselves.'

'No way,' said Morris tensely. 'I'm seeing this right to the end. I want to be there when they arrest Capone and his team. That would give me a particular pleasure, I must admit. The bosses told me to back away once I had located the team, but I need to confirm Tolo is the place 100 per cent before I do so. Phone Harrison and the others if you want. After Cain, I'm going to call him myself anyway.'

'OK, you can give him the good news then. You can mention I'll be sending a full report in the morning.'

'Right. OK, let me collect this stuff up and get back to the hotel. Phone Cain. Quick beer later. I'll probably head back tomorrow, now that we are done here.'

'If you decide definitely, let me know as soon as possible and I'll get the jet arranged. See you in the bar at about six? I'll have updated all my files by then, I reckon.'

'I'll be there—and I'm buying tonight,' said Morris, heading confidently towards the door.

Morris felt very good as he headed back to the hotel. He could be back in Scotland soon—hopefully see his kids and collect his bonus in a few days. He was looking forward to updating Cain with his discoveries.

Cain had just finished his room service breakfast when the phone rang.

'Ah, Sam!' he said. 'I was just about to phone you. How's everything going out there in Singapore?'

'Better than I possibly expected,' replied Morris. 'I think I have the location for the cheat school . . .'

'Tolo?' interrupted Cain.

'Eh, yes,' said Morris. 'How the hell did you come up with that?' There was a moment's disappointment in his voice, which was soon forgotten in the general enthusiasm that he was feeling, as Cain updated him on what he had found in S. Africa. Morris in turn informed Cain all he had learnt that day.

'Good stuff. Quite amazing actually. Anyway—when are you coming back? Do you think you could make it back soon?' Cain enquired.

'Aye, now that I'm pretty well done here, I could fly back tomorrow. Why the urgency?' said Morris.

'Look, I know you are working for the bosses and are on a good deal, but I trust you and I'm going to ask you not to tell them all this latest stuff. Have you contacted them yet?'

'No, you know I'd always tell you first. What's up?'

'Good you haven't called. I just feel we were the first to be hit, and if possible, we should try and sort it out ourselves. I want us to go to Tolo and see if we can stop the team ourselves. I'm also worried about that Harrison and what he might do.'

'He's not that bad, I hope. We're not dealing with the old gangsters here. But you're right, I had the same thoughts. I'd like to be there and finish it all off, if possible, but in case I want to go there to confirm it is the place, both of us together—no one else—would be the best way, for me anyway . . .'

'I had a wee hope that would be your attitude—so you'll come?' Cain said.

'Sure I'll come, but the guy out here, Campbell, expects me to contact the bosses today and update them. He is compiling a report just now, which he will send tomorrow morning at the latest.'

'That should be OK. You get back as early as you can. Get the jet to take you to Milan, and I'll meet you there, say at the nearest coffee shop to the International Arrival Gate—and we'll get up to Tolo pronto. By the time Harrison and the others organise themselves for whatever they want to do, hopefully we will have sorted it out and there'll be no need for any rough stuff, if that's what they have in mind.'

'Right, I'll get Campbell to arrange the flight tomorrow morning. I'll say destination London not Madrid. Whatever happens, just wait for me. Don't go up there yourself.'

'I'll wait for you, don't worry,' replied Cain. 'This is about you as much as me.'

'What do you plan to do when we get there? Tell them they have been naughty and please stop?' Morris said.

'I'll tell you when I meet you, but I think we will have no problems curtailing their activities. I can be very persuasive when called upon.'

'It's going to be a bit weird, though, walking into Tolo—is there any danger, you think?' said Morris.

'Can't imagine. These are roulette cheats, not murderers. We'll be OK.'

'Right, see you at Milan Airport. I'll text you once I get the details of the flight. Another busy day ahead, but we are near the end of the tunnel now—at last. Ciao!'

Cain booked another night in the hotel and spent the day planning for Tolo. In fact, he didn't have a specific plan in mind, but felt if he could get a head to head with someone high up in the team, a few threats and reminders of who they had stolen from would prove sufficient to curtail any future Blitzkriegs.

He read, had some lunch, a swim, made some notes, had a couple of drinks before dinner, and was in bed by midnight. The hotel had booked him a flight to Milan for 08.00.

In Singapore, Morris finished his packing for the morning. He had phoned Campbell, who had collected all the information for his report and had done a draft copy saying he would 'polish' it up in the morning and send it off to the bosses.

'OK,' replied Morris, 'I haven't called them either. Want to figure a few things out in my head, make sure I can answer any questions. Any chance you could delay sending off your stuff until I phone them in the morning? I don't want them to think I've been slow off the mark.'

Campbell paused for a second, looking out his office window with a shrewd smile on his face.

'I suppose, but we have to move quickly, you know.'

'Yeah, yeah, I know. By morning I'll be set. I'm sure. I'll get back to the United Kingdom as soon as possible tomorrow. Now that it looks all over, I want to see the kids. I'm totally spent. Can you get the jet first thing?'

'Sure, it's reserved for you, you know. Till further notice, nine in the morning?'

'Maybe a bit earlier, five OK?'

'Right. Where to? London? Or can we drop you off in Italy perhaps?'

Morris was taken by surprise.

'Come on, I'm not daft. I know what you are up to. You want to get back and sort it out yourself. I had a feeling when you were asking me to delay the report but was sure when you asked for the earliest flight.'

Morris didn't know what to say. Eventually, he raised his hand even though Campbell was not present.

'OK, you are right. I phoned Cain, and we both agreed that we should go to Tolo ourselves and try and sort it out, not for any glory or anything. The main reason is that we feel it is our right—since we were hit first—and the second reason is that Cain is worried about what Harrison and the rest might do if they have the location. Hopefully, we can get it all sorted before they send in the troops or whatever they have planned. In any case, we need to try and confirm that Tolo is the actual training centre.'

Campbell nodded and thought for a bit.

'I can see all that—sure. What happens if you go in there and screw it up? Remember, you are on a decent bonus. That could be lost if it all goes wrong.'

'True, but I feel it's something I have to do. They took my casino for money on my watch, and I don't like that. It's personnel. I'm sure you can see? In the end, the money is of secondary importance.'

'OK, but I have my own job to think about. I'll send the report off tomorrow at noon. The earliest that they would be expected to organise some form of retribution would be by the next morning. Make sure you are out of Tolo quick. And if you do sort it out, don't delay. Get on the phone to Harrison and the others immediately.'

'Yes, don't worry about that. I just want to know it's finished and get home.'

'Noon tomorrow at the very latest—OK?'

'Got it, got it, and thanks. Right, I'll see you in the bar in a bit . . .'

They met in the bar just after six and went over the day's events again. Campbell asked the same question that Morris had relayed to Cain.

'What exactly do you plan to do?'

Morris shrugged.

'Cain wouldn't tell me. He's probably trying to figure it out himself. It's a unique situation. Perhaps we'll go into Tolo and see every one of the scammers—perhaps none. Maybe they don't actually live there. I'm sure we'll be able to find the casino though, and that might help us. If we can't clear everything up, Cain will contact the bosses and let them deal with it.'

'Wouldn't mind being with you on this one. It should be very interesting, at the very least,' Campbell said.

'Yep! God knows what will happen.'

They had a couple of beers and ordered some food. A couple of hours passed. Morris left, resisting several offers from girls as he left the bar. Looking back, he saw Campbell move from where they had sat and position himself on a table where a thin Chinese woman sat, her long silky hair sliding down to her hips at exactly the point where her hot pants reached up to. Without thinking, Morris focused on the girl's Adam's apple. He saw no protrusion.

'Good choice,' Morris nodded, smiling, 'might delay the report as well . . .'

# Chapter 16

He was on his way to Milan at just after 5.30 after a slight delay. He nodded off in the plane and dreamt that he was Clint Eastwood walking along a dusty road into a deserted town shooting at various heads that would appear from a window or from behind a door. He never missed, and as the victims fell to the ground, they would drop money and cash chips. In his dream, he was concerned that they all looked like young boys—but he had had to shoot them. He could even hear the high-pitched screeching echoes of the bullets as they were fired—in that unique Spaghetti Western-type sound—even though his shots were all direct hits. He had noticed Cain doing exactly the same from the other end of town. They had met in the middle next to the only survivor, who was scrambling in the dust for his life.

'Take me to your leader,' Morris had heard himself say. 'We know who you are . . .'

Strange dream, he admitted to himself on waking up. He felt pretty refreshed, had some breakfast, and in what seemed an incredibly short time was landing in Milan. He found the nearest coffee shop as described by Cain and positioned himself at the periphery of it so that he would be noticed easily enough. He bought himself a newspaper and waited.

Two hours later, he saw Cain coming through the arrival gate and beckoning him over.

'You look pretty fresh,' commented Cain. 'Sleep on the plane?'

'Yeah, nearly straight through. You OK? What do you want to do? Do you want to get a train or hire a car or what?'

'No, taxi time. Let's go. Let's try and get this over by the end of the day.'

'Sounds good to me,' agreed Morris.

As they set off towards Tolo, Campbell's e-mail report had arrived in each of the big boss's Inboxes. After South Africa, they had dispersed to various locations, with only Harrison staying in Durban to sort out the problems at the International. He was in front of his computer when the report arrived, and as such, he was the first to read it. He did so with profound interest and in the end satisfaction.

'Nice one, Campbell,' he muttered. Getting Morris out to Singapore had worked as well as they had hoped, and now they had all the names and likely locations. He hadn't heard of Tolo before and was interested to be informed that it was a hotbed of casino cheats, with its own, albeit closed casino.

'Right,' he thought, 'how to proceed?' He had had a few ideas already, but he believed he could now focus on the job more clearly. An idea came to him and he made a call to his 'Special Operations' manager, Stuart Rutherford, outlining the plan forming in his mind.

'That will go down nicely,' he thought to himself. 'Should scare the hell out of them.'

He received an e-mail from Pullman asking him if he had received Campbell's report yet, but he ignored it for the moment . . . He wasn't sure who he wanted on board yet. In the next two hours, he also received communications from Ling and Kruger, but those too went unanswered. Eventually, he decided to phone Campbell and speak to Morris.

On the second attempt, he got through.

'Hello, Campbell,' he said bypassing formalities. 'Got your report—good stuff. Like the questions Morris came up with. So we have all the names and the town where they all trained presumably?'

'Yes, but it isn't certain that Tolo is the town or that the cheats are actually based there. What are you thinking of doing? Passing it on to the Italian authorities?'

'You think they would be interested? They're all bent anyway,' Harrison replied with a snort.

'What? Are you going to send in some boys? What do the others think of that?'

'That's my business!' Harrison raised his voice. 'Don't ask me smart-arse questions, would you. I'll sort it out any way I feel fit. You've supplied the information, remember. Anyway, is Morris around? I've been expecting an update from him personally.'

Campbell, in anger, said nothing, save, 'He left this morning.'

'So soon? Where to? England?'

'Guess so. I just booked the jet for him and told him to take him to wherever he wanted. So I guess he'll be back in the United Kingdom now. Give him a call. I don't know . . .'

'Yes, I think I'll do just that. Didn't expect such good results so quick, but I'm thinking now that he should have contacted me sooner. What's he up to? Is Cain back in England too?'

'No idea about that,' replied Campbell. 'I'm sure Morris knew that you would be getting all the information from my report. He's probably waiting for a call from you telling him how to collect his bonus.'

'He gets that when the threat to Singapore is eliminated once and for all. I'm paying him nothing unless we cancel out that threat permanently. Campbell, have you any idea how much it would cost to set up an audio system in my place and

139

how much we could lose in lost business in that time? We could even lose our clients totally if they started going to other casinos.'

'I have an exact idea of the cost, Mr Harrison. It was me who insisted that, despite the expense, audio was needed, precisely to prevent the sort of threat we are facing now. Even if this problem is sorted, you will still need roulette audio one day.'

'In the future, yes, but just now isn't the right time. Investment problems, stuff you don't need to know about. Make sure your casino is safe while I sort out these bastards. We're vulnerable, and I feel something in my bones that they are heading your way soon. Are all your Surveillance guys ready? Put extra guys on if necessary for the next couple of days. After that, the problem will have been dealt with. Keep in touch,' he ended the call.

'Investment problems?' thought Campbell. He had heard a few rumours about the Harrison and JP overextending themselves in the rush to open the Seven Winds. Maybe it was true after all. He had wondered time and time again why they hadn't installed the audio they so desperately needed. After all, twenty million for these guys was not a fortune.

He reached for his phone and called Morris.

'Morris, it's Donnie Campbell here. Has Harrison phoned you? No? Well, I think he's just about to. Look, I think this is heating up a bit too quickly. He asked where you were, and I can see that once he received my report, he was wondering why you hadn't contacted him prior to that. I think I fobbed him off on that one. He didn't want to give me any details of his proposed solution to the problem and got a bit tetchy when I asked. He's also really panicky about Singapore. He's worried because he realises how vulnerable it is. He also hinted that the bosses have debt problems. That would explain his fear, but I have to tell you that also makes him even more dangerous than normal. He also said that you weren't getting paid until the threat was "eliminated once and for all", in his exact words. I'm telling you—although I shouldn't—because I'm getting worried now. He is a very dangerous man and has contacts to match. I think you should get the hell out of there now. Where are you at the moment, in a car?'

Morris had been listening intently saying nothing.

'Yes, we're nearly at Tolo now. Thanks for that, Donnie. For the first time, I'm getting worried myself. I think I underestimated this guy's paranoia. He sounds even a little mad. Maybe we'll end up warning the Tolo guys in the end. I don't want anything to do with serious repercussions, which it sounds like he has in mind. I don't even care much about the money at this moment. I feel I'm getting drawn in. Look, thanks again, Donnie. I'm going to discuss things with Cain. Our conversation never happened, of course.'

'For sure. As far as I know, you are back in the United Kingdom,' echoed Campbell, finishing the call.

Cain had seen the serious look on Morris's face becoming more strained as each minute passed. He told the taxi to stop at the nearest rest place. This happened to be at a petrol station, which he informed them was barely half a kilometre outside Tolo itself. They paid him, saying they would walk the rest of the way, and he drove off with a shrug. 'Milan to a petrol station outside Tolo—fair enough.'

Cain and Morris got a sandwich and a drink and sat at a table inside the station.

'Right,' Morris said, 'I think it is time you told me what you had in mind for Tolo. Maybe we should get back home. Looks like real trouble ahead.'

'After I've paid for that taxi? You must be kidding!' replied Cain, trying to lighten up the mood. 'Here's what I have in mind . . .'

Just as he started, Morris's phone rang. The caller was not identified, but he was not taking any risks and did not answer it.

Harrison let out an expletive as he failed to get through. He had just spoken to Pullman, who had asked him what they should do. He too was getting increasingly worried about Singapore. The fact that Capone had been a casino manager implied that there was every chance that he may have heard about the audio problem through the grapevine. 'We have to act soon,' he pleaded. 'You know I can't take a big hit. I'll go down.'

'You're not the only fucking one!' Campbell shouted down the phone.

'What do the others say we should do?' asked Pullman.

'Haven't replied to their emails or answered their calls. The other two are a bit soft, if you know what I mean. Don't think they would go all the way if they had to. They can take a financial on Singapore more than we can. Not such a big deal to them.'

'No, it's you and me, Arron, like it always really was.'

'Sure, sure. We are going to kill them all if we don't get what we want. Rutherford is putting things together. But I have thought of something a little less messy—I know it's not like me—that hopefully will put them off for good. Quite an inspirational idea. I'll think you'll like it. We don't even have to kill anyone, in fact.'

'Really? What will we do?' asked Pullman.

'I'll keep it as a surprise. Look. I've got to get organised . . . I'll call you back soon.'

He then made about a dozen calls in an hour, at the end of which he called back to Pullman and announced excitely, 'OK—game on. Everything's set up. I leave for Milan tomorrow morning. Can you get there by afternoon tomorrow? Where are you now anyway?'

'Spain, checking out the proposed site of the new casino. Yes, I'll be in Milan tomorrow for sure. I'll leave a message at the information desk and wait for your call.'

'Don't contact the other two yet,' Harrison urged. 'Don't take their calls. In the end, they'll be glad we sorted the problem without them having to get involved.'

'What will you say to that Morris guy, or Cain, if they call?'

'I'll tell then thanks for the information and the money is in the post. I'm sure they will be happy with that. We don't need them now anyway . . .'

It was a hot day as Morris and Cain walked into Tolo. The first thing that caught their eye was a sign saying Hotel Apollo and a sign indicating there were vacancies.

'We will make base there, book in for a couple of days saying we are tourists, ask about the spa, that sort of thing,' said Cain.

'We can't just walk around town with our suitcases. That's true,' replied Morris.

Walking into the town and the rundown hotel, they immediately realised that they were standing out like sore thumbs. The place seemed deserted. Even the receptionist seemed to almost jump when they came through the door. However, she didn't seem particularly suspicious as she booked them in. She introduced herself as Maria. They asked a couple of questions about the spa and asked if it was open at that time. It was.

'Are you English?' she asked in that language.

'No, Scottish,' Morris replied. 'Where did you learn English so well?' he continued.

'We all speak very good English here, apart from the older people. Our good mayor insisted it be taught in the school. He said it would give us a better chance of improving ourselves.'

'Yes, that's good. I see the town looks quiet now. Don't many tourists come? We were told the spa has great healing properties. My old friend here has a back problem. Do you think the spa is good?' asked Morris.

'It is very good. It is about the only thing the tourists come for now. We used to have a casino once.'

'A casino here, in this small town? Really? When was that?' asked Cain.

'A few years ago,' Maria said somewhat sheepishly.

'Can you tell us how to get to the spa please?'

She instructed them before Cain spoke again.

'Hey! I want to take a picture of that old casino. Tom will never believe there was one here once. Is it still standing?'

This time, both of them noticed a definite nervousness in her voice.

'Yes . . . they keep it in good condition because . . . because . . . they hope one day it will open again.'

'That would be good for the town. Is it near the spa?' asked Morris.

'Exactly next to it,' she said, trying to smile again.

'OK, great! We'll go and unpack and then get up there for a swim. Do they do massages?'

'Yes, but not today. Tomorrow—sorry.'

'No problem, we'll get one tomorrow. Good restaurant somewhere?'

Maria pointed over the street. 'Mario's, see there—best in Tolo. Make sure you tell them that Maria sent you.'

'OK, we will. See you later.' Cain and Morris both smiled.

She smiled back. She had been worried for a few minutes when they mentioned the casino, but she felt they were genuine enough. She decided not to make the phone call she had been thinking of making. Be wary of strangers, Capone had said, but she believed they seemed genuine enough.

Morris and Cain unpacked and were soon heading off towards the spa. At a rundown tourist store, they found swimming shoes, towels, and trunks and placed them in their bags.

The town was eerily quiet.

'Not what I had anticipated,' said Cain. 'Haven't seen a male since the petrol station.'

'Doesn't seem to be even any women around and just a few tourists by the looks of it,' Morris replied.

'Mid-afternoon. I suppose they'll be having a siesta. We'll see later. Let's get up to the casino, and we'd better have that swim, in case the girl asks us some questions about the place later.'

'Looking forward to it anyway. A massage would have been nice though,' replied Morris.

'I'm sure Linda will sort out all your old muscles when you get back.'

'Boy, that sounds good,' Morris smiled. 'Maybe in two days. Lovely.' He shivered despite the heat.

The spa too was rundown. Only a handful of individuals were swimming in the pool or getting blasted by jet sprays. However, they enjoyed the experience and left feeling refreshed, their skins soft and smelling of the minerals contained in the water.

'OK, we've done the tourist bit. Let's have a look at the casino,' Cain said as they left. 'Must admit I don't see the town showing any signs of newfound wealth. In fact, I don't see the town showing signs of anything much at all. Not what I expected.'

'Yeah, you're right. It's bloody dead. The scam team must live elsewhere. I guess they just came here to train. Mind you, where are the young men who do live here? I don't think I have seen more than a handful of males between eighteen and fifty, mostly old guys.'

They had a quick look around, but no one seemed remotely interested in their movements. They stood next to the casino, and Morris took a few pictures of Cain smiling and pointing towards the casino sign. They moved round the side after checking that no one was watching and peered through the window.

'Well, would you look at that!' declared Morris. 'Must be a dozen tables, all looking clean and recently used. The chips are still in the float as well. Not so long since this place was used—the "Lions' Den", so to speak.'

Cain strained to have a look.

'Damn it, I hoped he might be here. Well, we were sure enough anyway about a training school, but it's nice to confirm it. I doubt trying to break in would help us at all. What do you think?'

'Not worth the risk. Right, we have got a feeling for the town. What about your plan of trying to locate the mayor?'

'Would have been better to get him here, red-handed, but we can ask around. He should be here. Where else could he be?' He turned towards Morris, who was sharing his nervous look.

Back at the hotel, they thanked Maria for her help with the spa, and after confirming they were going to eat at Mario's, Cain spoke to her.

'My back is feeling better already. That is the best spa I have ever been to. This place shouldn't be so quiet. Look, Maria, I am a tourism journalist, and I think I can help bring some more visitors here.'

'That would be great,' she smiled again. She smiled all the time.

'Nothing wrong with that,' thought Cain, charmed by the girl's lovely demeanour.

'You mentioned the mayor before. He seems to want the best for the town. I'd like to meet him, see what plans he has for the town.'

'He is very good and he has plans to help us,' came the quiet reply.

'That sounds good. I would like to meet him and discuss this with him. Many people read the magazine I write for, and I can really help the town, I think.'

'That would be nice,' her white teeth flashed again. She hesitated and then reached for the phone, but then stopped. 'I'll try and contact him while you have dinner. I'll come over and tell you if I can find him and he can meet you tomorrow.'

'Tomorrow would be great, but tonight even better, if possible, of course,' Cain said.

'Go and eat. I'll try.'

They went to their rooms, dumped their holdalls, and were back in Reception moments later. Maria had gone. An ancient-looking lady sat instead, peering towards an old box TV showing an even older black-and-white comedy.

'She seemed to panic a little—that Maria,' said Morris. 'Did you see her reach for the phone and then change her mind?'

'Yes, I'm sure she is somewhere getting instructions on what to tell us now.'

'Anyway, a beer before dinner?'

'Hadn't thought of that. Good idea!' Morris said. 'That spa has given me a good thirst.'

It took all of his nerve to remain calm when they walked into Mario's. There was no way he could have anticipated what he would see and no possibility of retreat. He managed to reach an empty table without drawing undue attention to himself or Cain. Sitting sipping coffee and watching football on the overhead TV was at least nine notorious roulette cheats. Morris tried not to stare, but as his eyes briefly swept the room, every face seemed to belong to a poussettisti, and most of the well-known ones, as well. The best in the business.

'Jesus Christ!' he said to himself, feeling beads of sweat on his forehead. It was surreal—as if he had walked into a place and Zeppelin, Sabbath, and Purple were all there at once, calmly drinking and chatting away.

Cain caught his eye. 'Hey, that looks like—'

'Quiet! It is, all of them are. It's a bloody scam conference! Try and act normal, if you can. Get some drinks in quick. I'm shaking like a leaf.'

There were one or two other tourist-looking types in the restaurant. The TV mounted on the wall was showing the news. When their beers arrived, they were consumed eagerly, and soon, two more were ordered. It took all of Morris's will power not to stare at the customers, who, apart from a quick glance at them on their entry, seemed to have no interest in them at all.

'OK, I'm a bit calmer now. What a shock! So what are these guys doing here?' Morris said.

'Well, I'd figure they are the scam trainers, the old pros relaxing after a hard day's work. Many more than I thought, though. I figured Ernesto and one or two others, max,' Cain said.

'They look so different from the photos. You almost come to see them as unreal when all you have seen is photos for twenty odd years,' said Morris.

'You have never met or seen face to face any of them ever?' Cain said, a little surprised.

'Yes, one at the back and one just under the TV—don't look. Inghazi and Ponzo. But that was years ago. They look much the same actually. Didn't interview them, just marched them out, as we used to do in the old days.'

'So they won't know you?'

'Unless they were in Durban for the presentation—no.'

'OK, that's good. We'll just hang on tight here. Getting a bit nervous about all this though . . .'

'Me too,' replied Morris, gulping his beer.

They ordered a starter and a half kilo of wine. Cain looked up and saw Maria approaching. He could see by her face that she was bringing bad news.

'Are you enjoying your meal?' she asked.

'Very nice, Maria. Any news from the mayor?'

'I'm sorry. I didn't know, but he is out of town. I'm so sorry, on business.'

'Will he back soon?' Cain persevered.

'His secretary didn't say. Maybe you want to talk to him about the town?'

'Ah! I think the mayor would have had more impact on my readers, you know, but I'll think about it, OK?'

She nodded, smiled, and left.

'She must smile more in a day than a Swiss person does in a month,' Morris said, liking her despite her probable deception. 'What now, then?' he asked Cain.

'God knows. I feel a bit daft, just thinking we could walk in here and sort the whole thing out in an afternoon by confronting the mayor and telling him we knew what he and his town were up to and forcing them to stop and even give back the money!'

'On the other hand,' Morris interrupted, 'we have seen the casino looks new and operational, which more or less confirms what we concluded about a training school, and now we have bumped into this lot, the cheat trainers. This is definitely the place.'

'So what have we got?' Cain said. 'The trainers are here, but we have hardly seen any young men around and certainly none to match the photos of the scam teams, so they do not live here. They did maybe when they trained and have now gone, or are they away on another job? So soon? Either way, can't see us doing much more except confronting these guys. Agree?'

'We wouldn't get anything from these guys, believe me. They could lie their way into heaven. They'll just deny everything. Look, if there is a chance that the young guys are away on another attack, maybe we had better get on to the owners and warn them of the possibility, wouldn't look good that we were swanking around here when a place was getting hit for millions!'

'Yes, I agree,' said Cain. 'Let's finish the meal, and I'll phone when we get back to the hotel, but I'm not phoning Arron. He'd probably tell me to poison the water or something. I'll try and get hold of Kruger. I think he's a bit more rational. The thing is we need proof to bring in the law. We know they stole, but can't prove it. There was always something blocking the camera view at the past-posting moment, except for the guys that Roberts caught red-handed, but they're dead. We can link them to the team, but that's about it. So,' he continued, 'the only real way we can get them, if we don't have a chance to rationalise with them, is to get them doing it again, with clear proof and coverage. In a way, we actually want them to go again, but when we are totally ready for them and can get enough evidence for a court conviction.'

Morris nodded in agreement.

'So we are done here. Make the call later and we will head off in the morning. Anyway, I'm glad we came. As you say, we've learnt a lot. Having seen how rundown the town is, maybe they thought stealing the money could help the place. You know, a collective decision.'

'What, you think the whole town is in on it?' Morris pondered.

'Wouldn't they more or less have to be? Hundreds of young—mostly ex-croupiers, suddenly all leaving town at once. I think everyone here knows and have been told to keep quiet. You saw how nervous that Maria got a couple of times. She knows. I'll bet on it. The barman knows, the waiter knows, the spa girl knows . . .'

'Well, what about the money then? If they all know . . . I'm sure they would want some sort of benefit for themselves or the town?' Morris said.

'Probably, otherwise they would have no incentive to remain quiet. Can't see the money has been spent. Nobody driving around in a new Mercedes or something . . .'

'Maybe they are still sitting on it. I don't know. If they are all in it together, how much do they want? Surely they would realise that they can't get away with it forever?' Morris added.

'Probably like a lot of things, it's hard to stop cheating once it becomes a habit. This mayor, though, despite having a cheating brother, seems a sensible type and intelligent. If they are all in it together, I'd see him trying to use the money for some good for the town. Probably still got a million to a million and a half. He could do a lot with that.'

'Didn't that Maria say he had plans?' Morris asked.

'She did. Maybe develop the town in some way. Improve the spa, a hotel. Maybe reopen the casino!'

'All possibilities. I agree,' said Morris. 'I've almost got some sympathy for them, if that is what they want to do. But whatever, they have to be stopped from hitting more casinos. We can't just let them go on. We need to lock then away, some of then anyway, or otherwise persuade them to stop.'

Morris went up to the bar and ordered a couple of beers. While he was waiting, some of the scam trainers approached the bar reaching for their wallets to pay the bill. One of them took a call, which was in fact, from Ernesto Capone. They were just behind Morris, so he could not help but overhear. The trainer was obviously greeting a friend, judging by the warm tone of his voice. He was speaking in a low voice, but could just be heard.

Morris thought he heard the word 'casino' being mentioned and unconsciously honed in, his hearing sense somehow enhanced. Just as he received his beers, he was sure he heard the word 'Singapore' or something very similar. He walked back to the table and placed the beers on the table.

'John,' he urged, 'a couple of the guys were at the bar and I'm sure I heard one of them say "Singapore" and maybe casino a few seconds before. That could be interesting. The town's deserted, and we hear one of the scam trainers mention Singapore! I think they could be going there. Shit! They could be there already! Why else would Singapore come up in a conversation in a small town like this?'

Cain started to move quickly. His brain was motoring up.

'Right, down these beers quickly. Back to the hotel and I'll start calling the guys. You had better phone Campbell and say what you suspect. I agree. Why else would Singapore come up in any conversation? Why there? So far away. Don't they know if they are caught, they'll go down big style? The Singapore government doesn't mess around when it comes to crime. Ten degrees below zero tolerance if you like.'

'There's no audio at the newest casino,' Morris reminded him of his call from Singapore. 'Without audio, they must feel that they are invincible and can never get caught. The Seven Winds has over 100 roulette tables. Can you imagine if they all hit them at once?! Shit, let's get moving. This one could make the two million in Durban look like the coins in a beggar's tin cup.'

They paid their bill as quickly as they could without drawing attention to themselves and headed straight over the road to the hotel.

'I'm going to call Kruger now,' said Cain, moving out on to the balcony. 'You?'

'Going to try and get Campbell and warn him. I'll try and impress on him that if they come in, we have to get evidence. Basically, we have to let them cheat and try and get them on the first attempt. Don't know if they will go for that. If they spot them, they'll want to grab them straight away. Remember, there's probably going to be dozens of them. They'd have to be very confident to feel that they could have that many under total control. But I'll try and impress the importance of what you said. Hopefully he'll see the bigger picture. Maybe if you push Kruger, he can make the other bosses see likewise and we'll get a result.'

'OK,' said Cain, moving on to the balcony.

# Chapter 17

Capone and his entourage of 142 people arrived in Singapore while Cain and Morris had been relaxing in the spa. Capone felt much less confident than when they arrived in Durban. It all felt too rushed. The scouts had only gone to Singapore two days back, and their initial report was that Surveillance and Security was strong, but they still had the audio advantage. He had an overwhelming feeling that the net was closing in. When he had received a call from Maria from the hotel telling him of the two guys asking questions and wanting to meet him, his fear only increased. They had only missed him by a day. The mayor had told her to say he was away on a business trip. And there had been no contact from the guys in Africa. They were young. Surely they would have phoned their parents by now, at least to tell them they were all right? He couldn't phone them. Their mobiles had been kept by Capone before they left, along with credit cards—anything that could be used to identify them. So where were they? How would they get home with their fake passports? Maybe they wanted to stay in Africa. After all, they were young and adventurous. Would they have tried to cheat on their own? Capone figured that likely, at least eventually, as he surmised that they probably had no more than a few tens of thousands on them. Surely they wouldn't start cheating so soon? But why hadn't they called? If they had been caught, he feared that isolated from the team and worried, they could eventually break and reveal all. If that was the case, the whole thing was finished. They had to get in and out of Singapore quick. He was reassured by the fact the three had not known the next location, but still, the information could be everywhere by now—maybe they had all the names of the scammers. They could only have the real names, he reassured himself, not the ones they would use in the casino. Those were fresh with new names, thanks to his forger pal in Alessandria. He started to realise that until he could find out what happened to the guys in Durban, they could not go back to Tolo. And those two guys asking questions about the casino and him . . . who were they? Journalists?

He gulped, deep in thought. He had discussed his fears with his brother for hours prior to their Singapore departure and hoped the plan they had come up with would work. Meanwhile, he had made some calls to relatives in South Africa to push them to get some information on the guys in Durban.

Capone and his group booked in using their fake passports at three separate budget hotels which were close to each other. He collected all the real passports and locked them in his suitcase. His mind was working fast and clearly, but the thrill of Durban had gone. Now the overwhelming feeling was fear, which he tried to push to the back of his mind. It was important that he appeared confident to the young guys.

The three Amari brothers, the scouts, had been waiting for him at the hotel, and after dropping off his case in the room, the mayor immediately went down to join them. They sat at a long bamboo bar. He saw the famous 'Singapore Sling' drink was on special offer. He was tempted to order ten, but settled for an espresso instead.

'Couldn't be more different from Durban,' Mario Amari said, shaking his head.

'We have had two trips now and nothing changes. Security is everywhere—plenty of staff, an inspector for each table. Once we figured out the Surveillance staff by their uniform, we waited near the staff entrance for them to leave, and there were something like fifty per shift! We had a quick look at the other casinos too. It's just as tight, if not worse.'

'Shit!' interrupted Capone. 'That means dozens of manned cameras, probably covering everything. It means we have to have a major distraction again if my plan is going to work. I thought as much, but was hoping we wouldn't have to use it. It also means we have less time. No two hours here, for sure. An hour max. That means we have to hit the tables in as many spins as we can, take a few risks, and get out. Have to go for the middle dozen as well. Constant cashing in like before, in case we are caught. Whatever happens, we are straight out of Singapore and then home—maybe.'

'Maybe? What do you mean? I thought this was the last place?' Mario said.

'Certain things are happening or maybe happening. We may have to lay low for a while. Not a word to the others from you three. I'm just taking precautions. Don't worry too much. Right, let's get down to the details. We go tomorrow evening. Here's the plan . . . the first group . . .'

Morris woke Campbell in the middle of the night, but he seemed alert enough.

'Where are you? Tolo, I'll bet,' Campbell said.

'Yes, I'm here with Cain. Interesting developments. We saw the casino. It's basically up and running, and we just walked into a restaurant full of casino cheats, who we guess are the trainers for the young cheat teams.' He reeled off as many names as he could remember.

'That must have done your head in. Bloody hell. Well, that settles it, for sure. What are you going to do now?'

'Cain is phoning the big boys right now. I think he'll miss out Harrison for the moment.'

'Sounds sensible. He phoned me earlier saying to be on double stand-by. He's sure their coming here. He's so paranoid . . .'

'Well, actually, he might be right for once.' Morris explained what he had overheard in the restaurant.

'Shit,' Campbell said, but feeling a growing excitement as the news sunk in. 'Coming here? Which casino?'

'No idea there, but the Seven Winds would be the most likely, I'd think. No audio, less-experienced staff . . .'

'Right . . . right. Well, thanks for the warning. Next step for you guys?'

'Maybe hang around here for a day, watch the trainers, I don't know. Cain will decide. Can't see us getting to Singapore soon enough. I'm sure you are going to get a visit within the next day. Both previous hits have been mid-afternoon to evening, remember? Could be the same there.'

'We are more or less full all the time. Could be any time,' Campbell replied, already getting out of bed and starting to get dressed. 'Phone me straight away if you have any more information,' Campbell concluded, ending the call abruptly, before Morris could suggest to him that they try and catch the team red-handed.

Cain had just returned from the balcony, in between calls.

'OK,' he said. 'I've phoned Kruger, who says he'll phone Ling and update him. He is taking it pretty calmly, as I would expect from him. He agreed that we needed to catch them in the actual act, but he doesn't think Harrison or Pullman will go for it, since it's their casino that is most vulnerable, being recently opened. He's been trying to talk to them himself, but he hasn't been able to get in touch with them for the last couple of days now. He thinks they might be up to something. Meanwhile, he suggested we stay here and see what is happening with the trainers: who is saying what, anything suspicious, etc. I said we would stay for another day at least. Did you get Campbell?' Cain enquired.

'Yes, Harrison has already phoned him and told him to be on the lookout. I don't think he knows anything, just paranoid about the potential hit. He'll be convinced as well that it's his casino that's the target. So, we'll hang around here for another day, fair enough. I'm going to phone the kids and Linda. Fancy a malt out on the balcony?'

'Good thinking, old chap. Can see me getting a few calls before we call it a day. May as well relax a bit and enjoy ourselves while we wait.'

Morris got a bottle from his case and got a couple of glasses from the bathroom and ice from the small, old-looking fridge in the corner, which was making a peculiar, grating, mechanical noise as it hummed away.

A few minutes after speaking to his kids and then Linda, Morris received a call. He peered down to see the sender; it was Campbell. He answered it.

'Foong just came in. All the guys from the hits in Greece and Durban were on a flight from Milan, which arrived a few hours ago. Just checking the hotels at the moment, not staying in any of the big ones. Couple of hours maximum, we should know where they are. We are all set at the Seven Winds—fifty extra staff called in on overtime. Reception is crowded with our guys, on the lookout, just in case they come straight away. Your end?'

'Donnie, I doubt they will use the same passports at the hotels, and Cain has contacted Kruger, who says he will speak to the other bosses, including Harrison, although he says he hasn't been responding to his calls and e-mails lately.'

Cain interrupted Morris asking what information he had been told. He then took the phone.

'Hello, Donald—is it? Look, time is of the essence. I have talked to Kruger, and he says he will try and contact Arron. Look—basically to stop these guys, we have to get them in the act. It's no use just preventing them coming in. We don't have enough on them just now. It's best you try and get a hold of Harrison, but it seems he doesn't want to be contacted, so—do you have Kruger's number? OK, phone him if you can't get Harrison. Where the hell is he anyway?'

'OK, I'll try and contact Harrison first. I'll phone now and phone Sam back.' Campbell ended the call.

Cain immediately called Kruger.

'Cain, here. Have you got through to Harrison yet? No! Well the team has landed in Singapore. If you want this to end, you have to get hold of Harrison or persuade whoever is in charge in his absence to let the team come in and then get caught. At the moment, the place is swarming with staff. They'd be mad to try it. They'll run a mile and then we'll have to start all over again!'

'I know, I know. I can't get hold of him. I know he's left South Africa, think to Europe, but I can't confirm it. Pullman is in Spain. Got hold of Ling, and he's fine with your plan, as long as this all ends after this attack.'

'Europe? Why not to Singapore, if any place?' asked Cain puzzled.

'Don't ask me. You are dealing with a madman here. If he takes a substantial hit at his casino, he's finished and Pullman too. In the end, he was a little guy who went over his head,' Kruger said dismissively.

'If you can't contact or persuade Arron, do you have the authority to order Campbell to back off and let the Italians make their moves?'

'Yes, there's a control procedure wherein matters of utmost security and if one or more of us is unavailable, those that remain can make the decisions. So Ling and I say it's OK, so it is. Campbell, our Surveillance and Security director, knows the score.'

'I know. I was just speaking to him. He's also trying to get hold of Harrison just now. I suggest you wait ten more minutes, and then if he hasn't spoken to Arron, he'll be calling you. Tell him to ease back the security and to make damn sure he gets the team with 100 per cent back-up evidence. If he has contacted Arron and he hasn't gone for it, you'll have to try and get Arron again and as soon as possible.'

'I'll try, but it isn't me that's going down. My casino out there won't be hit. In the end, it's his problem.'

'I know, but we can't let them get away again. Could be one of your places next, somewhere else.'

'OK, OK . . . you're right, I guess . . . I'll wait ten minutes and then tell Campbell to ease back.'

Cain ended the call and had a slug of malt. He'd had enough of all this shit.

'One more day,' he said. 'One more day and this Blitzkrieg scam is kaput, or it had better bloody be!'

Morris nodded, 'You'll be in Lochinver in a day or two at most—relaxing with Magda. Cheers!'

'Aye, cheers!' Cain replied, taking a more modest slug of malt.

They sat, more or less silent, for fifteen minutes and then Kruger phoned and said, 'Right, I couldn't get Arron nor could Campbell. I told him to ease up and told him the reasons. I said I would cover any losses they made as a result, so he'd better be good and get these guys the minute they hit. He felt better after that and told me he'd lay off the official security but get plain clothes involved more. He's going to have them hanging around the roulettes, ready to nab them. Says he'll try and time it so that the individual teams get one hit each, and then he'll round them up. The Singapore Regulatory Authority have been informed and will be ready to come in and take them away at the right moment. Campbell says he'll pull the casino shutters down, isolating the guests and restricting escape to the emergency doors, which will be covered. I'll say one thing, this Campbell is on the ball.'

'I'm sure it will go OK. Good. I'm glad that has been sorted,' Cain said relieved. 'So, basically, the next time I hear from you, I trust you will be telling me that more than 100 Italian cheats have been locked up and will be facing trial and lengthy sentences. Great—job done. Then we can get back to what we used to do before this madness began.'

Kruger finished the call by confirming he had asked Campbell to keep them updated as things developed. Morris was actually talking to Campbell at that moment about his plan to capture the team and was as impressed as Kruger had obviously been.

'Let them in, little security presence, but heavy undercover Surveillance, one cheat move per team, if possible, shutters down, police in, lock up, and it's all over,' Morris repeated to Cain after finishing his call.

They both stretched over, glasses coming together. A sudden gust of wind passed over the balcony, disturbing a nearby tree, whose leaves shimmered and danced wildly, creating a reassuring rustling sound.

'Time for bed,' said Morris. 'Another long day. The book is closing tomorrow. I can feel it.'

'I'll stay up a bit,' said Cain. 'Listen to the wind and leaves with a glass of malt. See you tomorrow.'

# Chapter 18

Harrison, along with Andrews (who spoke Italian), arrived in Rome at 07.30 and, by 8.00, had met up with Pullman. They took a taxi to a warehouse on the outskirts of town. He recognised the face of the solitary figure waiting outside the massive door. It had been a while since they had needed his services. Stuart Rutherford was over two metres tall, was bald, and had a handlebar moustache dropping down to his chin.

'The bodies here?' Harrison asked immediately, the same time as shaking Rutherford's hand.

'Yes, came in last night. The morgue people in Port Elizabeth will shit themselves when they find that three bodies that were under their authority have been borrowed!'

'Any trouble getting them?'

'Not in the slightest. Easiest break-in I've ever done—no staff around, on to a trolley, and out to the airport. What are your plans for them?'

'You'll see in a few hours,' said Harrison with a twisted grin. 'But you'll be there don't worry.'

'Right, the helicopter is behind the warehouse—ammunition—men—all set. Ready to go when you are,' Rutherford added.

'Fine,' said Harrison. 'I've told you the basics. We just go into this Tolo town and scare them off with a little show and a few threats. We shouldn't have to kill anyone. Sorry about that, Rutherford,' he said in mock apology.

'Shame, it's been a couple of months. I'm missing it!' replied Rutherford.

Harrison couldn't tell if he was joking or not—not that he cared much either way.

In the warehouse, he met the crew that Rutherford had assembled. Tough enough looking to scare the shit out of the Tolo residents, he was sure. There were ten guys and two dark vans. The helicopter and pilot were waiting for him.

Harrison spoke to those assembled.

'Right, you guys drive up to the outskirts of the village. When you see the helicopter fly over, make your way to the town square, which you can't miss, right in the middle of the only road. Big fountain there apparently. I'll be getting out of the helicopter, and then we find the cheats if they are there or those that trained them. Failing that, we'll beat up a couple of villagers, just enough to tell them all that we know who they are and we can extinguish their threat permanently at any moment. If the team is away, we'll make sure they are phoned and stop any attacks they were thinking of. Simple, really. We'll be back here in a few hours, and you'll get your money then. OK?'

There was no dissent. As far as these guys could see, they were getting five thousand euros each for scaring a few village folk. Easy money . . .

Harrison, Pullman, and Andrews got into the helicopter and headed off towards Tolo. The three ex-past posters, Rossini, Zapalate, and Nero, stared upwards, their faces a deathly white, the rest of their bodies covered by sheets. Half an hour later, they spotted the outskirts of Tolo and landed and waited until they saw the two vans approaching a couple of hours later. The bodies were defrosting rapidly, and the living passengers in the helicopter had thought it best to get out and wait for the rest of the team outside.

There were few cars on the road, and they easily saw the vans approaching at high speed towards Tolo. Harrison and the rest got back in and were soon flying 100 or so feet above the town. It was early afternoon and not too many people were around, so Harrison told the pilot to circle around a few times. It didn't take long, and soon a large crowd had gathered below, wondering who was paying them a visit and why the helicopter was circling without landing. He saw a few older people run rapidly away on seeing the machine.

'Monster coming to get you,' Harrison said, laughing.

He then pulled Zapalate from the floor with the reluctant help of Andrews, who was looking a bit squeamish by this time. Pullman opened the door and Harrison aimed for the centre of the crowd. The body tumbled out, and as it approached the ground, people scattered at the last minute. Some screaming could be heard above the noise of the helicopter, and one or two could be seen retching.

'Perfect!' smiled Harrison, returning to slide Nero and Rossini towards the door and releasing them too. On the ground, it looked like panic was ensuing.

'OK, land! Land right below—now!' he had to scream at the pilot, who did as he was told. He hadn't been told about dead bodies and was feeling sick as he directed the helicopter down.

As they landed, the vans arrived and came to a halt next to the fountain in the middle of the square. The ten heavily armed men came out, making as much noise as possible. The three bodies lay crumpled and broken on the road. No one was near them, but everyone was looking at them. Silence slowly descended as the helicopter blades came to a stop, and Harrison waited until there was totally quiet before speaking with Andrews, acting as his translator.

From the balcony shadows, Cain and Morris looked down in amazement at the unfolding drama.

'Jesus Almighty!' declared Cain. 'It's Arron. What the hell is he doing?'

Morris was staring intently.

'He's here to shake everybody up . . . I bet these are the guys from the casino and road accident in Durban. He's dumped the bodies from a helicopter. How could he do that? Nobody here even knows they were dead. Their mothers are probably down there . . . Jesus . . . this could get nasty.'

Just at that moment, a sudden wailing could be heard, and a middle-aged woman ran from the crowd towards one of the bodies, followed by a second, this time with a man.

Harrison even looked like he was grinning slightly, as he ignored their grief.

'These are the bodies we have brought back for you from Durban. You can thank us later. We are sure you are glad to have them home. Sorry they fell out of the helicopter, they slipped, but you see what happens to bad people.'

Andrews was translating as best he could but becoming increasingly nervous. He hadn't been bothered about dropping the bodies, but if they were people's kids . . . He had been in a few tense situations with Harrison, and he felt this one was rapidly escalating. Italian kids dumped naked in the street. Arron had told him that he had not killed them himself. 'But,' Andrews suddenly thought, 'did these people know?'

His voice started to lose a bit of control, and he was glad for the armed back-up standing around the fountain.

'Now let this be a lesson to you all,' he managed to continue. 'I know you have been stealing from casinos, and as far as I'm concerned, you are all involved. Now understand, if any more casinos are attacked, we will be back and there will be hundreds of bodies lying here dead. We will spare no one. Now, I want to know where the team is now—are they in Singapore?'

There was a wall of silence as people averted their gaze to the road.

'Thought so, thought so . . . What do you call it? Omerta or something? Silence . . . OK . . .' Harrison said.

He walked towards the crowd and pulled a girl back by her hair towards the centre.

Cain realised with a start that it was Maria. Without hesitation or thinking, he moved from the balcony.

'What are you doing?—He's mad!' said Morris, grabbing his arm.

'We have to help. He could kill her!'

'I know. That's why you can't . . .'

'I'm going . . . I'll talk to him . . .'

Morris sighed and said, 'Shite.' Resigned, he headed down the stairs with Cain.

Below, Harrison was shouting, and Andrews, still translating, was looking frantically around.

'I'll ask again,' he said, pointing a gun at Maria's head. Her natural friendly disposition had been replaced by a look of absolute terror.

'Singapore,' someone shouted. 'It's Singapore!'

'Thought so!' Harrison said, then asked Andrews to ask. 'Now, which casino?'

One of the crowd caught a signal from the restaurant and bar, where the trainers had congregated on seeing the helicopter hovering overhead. They knew trouble when they saw it. They had collected their guns, which were kept in a drawer behind the bar, and sat waiting around their tables with the guns held underneath.

'The trainers will tell you. They know everything. They are probably in the bar,' the man in the crowd said, pointing the direction.

'The scam trainers? Oh yes! I want to meet them,' Harrison said. He signalled for the team to follow him to the bar and still clutched Maria as he moved towards it. Andrews made a last comment to the crowd, 'Now everyone remember the message I gave you and go home now.'

The crowd dispersed, many running rapidly. The mothers of the dead boys were the first to leave, heading home with grim determination etched on their faces.

By the time Morris and Cain got to the square, most of the people had left and Harrison et al were already entering the bar.

When they got there, Cain immediately shouted, 'Arron, it's me, Cain! What the fuck are you doing?'

'Cain and Morris!' Harrison replied. 'What a surprise! Had a feeling you would pay Tolo a visit. Well, I'm just cleaning up the mess. Now look who we have here sitting all in a corner. It's the trainers, guilty as charged.' Still holding Maria, he asked Andrews to speak to the trainers.

'We speak English. What do you want?' said one of them calmly.

'Of course you do, except when in interview rooms. What Singapore casino and when? Simple questions. Tell me now or this girl will join her friends on the road,' Harrison said, raising his gun.

The trainers all seemed to move their chairs at once to face Harrison and his crew, although they did it slowly. Rutherford's hand went to his side, his eyes darting everywhere.

'There are so many casinos in Singapore. I can't remember,' said the trainer in mock forgetfulness. 'Which one could it be?'

Harrison had raised the gun towards Maria's head again.

Suddenly, Cain saw a look on his face.

'He was going to do it . . .' he decided, and without thinking, he lunged for Harrison and Maria broke free. Harrison fired his gun, which shattered one of the bar's windows.

Suddenly, the trainers had all pulled guns from their pockets or laps and blasted their shots all at once into the crew, who returned fire even as some of them were wounded. There was a huge explosion of noise. Morris dived for cover, trying to pull Cain and Maria with him. The noise of the shooting overwhelmed every other sense as they crashed to the floor. It was all over in what was a few seconds. Most of the crew and all of the trainers were on the floor—most of them dead—others twitching and crying out.

'Holy shit!' Harrison yelled. 'Wow! Gun battle in Tolo—shoot-out at the OK Tolo!' Somehow, he had escaped injury. Pullman and Andrews were not so lucky. Both lay dead on the floor. Harrison went up to one of the injured trainers.

'Which casino? Which fucking casino?' He put the gun in the man's mouth and pulled the trigger immediately.

He then went to the next injured body and asked the question again.

'The one with no audio, the new one!' the trainer screeched.

'Thanks,' Harrison said, then shot him as well. 'Why didn't you just tell me when I asked nicely?' He turned to the remnants of his own crew. 'Finish the last couple off—leave these three. She can spread the word, and the guys could be trouble if I knocked them off too.' He got out his phone and called Campbell, confirming that the Seven Winds was about to be hit.

There was only one trainer left alive at that point, and he was quickly dispatched by Rutherford. Harrison strode to the door with the rest of his team, but stopped at the entrance. An old woman was staring at him with pure hatred in her eyes, a shotgun levelled at his stomach. Behind her was a small crowd of mothers and grandparents, all holding old rusty-looking shotguns.

'I am Paulo's grandmother,' she said slowly. 'This is for him and for the others!'

Simultaneously, six shotguns were fired.

Harrison was nearly cut in half. 'Asta la vista, baby,' he thought for some reason as the blackness overwhelmed him.

After that, the crowd moved to the bar door as the remaining members of the crew that were still moving were dispatched with. Rutherford was the last to die.

After that, there was stillness—only Morris, Cain, and Maria appeared to be alive. The townsfolk helped Maria to her feet. She was fine but shaking uncontrollably. Cain, however, remained slumped over Morris, who tried to raise him slowly.

'John, are you OK, mate? John—shit!'

He had noticed the wound in the head and looked immediately at Cain's chest, which was moving rapidly in and out. He was still alive, thank God, but the wound looked bad, as blood trickled steadily from it down his cheek.

He called for help, and the old grandmothers appeared and started to attend to Cain, who was now moaning. None of them spoke English, so he called for Maria, who had one look at Cain.

'He needs a hospital and quickly. The nearest one that can treat that sort of wound is in Milan. We have to get him there.'

'The helicopter. It could still be there. Can you check? If it is, take some men and guns and hold the pilot until we can get John on.'

Maria nodded and left.

The pilot was sitting in his helicopter reading a magazine. He had headphones on and the engine was still on. He had heard, or seen nothing. He looked up, saw a gun in his face, and a few minutes later, the locals were helping Cain into the helicopter. He was laid down where the three dead bodies had been on the trip into Tolo.

'Where are the others? I can't leave without them. I won't be paid!'

'All dead. Now get moving to a Milan hospital. Land on the roof if you have to,' shouted Morris.

The pilot didn't hesitate. He had done a couple of jobs for Harrison before, but there had been no violence. He should have backed out when he saw the three dead bodies being loaded into the chopper and then the guns. He had needed the money though and had gone ahead. He cursed himself now—all of them dead, if the guy had been right. 'Something had gone badly wrong,' he concluded ruefully.

There was a car park at the back of the Milan hospital which he located via his map and with space enough to land, and on setting down, Morris got out, carried Cain using a fireman's lift towards the entrance. The pilot took the opportunity he had and took off immediately. Morris didn't care. He only had one priority—to try and save Cain. He staggered in, and the staff soon surrounded him and Cain. He was told to sit down and wait. They brought him a glass of water. A bottle of malt would have been preferable.

# Chapter 19

Capone was holding a final meeting with the scam team at seven thirty in the evening when the phone rang. It was Maria, who told him of the events that had unfolded in the town, mentioning that Harrison had been told which casino had been targeted in Singapore. He could scarcely believe it. At least his brother was with him, but Rossini, Zapalate, and Nero thrown dead from a helicopter and all the trainers. His mind raced. So they had been identified . . . What now? Call it all off, he initially decided, then realised that they could not go back to Tolo then and maybe forever. They would all be killed. 'Why had they reacted like that . . . ?' Who were the two journalist guys that had come to Maria's rescue? All he could tell Maria was that he would sort everything out, to contact the family of those killed, and that money would be available for the funerals, to tell the police that they had no idea why the killers had come to town, and that the shotguns had been used in self defense.

'They may ask for me or even wonder where all the rest of the men are. You can say we are in France for Milan's Champion League game, which is on tonight. Just keep it simple. If they mention casino scams, just deny it, OK?'

Maria listened and tried to remember the instructions, although shock was setting in and she found it hard to concentrate. She could be very easily dead, she realised, and started to shake in fright again.

After he finished the call, Capone told the team that he had to sort something out but to reassemble in the foyer of his own hotel in half an hour. He had a lot of quick thinking to do. They knew they were in Singapore—and expected at the Seven Winds Casino. They would be ready for them. They were finished, but they needed money, more than ever. He sought out his brother, finding him in his room, and updated him on all the events.

'What can we do now?' Marco said in exasperation. 'We will be caught. We have to call it off. Where will we go? We will be arrested or killed if we return home . . .' he added.

His brother tried to reassure him, putting his arm round his shoulder, thinking how lucky he was to have been included in the team but at the same time horrified that all his old colleagues had been massacred, every one of them, a bloodbath in Tolo.

'We have to hit quick and escape. You are right. We cannot go back to Tolo just now, possibly for a very long time. We have to get to somewhere and stay, but we need money for that. Can you get the rest of the money from the bank transferred?'

'I can, but I won't. That money is for the town. They need it more than ever now. No, we take fresh money, enough to get out of here and survive until we can figure out what to do. We have to decide now where we are going to go. Malaysia, Thailand, Brazil—shit . . . I don't know. As long as we get out of Singapore quickly, we can go anywhere and then move again later. We can't use our return ticket to Milan. The police will surely be waiting for us at the airport. So let's just book flights for us all for whatever is available around midnight, when we should have finished. But the thing we have to plan is how can we hit them and get away with it?' the mayor concluded, shaking his head in desperation.

'OK, OK, I'm trying to think,' replied Ernesto. 'We are expected at the Seven Winds, right? You said one of the trainers said so and was then shot. So they know. We have to presume the bastards informed Singapore before they were all killed. OK . . . OK, maybe we go there—some of us—the Greek team. I'll go with them again, and I'm sure they'll watch us like hawks once they see we are the same team that knocked out Greece. Maybe the other guys can go to the two other new casinos, which hopefully shouldn't be expecting us now and try and make a quick hit—half hour maximum,' Ernesto concluded.

'So the rest of the team try and get just enough to get us out of here while we figure something out,' nodded the mayor. 'You guys draw attention to yourself, maybe make a couple of slightly suspicious moves but no actual cheating. At the most, they'll just ask you to leave the casino. They can't lock you up till they have proof. When we are finished with the other casinos, we'll meet up at the airport. I'll tell my teams to only make a move if they are 100 per cent sure. The other casinos could have been alerted that we are in Singapore too, so we have to be very clever and above all, quick.'

'Yes, that could work. Seems the best idea, but I'm worrying about the airport. Maybe they'll try and stop us?' Ernesto said.

'But they'll have only the names from our fake passports, not the ones we'll be using at the airport,' Marco reminded him.

'All right then, sounds possible. What else can we do? Look, I'll go down and get Reception to organise tickets—anywhere, right? About midnight?'

'Yes. Another thing, we can't tell the teams about all that's happened, not just yet anyway. They wouldn't be able to function . . .'

'Some of their fathers are dead though,' Ernesto complained.

'I know. As soon as we are out, I'll tell them all, but we can't tell them now, nothing except the fact that our plan has changed. Go and get those tickets now.' The mayor handed over his credit card to his brother. He decided to phone Maria to see what was happening in Tolo. She informed him that the police had arrived but had seemed to be totally baffled as to why a shoot-out had occurred in a small town. What had some mercenary group been doing going berserk in Tolo? Why had they dropped three bodies from a helicopter? No references had been made to casino cheats, although it wouldn't take long for them to discover that most of the dead cheats had police files on them. Maria said everyone was doing a good job keeping tight lipped but were now worried about the boys In Singapore.

'Tell them not to worry. Maria . . . we are going away for a while, don't even know where just now. Look, you are in charge of the town. As soon as I can, I'm going to call Toni at the bank and authorise access of the funds to you. Have a town meeting and invest in something, perhaps reopening the casino would not be the best idea . . .' he said, trying to affect a laugh. 'OK, I'll contact you soon, and Maria, . . .' he said.

'Yes?'

'You make me proud to be your father . . .'

A half hour later, he had gathered the team together and gave then details of the change of plans.

'The team that hit Greece, the best-known ones, will go with Ernesto to the Seven Winds. Use the same passports as Greece. They'll be ready for you anyway. Stay till ten. Play a bit, maybe a couple of suspicious hand movements to keep Surveillance interested, but do not cheat. Do you all understand? If you do, you will be caught, so don't. Then at ten, just walk out and get a taxi to Changhi Airport. We meet outside, where the taxis are. Do nothing, right? It is vital you do not cheat. Act suspiciously to draw attention to yourselves, but do not add any bets to the numbers. Is that clear?' he said forcibly.

'OK, OK . . . we got the message,' said one disappointed team member.

The mayor could see there were several miserable and confused faces around, but they nodded in agreement to his request. He dreaded having to tell some of them of their fathers' murders and tried to push it from his mind.

'OK, are we ready? We meet at the airport at 11.15 at the latest. You have to be there. No show, you don't go! Like Durban, we are out as quick as possible, before they can collate the evidence against us. Any questions? None? OK, off you go with Ernesto here. Remember, 11.15 at the airport!'

The Greek group stirred themselves and left. The remainder listened to Capone as he outlined his plan.

'We will split into two groups and hit the other two casinos, as best we can. The scouts have only visited them for a short while. We have had to change our plans, which I'll explain to you later, so we have to go in, sum up our chances quickly, and make a move if we can. Target any busy tables with a high value. We do not have much time and need to get as much money as we can. You have the lookouts and the runners. Try to get American dollars but Singapore ones are OK if it's a problem. But, as before, don't take any unnecessary risks, and keep cashing out, OK.'

He realised he was speaking very quickly, and he was sure it all must have sounded a bit panicky. He tried to calm down a little.

'Remember, eleven thirty at the airport,' he mentioned again. 'OK, OK, let's go. I'll be going with our few "untested" ones. Here is your big chance—what you have been waiting for. It's eight thirty now, so in and out by nine thirty, ten.'

They hailed taxis and set off to the two other new Singapore casinos . . .

At eight forty-five at the Seven Winds, Foong had reported to Campbell that they had not been able to match up the Italian flight names with any bookings in any of the main hotels.

'Still looking. We have men asking around the smaller places . . .'

'Probably using false IDs,' surmised Campbell. 'Anyway, the main thing is we know they are here and coming our way. I've told the other casinos, they can relax a bit now. Some of the guys were worried. We are ready. Up here, we are fully manned and ready to record every roulette table from every angle. On the floor, it looks like the place is almost unsupervised. Security reduced to the bare minimum, except the undercover guys, of course. They will think it will be a stroll in the park and make their move. That's when we get them, not before, remember. Then this Blitzkrieg scam will be over.'

'When will they come?' asked Foong.

'I'd imagine tonight. They seem to favour a quick in-and-out policy, judging by the previous places, so we have to be alert and ready from this minute till it's over. No dinner breaks, coffee breaks, nothing.'

'So we just wait?' said Foong.

'Yep, just wait. They'll be here soon. I can almost feel them.' It was at that moment that he received a call from the Reception office.

'Mr. Campbell, it's me, Tanya from Reception. Just to tell you that two Italians are registering now. I'm going to phone Surveillance now—looks like there's a lot of them, maybe forty plus?'

'Right, just act normal. Surveillance and I will handle everything. Don't give then any problems registering. The passports may be false. Just ignore that, like I told you before.'

He got on to one of the Reception cameras and zoomed into the large group that were registering at the various Reception points. He did not need to check the names against the lists he had. It was clear that this was the same group that had hit Greece. The excitement pumped through his body. He quickly left his office and entered the Surveillance Room, which was full of employees now chattering excitedly. He did not need to ask if they had noticed as well—it was obvious they had.

He approached the Surveillance manager, David Webster.

'Remember, Dave, we really need the footage, and it has to be good.'

'I know. You've told me a thousand times!' came the smiling and confident reply.

'Look around! We have 110 cameras trained on the roulettes from all possible angles. If a fly landed on the table, we'd see it. How many moves do you want before we stop them?'

'Ideally, just one from each team, but it may not work out like that. We can't pull the first team till all, or most, of the others make their moves too. I'll stay here, if you don't mind. I've got the all-clear to bring down the shutters if needed. Then, there will be no way out. After that, we just isolate the teams, get any money back, and hand them over to the police. Security and the Police are alerted. Arron, I can't get hold of, but I've got the all-clear from Kruger to hold off until we've got proof. Foong is phoning the police, and they will be ready to be here in minutes.

'I'm hoping Arron will be fine when the guys are all safely locked up. You know how many times he's phoned here? Up until a couple of days ago, that is,' said Webster.

'He's got financial problems with this place. Once they're locked up, I'm sure he'll calm down, back to his usual, only mildly paranoid, self,' replied Campbell.

As he looked at the various monitors, he could see that the Italians had finished registering and were now entering the casino itself. They were splitting up into groups of three or four, and a quick count showed there was about twenty groups.

'Shit, man!' Campbell exclaimed. 'There's Capone himself—why has he come? Watch him, David!'

'It's him all right! Trying to distract us from the others, no doubt! What does he think we will fall for that again?'

Nevertheless, Webster instructed one of the operators to watch him like a hawk. 'Here they come, here they come . . .' one of the operators could be heard chanting to himself excitedly.

At his targeted casino, Marco Capone and his team were going through a similar Reception process. Although it was a relatively new casino, everything looked tight, as he expected from one of the top casinos in the world. He felt that he was walking into a trap, but what could they do? This was the ultimate test for his young team—at least they didn't appear nervous at all.

On entering, he saw the lookouts take their position and the runners standing behind the three-man crews. 'All OK, so far,' he thought. Plenty of busy tables: still a chance to get some money, he reckoned.

Like Durban, he found that the busy bar overlooked the roulette pits, and he grabbed a stool and ordered a Coca Cola. It was nine. They had about an hour, tops. He had seen the table limits as he approached the bar. They were very high, which was very good for them. He tried to relax, a little encouraged by what he had seen so far.

Within a few minutes, he saw the first runner approaching one of the cash desks. He looked around rapidly—no movements that looked suspicious—the runner passed him, and the money was slipped into his jacket pocket in a second, and then he was back to the table. They had decided that he would collect the money as it came in, in case they had to get out quick. At least then, the other teams would get some cash to help their escape. What had been given to him looked and felt like it was about 25,000 dollars. Nice start. He saw another runner moving from their table and another. He looked up at the lookout at the casino entrance—no problems there. After half an hour, he had received what he figured was about 300,000 dollars. He looked at his palms, which were soaked with sweat. His heart was pumping and he felt faint. It's enough, he reasoned—go. He saw the lookout glance over at him and raise an eyebrow. He too looked like he felt it was time to go. He saw the pit bosses start to do the hourly results estimates. In a few minutes, it would be clear that hundreds of thousands of dollars had gone out in the last hour and they would want to know where from and who won it.

'Time to go!' he said quietly. He nodded his head at the lookout, who immediately initiated the pre-arranged 'tired arm' stretching movement. Capone paid for his drink and headed for the exit. Within ten minutes, the others should have cashed out their last chips and joined him outside. As he left, he saw a pit boss shouting at a puzzled inspector, who was staring into one of the roulette floats and shaking his head.

'What do you mean you don't know where it went! I'll just say that to the manager, will I?—"We lost 90,000 dollars and I'm afraid it just flew off the table by itself . . ."!'

Capone almost smiled. He even felt sorry for the inspector as he headed out of the casino. He breathed deeply. 'God, that had been exciting!' Nerve-racking, but thrilling.

Within a few more minutes, the rest of the team had joined them, and they were on their way to the airport, their luggage left forever at their cheap hotels. They had enough money to buy new clothes, wherever they ended up.

As the taxis made their way to the airport, at the Seven Winds Casino, an operator was watching Capone's every move. He walked around for a while, smiling and talking to the staff, just as he had done in Greece, Campbell thought, recalling the report. 'Wasn't he being a bit obvious?' Campbell was sure he was doing it to again to distract attention from the cheats at the tables. He noticed that Capone had used the Wiseman name again when registering. Campbell thought Wiseman was being a bit naïve if he thought a casino would fall for exactly the same trick again. The names of the others were all the same as in Greece too. 'Sloppy,' he thought. Maybe the Surveillance world had given them too much credit.

By then, the other scammers in groups of three, with runners standing behind, had settled at their particular tables and were buying in for chips.

'Pattern—same as before!' Campbell called out. 'Everyone ready! All the cameras zoom in from behind. It's going to happen any minute. Remember, it will be third dozen, twenty-five to thirty-six. When you see the past post, call it out and save the footage immediately, then ask Dave what you should do next.'

The room had gone completely silent as nearly sixty Surveillance staff peered at their monitors. All of them wanted to be the first to catch the past-posting moves. Five minutes passed. Nothing had happened. Ten minutes passed. Again, no moves had been made.

'Nobody has seen anything yet?' Campbell announced to the room, the only reply being muttered negatives. Cameras were zooming in and out when each winning number came in, but after half an hour, it was clear that, as yet, none of the teams were attempting to cheat.

'What the friggin' hell is going on?' Webster called out in frustration. 'They come to Singapore and just sit and watch the ball going round and round . . . !'

Suddenly Campbell called Webster aside.

'This is only half the total that flew here. Where are the rest? There may even be more . . .'

'What? Do you think they are waiting for the other seventy to arrive here? That doesn't make much sense,' asked Webster, slightly puzzled.

'No, I don't mean that. I think this could be another diversion. Phone the other casinos' Surveillance bosses now. Ask if they have had any Italians registering or have anything suspicious to report. Quick!'

'Right!' Webster replied and moved to his desk.

In ten minutes, he came back, almost running towards the corner where Campbell was standing.

'You won't believe it! Lightwood says they have lost 200,000 in the last hour. They're not sure who took it, but he confirms that more than thirty Italians came in about that time and they all seem to have left! And Boulder says they are down about the same and are checking their registrations now.'

Campbell almost laughed and would have, if he didn't feel so stupid.

'Somehow, they must have figured we would be waiting for them here. Shit! We'll have to do some serious damage limitation later. Lucky it doesn't seem to be too much money. Forget Harrison and Pullman, it's Kruger and Ling who own these casinos, and they are not going to be impressed. Arron will probably laugh his head off, though, knowing him.'

One of the operators called out, 'They are on the move. Look like they are leaving!'

'Knew it, a bloody distraction again,' said Campbell.

'Can't we just grab them now? Force them to confess?' asked Webster in desperation.

'Confess to what—entering the casino and not cheating? We needed the footage, damn it . . . Now, unless the other places have got hard evidence, we can't get them into jail—bloody disaster! Now they are free to try again somewhere else and we have to start all over again.'

'Shit!' said Webster.

'Yes. Shit, shit, shit! . . . Now I've got to try and get through to Harrison and Kruger again. Better give Morris a call too and tell him the disappointing news.'

'What about the passports?' asked Webster quietly.

'What do you mean?' replied Campbell with a quizzical look.

'Can't we at least get them for having false passports? Use that to make them at least confess to the cheat moves? Worth a try . . .'

Campbell thought rapidly. It could work, damn it!

'Get the shutters down!' he said a little louder than he had intended.

Webster grabbed a radio and announced as clearly as he could, 'Delta 1, this is Kilo 1—Tango 1—repeat, Tango 1.'

'Roger,' came the crackling reply.

'Come on, come on!' Campbell and Webster both called out, as they willed the shutters to descend and block the exits. Through the rover cameras, they could see the Italians moving as one towards the casino exit.

'Come on, you bastard!' yelled one of the operators, thumping the desk as he got caught up in the excitement.

Suddenly, a mechanical grating noise could be heard as the massive metal shutters, normally used for emergencies such as earthquakes and fires, started to descend.

The Italians stopped in their tracks and seemed to hesitate for a second. Suddenly, they rushed towards the shutters, which had nearly reached the ground by the time they had got close to them. With just a few feet to spare and in unison, most of them dropped their shoulders and ran through, the last few having to dive and slide through.

'Shit! Get Security to get them!' Webster shouted.

The Security operator called through the radio, but there was no immediate reply from the Security manager. By the time he did respond, Campbell could see from an external camera that the Italians were out of the casino and hailing taxis on the road.

'Nothing we can do now. Bastards!' he shouted and kicked a waste paper basket, which flew over the room.

'There's one of them left inside,' said one of the operators excitedly.

'What? Where?'

'There,' came the reply. 'The older guy, Wiseman.'

Capone was standing next to the shutters, next to some bemused customers, shaking his head with them.

'OK,' said Campbell. 'Better than nothing . . . Let's get him.' He turned to Foong. 'Get the police in and ask them to meet us in the Security Room.'

'Right,' Foong said, reaching for his phone.

Five minutes later, Capone was sitting in the Security Room. He calculated that it was the twenty-first time he had been in a similar situation. He was calm. Two security guards were standing over him.

Campbell, Foong, Webster, the Security manager, and two police officers entered the room and sat down.

'Hello, Ernesto. How are things in the cheating trade?'

'Excuse me, I don't understand?' came the reply in an American drawl.

'Look, let's not waste any time,' Campbell said with a mock sigh. 'You are part of a large cheating team. You came with them. I know you didn't cheat today, but some of your friends hit the other casinos. Maybe you'd like to tell us all about your activities and we can reach some agreement. Otherwise . . .'

'I still don't understand, I'm afraid. I'm sorry, what's happened?'

'OK, enough's enough. Can I have your passport please?' he said, reaching over, displaying an impatient give-me gesture with his hands and arm.

'Sure, no problem,' said Capone as he reached inside his jacket pocket.

Campbell could see straight away that it was an American passport. All the others had fake Italian ones. He started to shift in his chair. Surely, his Wiseman passport was fake too? He didn't open it, saying immediately, 'Look, we know who you are, Mr. Capone. This is a fake passport.'

'Oh, for Christ's sake,' came the weary reply. 'Not this Capone guy again. He must be my doppelgänger. I was hauled into a Vegas casino office once and accused of being this Capone, whoever he is. Look at the passport. My name is Wiseman, American Jew—not some Italian gangster or something. Must have an Italian walking around that looks just like me—poor guy!' he laughed.

'This passport is fake . . . You're Capone,' Campbell said, getting a little irritated.

'Check it out, if you want. It's a genuine all-American passport. I've never even been to Italy.'

'But you've been to Greece, haven't you?' said Campbell, immediately regretting it.

'Yes, I was, just last week, in fact. And I assure you that no one hauled me into any goddamn office when I was there. If I was a cheat, why didn't I do something there? Answer me that, pal?'

The room went silent. Campbell, caught out, was unsure what to do. He asked Foong to take the passport and have it authenticated.

'Wait a minute,' Capone interrupted. 'I've got a flight to catch at midnight. How long will this take?'

Campbell jumped at the chance. 'Where are you heading to? Have you got the ticket or booking reference? Back to Tolo, I'll bet—via Milan.'

'Tolo? This is getting a bit stupid,' Capone said, but he saw his chance. He reached into his pocket and produced his individual booking reference slip. He handed it over to Campbell, whose shoulders slumped on reading that the destination was Perth in Australia.

He slowly handed it back as Foong came back in the room shaking his head. The Wiseman passport was genuine.

'May I go now?' Capone said in a rhetorical tone, sliding his chair backwards. 'As you can see, my flight is in just over an hour. And by the way, I hear you guys have a blackball list or something. Can you send out the word? I am not Mr. Capone, or ever have been. OK? Next time I'm hauled into an office, I'm going to sue for harassment. Goodbye!'

There was nothing Campbell could do. It was a valid passport and he hadn't cheated. He let 'Wiseman' walk.

The room remained silent for a moment, some looking at the floor, some shaking their heads. Then Campbell remembered and turned to the Security manager. 'Why didn't you respond immediately when I said to stop the team leaving?' he said with a hint of resignation. 'We could have stopped them.'

'I left the radio on the table when I was activating the shutters,' came the meek reply.

'Fine, fine,' muttered Campbell, leaving the room. 'Fucking fine . . .'

Capone felt quite pleased with himself and his acting abilities. Compared to some of the interview rooms he had been in, that had been almost enjoyable. He particularly liked the bit where he had threatened to sue them—couldn't wait to tell that to his brother and friends, before remembering with a jolt that nearly all his friends lay dead in Tolo. He looked at his watch as he got into the taxi. He told the driver that he had a plane to catch and there was a big tip for him if he could get there as quickly as possible.

The taxi driver asked for the departure time, looked at his own watch, and replied, 'No need for speed, sir, or extra money—plenty of time.'

'An honest man,' thought Capone. 'Now there's a novel sight,' he smiled and continued to do so when he recalled the look on Campbell's face when he saw that he wasn't travelling to Italy.

Campbell had retreated to his office and tried to get through to Harrison. Someone answered and he heard a lot of background noise. He didn't recognise the voice, but recognised the Italian language.

'For Christ's sake,' he said, ending the call, before the Italian policeman who had picked up the phone could say anything more. He then dialled Morris, who answered immediately.

'Hello, Sam. It's Donald Campbell here. Got a lot to tell you and it's bad news—'

'Me too,' interrupted Morris. 'Cain has been shot—shot in the head. Still alive, thank God. There was a bloodbath in Tolo . . . You know about Arron, yes?'

'No, what happened to him? We've been trying to contact him most of the day. I just phoned his number and it sounded like someone was speaking in Italian or something?'

'He's dead, I'm afraid and Pullman too. Harrison went crazy, attacked the scam trainers. There was a shoot-out, and he got blasted by an old grandmother. He came with some gang. They're all dead as well, so are all the trainers. You know the three guys in South Africa? He dropped them naked from a helicopter on to the town square, would you believe?'

'What the hell!' replied Campbell, his mind all over the place.

'Yes, Arron threw them straight on to the road from the helicopter. He was mad.'

'Where are you now?' asked Campbell.

'The American hospital in Milan. Good treatment. They say Cain has a 50/50 chance. What's happened at your end? Everything wrapped up and finished, I hope? But what did you say about bad news?

'It is. Pretty exciting over here too, but no dead bodies. They came here— Ernesto Capone with a group, but they just sat around and didn't do anything, but they hit the two other casinos for about 300,000–400,000.'

'Shit! So they used Capone as a decoy again, like Greece in a way. Thought they would have taken more than 300–400?'

'Yes, we seem to have got off lightly, for some reason. Capone was here along with the others. We tried to stop them and maybe get them for false passports, but we screwed that up. Capone produced his Wiseman passport, which the police verified as genuine and swore he had never heard of Capone, and he produced a flight booking reference to Perth.'

'Perth? Why there?' said Morris in surprise. 'Do they plan to carry on? Hitting the Australian casinos? The Crown Casino is there. I'd better send a warning e-mail. Didn't the other casinos there pick up on anything?'

'They didn't really have any specific notice that the team had arrived in Singapore. We were so sure that it was our place that was going to get visited, we practically told them not to be on alert. And then Harrison made a quick call confirming it. Another bit of a cock-up there too on my part. It was the audio. Arron was sure they knew about it. We were the only logical choice, he believed.'

'Well, actually, I think he was right. Harrison put a gun in one of the trainer's mouths and was told that it was the one with no audio. One of the Tolo people must have phoned Capone with this information, and they changed their plans accordingly, thinking that one of the gang before they were killed, or myself, would have contacted the Seven Winds. So, Harrison did manage to call you before he got killed. I was pre-occupied with Cain, to be honest. It didn't even cross my mind to contact you, not that it would have made a difference, as it turns out. So we are back to square one again—this has gone on too long. Strange that they have headed straight to Australia. Normally, they go back to Italy, at least for a while.'

'Would you go back to Tolo if you were in their shoes?' asked Campbell. 'The police will be all over the place asking questions, or maybe they got scared after the shoot-out and decided to go on the run.'

'Arron's dead now, so the killing is over,' said Morris firmly.

'Yes, we know that, but do they? They probably think that Arron was sent by us all to stop them by whatever means, so they may just be a little reluctant to go home.'

'So Australia is just a convenient hiding place?' concluded Morris.

'I'd guess so, but it doesn't mean that they won't make an attempt while they are there. They must think they are pretty well invincible at the moment. Although the killing would surely have alerted them that we're not far behind.'

'No, I don't think they have gone to Australia to go for another casino, but of course, we can't make that presumption. With the Blitzkriegers, you never know,' said Morris.

'I know the manager at the Crown in Perth—Bob Minto. I'll give him a heads-up,' said Campbell. 'Now I have to clean up all this shit here—get a report done. I'm not going to come out of it smelling like roses, that's for sure.'

'At least you didn't lose any money from them where you were . . .' Morris said.

'True, but the rest of it won't make good reading. Remember, I'm supposed to monitor all three casinos, not just the Seven Winds. We, I, could have handled it better, and the other casinos won't be impressed at all with our lack of information. No Arron or JP to send the report to—weird. Just Kruger and Ling left of the big four. OK then, better get started. What are you going to do?'

'Speak to the doctors and see what they say. I've phoned Magda and she's waiting for an update. Wants to come out, but I said if we can possibly get him transferred to a hospital back home, we will. If that transpires, I'll accompany him back, and then Magda can be with him after that. Good luck. I'll be in touch. Give me a call if you hear anything about Australia or Tolo.'

'Sure, sure,' Campbell said and put the phone down. He let out a long breath. It had been some day. He phoned Minto in Perth and then started to attend to his report. He found it painful.

# Chapter 20

The Blitzkrieg scammers were in the air and on the way to Perth, and the Capone brothers sat together trying to decide what the hell they were going to do next.

'That's enough. We were lucky there,' said the mayor firmly. 'We have to go somewhere and hide. I have a responsibility to these guys, don't want them to end up shot or something. They know who we are. They were waiting for you at the Seven Winds. It was a trap. Luckily for us, we knew that they knew that it was that one.'

'Yes, but we hit the other two without anything being noticed, and presumably, they were waiting for us too,' said Ernesto.

'You'd figure, unless they were told they could relax, but anyway, it's all too risky now. We have enough money, I think, at least for a while. Finances are not the problem now. It's how we are going to stay alive.'

Ernesto thought for a moment.

'Why don't we offer them a deal? Leave us alone and we'll stop.'

'Oh yes, I'm sure they would go for that,' replied his brother with some sarcasm.

'Actually, if you think of it—why not? I remind you that they haven't caught us once, except possibly the International. As far as they know, we are so good we could go on forever.'

'But that wasn't the plan. The idea was to get enough money to get the town going again, and now we have lost some of our young men, your friends, and we are being hunted down.'

'I know that was the plan, but they don't. They probably think we will continue for as long as we can. So we contact them and tell them it's finished. They'll be relieved, believe me.'

'And the money. Three million,' said the mayor, but he was starting to see the logic in what his brother was saying.

'Chicken feed! They make that in a few hours. I think they'll swallow their pride and go for it, just to get us off their backs.'

'If three million is nothing to them, why did they kill three of our boys and attack Tolo?' Marco said.

'I agree that was crazy. Can't think that these smart business guys would want to get involved in murder. Talk to them. Maybe it was something that just went horribly wrong. I'm sure there must be an explanation.'

'Maybe they never planned to kill all those people. I agree it was the last thing we could have expected. OK then—I can make a call, but whom to?' the mayor said.

'Start low down, put the feelers out. Maybe the manager at the Durban place or the Greek casino?'

'Wait a minute!' said Marco. 'I've got a business card from that Greek casino guy, the one who made the presentation in Durban. I told you I bumped into him. It's in my wallet, I think.' He searched for and found the card. 'Here it is—Sam Morris—casino number and personal mobile.'

'There you go. Phone him when we land. Maybe ask for another million more!' his brother laughed sarcastically.

'God, if we could just get back to Tolo, that's it. I'm retiring . . .' said Marco wearily.

From a desperate situation, they both saw a possible solution to their predicament. Two hours later, they landed in Perth and booked into an airport hotel. They hoped that their stay in Australia would be the shortest any tourist had ever spent in the country.

Morris had seen the doctor, who told him that Cain had a good chance of making it but would likely remain in a coma for a lengthy period. The bullet had gone through his eye and had exited next to the ear.

'Whatever happens, he's likely to suffer brain damage, to what extent, we don't know. In a couple of weeks, we should have a clearer picture.' He was adamant that Cain remain in the hospital after Morris asked about the possibility of a transfer to England or Scotland.

He updated Magda, who immediately said she would be out 'on the next plane', and then he thought of what he should do himself.

It was no use hanging around the hospital. The scam team were still loose and maybe even ready to go again. He had some food, phoned his kids, telling them he would see them as soon as he possibly could. He left the hospital and ambled around the streets, glad of some fresh air.

He was about to phone Linda, when the phone rang.

'Is that Mr. Sam Morris?' He thought the voice sounded faintly familiar.

'Yes, it is,' he replied.

'Well . . . this is Mr Capone. You may remember me as Mr. Lorenzo when we met at Durban?'

'Mr. Capone, you say?' said Morris astonished. He recovered quickly. 'What do you want? You know we know where you are—Perth in Australia.'

'I know you know. My brother informed a man at the casino.'

'Right, right . . . OK, what is it you want? You are all in serious trouble. We'll get you soon, and you'll all be going to jail.'

'Well, many of you will be going with us. You have killed at least twelve people from my town.'

'We have not killed anyone. That was a mistake. I was there to talk with you. A man went crazy. It was nothing to do with me or my bosses.'

'The three youth dropped from the helicopter—how could you do that?' said the mayor, finding anger rising in him.

'What? They were killed in a road accident in South Africa after being caught cheating at a casino. Look, the guy in your town had lost his mind. His name was Harrison. He had money problems and was scared that you were going to go to his casino—which you did—in Singapore.'

'Killed in a road accident. I didn't . . . know,' said Marco.

'You didn't know. Well, as they say in Scotland, "You ken noo."'

'What?'

'Never mind. OK, you didn't know. No casino person killed them. They died in the road accident and their bodies must have been stolen and flown to Italy. I can only think the madman wanted to scare you to stop. I am telling you now—you must stop. Maybe there are other casino owners who would act the same,' he said, although he doubted it.

'We want to stop. That is why I phoned.' Capone said. 'We will stop if you guarantee we can live in peace and can keep the money.'

Morris clenched his fists but remained calm.

'Well, I cannot speak for the big bosses, of course, but I can contact them and present your proposal. I don't know about the money though . . .'

'Mr. Morris, we need the money for the town. I must tell you, I am an honest man, although my brother and his friends took the wrong path, I admit. Tolo was finished. Everything had closed down. We had no money. The only idea we could come up with was to take some money from two or three casinos and then use that money to help Tolo. Singapore was the last one and would have been, no matter what happened. This is the truth. But the killings have changed everything. We cannot go back to Tolo if our lives are in danger. The other side is if you don't guarantee our safety, we will have to carry on, and I remind you, we are very, very difficult to catch.'

For some reason, Morris believed him.

'Look, I think we can do something,' he said. 'It will be tough. How will I know you will never cheat again?'

'For a start, I give you my word. Also, if we are in Tolo, if anything did happen, you would know where to come to get us.'

'Can you guarantee all the men in the town will abide by your word?'

'Absolutely!'

'The three in Africa didn't.'

'That was unfortunate. You caught them, though. One or two individuals can be caught just by drawing attention to themselves. The great thing with our plan was the numbers involved, the organisation, the speed, and the diversions. One or two people cannot do this.'

'I agree there. It was some plan. Was it you who came up with it?'

'It was after someone gave me a lead in that direction.'

'If I do get a guarantee, I also want a promise that you and your town tell no one, give some other people ideas.'

'Don't worry. I won't write a book about it or something. Tolo is a close group. They will listen to me. Again, you have my word.'

'Well, then, I think this would suit everyone, accepting that the bosses of Greece, Durban, and Singapore can swallow their pride and the hole in their wallets. It can maybe be done. I'll need several hours to make many calls. I may have to go to a meeting. Perhaps they will want to meet you personally.'

'I can come, no one else from the team. As soon as you can, I want you to tell me it is safe for us to go home. We are at the airport and ready to go. Phone me back as soon as you know.'

Morris ended the call. He had definitely not expected that. But it seemed a great solution—three million dollars—nothing. Kruger alone was worth three billion. He would accept three million, he was sure, even reimburse the affected casinos by himself to calm things down.

'Right,' he said to himself. 'Let's get this finished!'

He phoned Kruger first and told him the whole story. He was shocked by the news of Arron and what he had done.

'Jesus Christ, he could ruin it for us all! This is big news, if it gets out. "Casino boss slaughters innocent Italians" . . . I was very closely associated with him, Christ's sake! Do you know the team hit one of my casinos in Singapore? They got away again! Are you any nearer getting the bastards?'

'Well, in a way, yes. We know they fled to Australia. Capone, there's two of them, the mayor brother phoned me a few minutes ago. They want to make a deal.'

'A deal?'

'Yes. Look, they're spooked about what happened in Tolo. Capone says they only ever planned to take enough for them to get people back to work in Tolo, apparently most of the businesses there were closed down in the last couple of years. So they wanted, or needed to get, money, and they devised this Blitzkrieg idea, using the old cheats from the area to train mostly the croupiers that were made redundant and some of their own kids. Capone says they want to stop, but they need the money and want a guarantee that they can keep the money and go back to Tolo. Otherwise, he says, they will have no choice but to carry on.'

'What!'

'Mr Kruger, it solves everything, apart from the three-million loss to the casinos.'

'Forget that. I see what you mean. If they carry on, it could be much more. Are you convinced by the offer?'

'I know they've deceived us before, but they are aware we are on to them, and just one case of past posting where we can prove it will be enough to get them jailed. Yes, I think it's genuine.'

There was silence for a full ten seconds, and then Kruger announced firmly, 'Fine, I'm with you, but I'll have to clear it with Ling first. Our rules say we have to be unanimous for these big decisions. I'll offer to write off the casino losses myself, if that will help.' He then asked some genuinely concerned questions about Cain, emphasising the 'if there was anything I can do' part, but in a sincere manner, and then he ended the conversation with a brief, 'Got to go.'

'Very powerful person,' Morris thought admiringly. Deserved all he had achieved—no doubt about that. Was this really it then? It was. Surely Ling would concur. He phoned Capone and told him the news.

'Thank you, thank you. It will never happen again, and I'm truly sorry for the trouble I have caused,' the mayor gushed. 'Hey, when we open the casino, you are invited as a special customer. I'll phone you when we open, but remember . . .'

'What's that?' asked Morris, also feeling a lot more relaxed.

'No cheating!'

Morris laughed loud, an emotional release, he realised, put the phone down, and headed for the nearest bar. He was already shaking his head as he entered in wonder and incredulity. The urge to see his kids burnt inside him like a furnace.

'This would make a good story,' he thought as he pulled the bar stool out and raised his hand towards the barman. 'God—I need a beer.' He drank his beer, went outside, and called Linda. The minute he ended the call, the phone rang. It was Kruger.

'I'm sorry. I tried, but Ling can be a stubborn bastard. He doesn't believe that this Tolo group will stop. He wants them all locked up and blames Arron's death on them. So, we are back to square one. Can you come up with anything, Sam?'

'Jesus Christ!' muttered Morris, letting out a sigh. 'I really believe it was a genuine conciliatory gesture from Capone,' he emphasised. 'I'll ask him to return the money—but what else can I say? Keep on running, because one boss wants to lock you up? Ling is being daft and stubborn. Right, I'll get back to you when I can.'

'Sorry we couldn't sort it out,' said Kruger with obvious disappointment. 'See what you can come up with. Remember, I'm with you on this one . . . but I can't go against Ling. It's awkward . . .'

After the call, Morris finished his beer and went for a walk in an attempt to think things out. He walked around and around the hospital, unconsciously not wanting to stray too far from it. He suddenly stopped as a plan started to shape in his head. The more he considered it, the better it seemed—or rather, he could not think of another way to end this cheating and chasing. He went back to the hospital, found some paper, and started to make some notes. When he had finished, he stared down at what he had produced and then reached for his phone.

Capone answered immediately. He and his team were back inside the airport arranging a flight home.

'Bad news,' Morris said straight away. 'However, I have come up with something that I think will get them off your back, and then hopefully, we can end this thing. Have you ever been to Las Vegas?'

# Chapter 21

Morris stayed another six hours at the hospital until Magda arrived. He did not want to leave Cain by himself, but he knew Magda would be next to him all the way through, whatever the outcome. The doctor had sounded more optimistic when he had last spoken to him. He left Magda sitting by his bedside holding Cain's hand and got a taxi to the airport. While he had been waiting for Magda's arrival, he had booked a flight to Vegas. The connections were poor, it was expensive, and he was already exhausted, but he had to get out there if they were all going to have some peace. He phoned Linda and the kids again at the airport and had some coffee while he waited the five hours until the first flight to London was announced. He then had another three hours to wait before the flight to New York and then, thank goodness, only an hour until the plane to Vegas.

A day and a half after leaving the hospital, Morris arrived in Vegas. He hadn't been there in years, but he fully expected it to be largely unchanged, which was perfect for his plans. Busy, high limits, and no Reception registration. He was surprised the scam team hadn't chosen Vegas over Singapore—until he remembered the attraction the latter held because of the lack of audio.

The Vegas casinos would have the real names and photos of the team, but they wouldn't have to register, so it would be up to luck if a Surveillance employee noticed them among the thousands of visitors. The chances were on his side.

'I'm a cheat for a day,' he smiled wearily to himself, 'but with a purpose!' he reminded himself.

He booked into the Riverside Hotel, although there was no river to be seen, phoned Capone, and crashed out. He slept for three hours, when there was a knock on the door. He knew who it was.

'Mr. Morris, nice to see you again. You remember, at the Durban conference?'

'Mr. Lorenzo or something, wasn't it? I even remember you had your badge half-hidden. So, you were there. Could have got you right there and then. I thought you looked a bit familiar. It was your brother I was thinking of.'

'Could have, but you didn't,' smiled Capone relaxing. He had been worried about a trap, and his team were all well away from this hotel, totally confused on why they had flown, not back to Italy, but over the Pacific to America. Most of them were asleep.

'Anyway, come in,' Morris said, ushering him into the room.

Capone sat on a chair near the window.

'I'm sorry for all the killings, on your side as well as mine. Things were never supposed to go that way,' the mayor said quietly.

'Thanks. Don't care a toss about Harrison, to be honest. I hardly knew the guy, but my good friend, Mr. Cain—who was with me when we met, is in a serious condition. He was shot when we were in Tolo.'

'They told me that someone attempted to save my daughter from being shot by that bastard. It must have been this Cain friend of yours,' said the mayor.

'It was. Your daughter, what was her name . . . Maria?'

'That's her. If something had happened to her, I don't know what I would have done. She is my only child.'

'Well, let's hope we can get this finished and you can get back to Tolo and I can get back to my own special girl and place.'

'Right, you told me enough on the phone to get me interested. Now fill in the details and I'll tell you if we can manage one more Blitzkrieg—is that what you are calling it?'

They sat for three full hours discussing Morris's plan, and at the end, Capone nodded.

'Should be no problem, or at least no more than we have faced so far. One thing, how do you know the bosses will be here in Vegas at that time?'

'I made some enquiries and was told by Surveillance guy at the seven Winds that they meet here on the second Friday of every month—to count their profits and catch up on their investments and takeovers. They have a suite in the Mirage, and as far as I know, none of them have missed a meeting in over ten years, only two this time though.'

'Good,' said Capone firmly. 'The second is tomorrow, so when do we go? Tonight? It would be better tomorrow. I have to organise the teams and brief them about the targets.'

'You sound like a military commander,' said Morris.

'That's exactly how I look at it,' replied Capone. 'Planning, good planning, cover all the bases. I'll get my scouts to get a report done. How many casinos in Vegas?'

'Bundles, but we are only hitting certain ones, the ones owned by Ling . . .' Morris said.

'And how many is that?'

'Seventeen, at the last count. Unless he has bought another one in the last few weeks or so. Hard to keep up with these billionaires. Would you like something to drink at the bar and dinner after? I would love to hear the whole story of how you set this all up and went through with it,' Morris said.

'At the end, at the end. I have a lot of preparation to do. Once it's all over, I hope we can relax then—even celebrate. How much do you think we will have to get?'

'It has to be a lot, enough to give Ling a real shock. I would say fifteen million minimum.'

'That's a lot of cheat moves, a lot. The casino will pick up on it. We'll have to keep moving.'

'Well, you do have seventeen places to get that amount, a bit less than a million per place. I'm sure you can do it!' Morris said.

'Thanks for the confidence vote. Are you sure you trust me?'

'Do I have a choice? What can I do?'

'Don't worry. I'm as keen as you to end this. Right, goodbye. Time to get organised,' said Capone abruptly.

'How did you find Australia?' asked Morris, trying to lighten the mood in anticipation of yet another nerve-racking day ahead.

'Nice place—good airport,' smiled Capone as he headed for the door.

Morris had a shower, a couple of beers in the lobby bar, a club sandwich, and was back in bed and asleep an hour later.

Capone was not so lucky. When they all were awake, he gathered the bemused group of young men. He still had not informed those whose fathers had been killed and explained to them that they had one last job to do.

'I cannot explain much just now, but after this attack, we will be free and able to do what we want back in Tolo.'

'Now get some food and more rest. Tomorrow will be long, and we fly back to Italy as soon as we have finished. That's a promise.'

'Or spend years in jail,' he thought to himself.

Most of the team moved towards the buffet at their hotel. The scouts remained behind.

'What's up, Boss?' asked Mario.

He updated them on Morris's plan. They stared at him intently.

'Seventeen casinos by tomorrow? No way! It can't be done!' protested Giuseppe.

'I know you can't scout these places as thoroughly as the other ones in the time we have. We just need some basic information on them, cash desk location, security arrangements—that sort of thing. Make sure you write it all down, as you'll get confused otherwise . . . I'll help too. So that's about four places each. I'll try and do the extra one. OK, here's the list of the places we go for. We are looking for the ones with the higher limits. Keep that in mind. If we find a particularly favourable place, we can miss one out and spend a bit longer in the good one, but it's important that we hit at least a dozen places. We have to show we can hit anywhere successfully,' he said, showing him the list Morris had supplied.

They split the destinations, agreeing to meet as soon as they could back at the hotel. They left. It was six hours later when they had all returned—Capone being the last.

They ordered some food, went through the casinos in order of perceived 'openness' to a hit, and then discussed the splitting of the groups and how they would organise the money collection for the expected millions of dollars.

'Right,' said Capone, 'first one is definitely The Roman Springs. High limits, poor security, good cash desk access. We sent in—what?—sixty guys there, fifteen groups with a runner each. An hour maximum and then they move on to this one, Crawfords. Maybe ten there . . .'

It was another three hours before the attack plan was finalised and all the details discussed to their satisfaction. Exhausted, they retreated to their rooms at three in the morning. By six in the morning, Capone had woken up and was feeling surprisingly refreshed.

'Last day of the Blitzkrieg,' he said as he hauled his feet from the bed, making a small gesture to God.

Morris didn't get up until ten and he too felt refreshed. It had been a long day the day before—full of nerves, concentration, and lingering shock from the Tolo shootings. He was happy with the gist of his plan and impressed with Capone, who he was increasingly prone to trust.

He phoned Capone's mobile and they discussed the plans for that evening in much finer detail.

'We only got into the casinos pretty late last night. Are the casinos busy all day?' Capone asked.

'More or less. I doubt things have changed since I was last here. They pick up in the evening after dinners and shows, but if you are ready to go, anytime after seven there should be adequate people camouflage, so to speak.'

'Good, because it's going to take several hours to get through them all. We are ready and are going for fourteen of the seventeen casinos owned by Ling. Now, we need a meeting place where I can drop off the money to you after each hit. I can't risk being caught with millions on me. Somewhere central to the casino locations?'

Morris listened to Capone as he named the target casinos and said he would phone him back. He left the casino and wandered out on to the strip, which was quiet at that time. If they started at about seven, hopefully they could finish before midnight. That was the same time that the bosses usually started their meeting. Good.

'Going OK, so far,' Morris thought. It was strange for him to be on the other side of the law, and he could feel the same adrenalin rush he got when he was catching a thief. He looked for a central location where he could collect the cash. Had to be somewhere with people around, he determined. He did not want to be alone anywhere with millions of dollars in front of him.

Noticing its pink neon lights, he saw a diner over the road. He got out his Vegas casino map and studied it.

'Could be good,' he concluded, walking towards it. He went inside and ordered a coffee and looked around. There was a corner booth, where high seats would hide any package that he would place around him or under his seat.

He asked the waitress if the place would be busy around seven and she replied that there would normally be a few in, but, 'you never know in Vegas'.

With the aid of fifty dollars, he was able to reserve the corner booth for seven, saying he had arranged to meet some important clients there.

'No problem, honey,' came the cheerful reply. Morris liked Americans. Their manners and sincerity seemed genuine to him.

He arranged to show Capone the place ten minutes before seven in the evening. The Roman Springs was a mere hundred metres away. Morris bought two suitcases and half a dozen very large carrier bags before heading back to the hotel.

They were ready—nothing to do but wait. Vegas seemed very quiet at that time. Morris bought the Herald Tribune and sat on his bed. Phoning Italy, he was glad to be told Cain's condition had improved further. He had a quick conversation with Magda, who was bearing up well.

Capone had divided his teams up, told them the casinos to hit and the timetable. His brother, normally used to deliberately attract attention, would not be going to any of the casinos. The casinos were well aware that where he went, the scam team followed or were nearby. His job was to book the flights back to Italy for any time after two in the morning and to help organise the money collection. Ernesto later reported back that the tickets were booked for three thirty the next morning, Vegas to Boston to Rome and Vegas, New York, Milan—two flights were necessary, as there were not enough free seats on either flight.

At the end of it all, even Capone found time for an hour's sleep. He felt good. He had prepared well.

Vegas was coming to life in its own special way as the night set in. The strip was lively as excited crowds made their way to the shows and to try their luck in one of the casinos. Thousands of lights illuminated the whole town against a pale blue sky. The night workers and hustlers were emerging from their daytime slumber and were eager to earn some cash. Morris met Capone and showed him the booth in the diner. The place was busy, but as they entered, the same waitress as before pointed to the alcove and gave a thumbs-up sign. Morris waved in thanks.

'Right,' said Capone. 'Let's get this done!'

'Excited?' asked Morris with a smile.

'You wouldn't believe how much,' replied Capone. 'What do you think of my new overcoat?' the mayor asked, opening one side of his rather large and heavy jacket, showing it contained at least six pockets.

'Did you get that made here? How did you manage that so quickly?' said Morris surprised.

'They say you can get anything in Vegas, so I went to a clothes shop and asked for a large coat with many inside pockets. The guy didn't even bat an eyelid. All he said was, "How many pockets would you like, sir?"' Morris laughed and shook his head. Capone continued, 'My brother always used to tell me that the greatest feeling he ever had was when he entered a new casino to try and rip it off. I never saw the attraction, but I can understand the sense of anticipation all right.'

'Good luck. I'll be here, waiting.'

At that moment, Ernesto entered, moved towards them, and sat down next to Morris, who looked slightly bemused.

'Insurance policy, you understand. Sorry,' said Capone. 'I trust you, but thinking of you sitting here with tens of millions of dollars by yourself just made me a bit uneasy. You understand?'

'Fair enough,' said Morris with no malice, and he laughed again at the absurdity of the situation: Sitting in a diner with the world's best known cheat, while his mayor brother and scam team hit more than a dozen Vegas casinos for millions. And then what they planned to do after—crazy! He reached out his hand, which Ernesto shook.

'Sorry to hear about your friends in Tolo. I was there. It was bad. If it was any consolation, they all died quickly,' he lied.

'Thank you for that. They were good guys, although you probably would not agree. I'm glad it was quick. They had a life full of daring and adventure, better than most have. Anyway, thanks.'

Marco left and the two men left in the diner's booth engaged in small chat, looked out the window, watching the lights and reflections of the strip.

'So you trained these young guys?' asked Morris.

'Yes, me and the others. It was ideal for us. We were known in so many casinos, and with all the advances in communication between them, we found we were getting recognised time and time again before we could get even close to a table. With the expenses of hotels and airfares, we were mostly losing money. So when Ernesto suggested we come and train the unemployed youngsters in Tolo, most of us jumped at the chance. Nearly all of us are from there or nearby, so it was like coming home to retire after our adventures, in a way.'

'Did you enjoy the training?'

'Fantastico! It was like seeing myself when I first started, and when they got so good that even I could not see the push, I was tall with pride. Compared to me, they were much better. I was not properly trained, or should I say not in such a methodical way. Remember, we trained them for two years. For the plan to work, they had to be so good—all of them—that the chances of being caught were practically nil. We achieved that aim. My brother talked about trying to open the old casino again, and we were to be used as managers, pit bosses, or trainers, when they needed new dealers.'

'You a manager!' Morris could hardly control himself as he envisaged Capone walking around the pit sternly watching the games and looking for cheats. He had to slap the table.

Capone looked bemused at first and then caught the logic and he too smiled and laughed.

'Sorry. I just can't see you as a manager—no offence!' Morris said, passing on his thoughts.

'I know, I know. It would be strange, but who better to be on the look-out for cheats!'

'Right enough, I suppose,' agreed Morris.

'Yes. "Casino opening. Managers and Pit Bosses needed. Experienced cheats preferred."'

They carried on in a similar vein, until they saw the mayor enter and slide into their booth, his frame blocked by the high seats.

'OK?' Morris asked, feeling a tremendous excitement building in him.

'Fine, fine, no problem. Takes a bit of organising, but the runners and the teams are doing fine.' He opened up the jacket he was wearing. Each pocket was stuffed with dollar bills, most of which looked high value in denomination. Capone strained, as he had to dig out the money, which had been jammed very tightly into the pockets.

'OK, four down, ten to go,' he said, sliding bundles of cash over the table.

Morris had opened one of the suitcases and slid the money in. 'How much do you think?' he asked the mayor.

'Not really sure. The Roman Springs had very good high limits, so we got a lot from there, the others OK. Maybe three, four million.'

Morris couldn't help but see Ernesto's eyes widening slightly and automatically thought, 'Down, boy.' There was no way he was going to go to the toilet and leave Ernesto with all that cash.

'OK, I'm off,' declared Marco and headed out again.

Morris looked around, brought a pen and paper from his pocket, and slid the suitcase under the table towards Ernesto.

'OK, we don't need an exact amount. Just take a bundle and tell me the denomination. They should be in bundles of tens or hundreds.'

Ernesto nodded and reached down and opened the case, taking out a handful of notes.

'Right, denomination is hundreds. One, two, three bundles of hundreds.'

Morris wrote down the amount on his pad: 'Hundreds × 300 = 30,000'.

Ernesto moved the first three bundles into the other suitcase sitting alongside the other one.

'Hundreds again . . . ten bundles of ten.'

Another ten grand was written down.

They had nearly finished estimating the cash when Capone entered again. After entering the booth, he opened both sides of the jacket proudly. He then showed the back of the coat, which also had numerous pockets. In total, there were twenty pockets, all stuffed to the brim.

'Have a look at this, guys!'

'Holy shit!' said Morris, suitably impressed. Ernesto looked close to having a heart attack. It took the mayor nearly ten minutes to get the money out.

'Still no problems?' Morris asked, hardly believing it was going so well.

'I told you they were the best,' said Ernesto proudly.

'Have you been to the Palace yet? Busiest in Vegas—huge limits.'

'I know, saving the best for last and in case we don't get enough from the other places,' Marco said, turning to leave. 'I'm exhausted. It's hard work, this—stealing millions. I've earned it!'

Morris and Ernesto carried on estimating the totals. The two suitcases were by then full.

An hour later, the mayor came in again. He simply dumped the money, and all he said was, 'Last one—the Palace,' blowing out some air and grabbing a drink of Coca Cola from his brother, before heading for the exit again.

An hour later, he came back. His face was red and sweat lay across his forehead, but he was triumphant as he pulled out cash from his pockets.

'Splendido!' he yelled. 'Splendido. We were right. The Palace had a 5,000-dollar straight-up limit. Ten thousand allowed on the splits or a 170,000 in our pockets per spin. We got them for at least forty spins, my friends!'

He sat down in the booth and downed a bottle of Coca Cola in one thirsty gulp. He stood up after a minute or so.

'Right, I'll get the team packed to go and ready to go. I'll wait for your call, Morris. Have you got enough to pay for your drinks?' he laughed, as visibly relaxed, he left the diner.

Morris and Ernesto carried on counting the money. In addition to the two suitcases, five carrier bags were stuffed with money.

Two hours earlier in the suite of the Palace, Kruger and Ling had been discussing the Blitzkrieg scam.

'The goddamn cheek of it—asking us to let them off the hook!' declared Ling indignantly. 'Unbelievable! Who do they think we are?—Some bit part casino operators? The thought that I would be willing to let anyone even take a penny from me for nothing. How do they think I got to where I am? By giving money away?'

'He was a bit of a pain sometimes,' Kruger thought. Ling was a highly intelligent and brilliant businessman who he admired, but Kruger was annoyed by his stubbornness at times. That was such a time.

Kruger and Ling moved on to what they really liked to discuss—how to make more money. The room they sat in was impressive. Beautifully furnished with the obligatory bar, the room also contained giant screens and various monitors from which they could analyse the hourly movements of their various Vegas casinos as well as stock market fluctuations. The room was divided into four quarters, each of which had been set up to show the individual casino performances of the four bosses. Harrison's and Pullman's monitors were blank, switched off in macabre respect.

Kruger's screens were showing that his Vegas places were having a good night. The bosses loved this monthly meeting. Walking around the room or sitting at the bar, drinking the finest brandy and seeing who could make the most money during the night. Kruger had been tempted for a moment to offer Ling a million-dollar bet that his casinos would out-perform Ling's that day. 'Call it intuition,' he thought to himself with a wry smile.

They walked around the room, talking amicably. The loss of the other two bosses was only seen as an opportunity to expand. Neither Kruger or Ling had liked Harrison or Pullman much, in any case. Andrew's demise had barely registered. It would be easy to get another 'butler'.

One of Ling's monitors was showing flashing red lights—a sign that the hourly casino profit had dropped badly. He ambled over to have a look.

'Bad hour—bloody hell! The roulettes dropped three million at the Roman Springs. Black jacks did OK. Anyway, what were we saying, Steve?'

He had just got back to the bar when another red light started flashing. He peered towards the screen but remained on his stool. When the third, fourth, and fifth monitors started to flash red, Ling and Kruger abruptly stopped talking and looked at each other, rising slowly and walking back to the screens and peering down.

'What the hell!' exclaimed Ling. 'The Palace has dropped 7.3 million and all on roulettes!'

Kruger walked along the monitors representing his casinos.

'My places seem to be doing fine,' he said with satisfaction and a smirk.

'Well mine aren't!' shouted Ling. 'I'm down nine million in the last two hours.' He reached for the phone. As he did so, another nine monitors seemed to switch on all at once. The room was bathed in a surreal, dull, red hue. Ling dropped the phone and ran around each of the monitors in turn.

'Oh my god!' he called out. 'Twenty million gone on roulettes. It's them! They are here! The Blitzkrieg is here! They must be! What can we do?' Phones started to ring. Ling was running around like a headless chicken.

'Could they be here?' thought Kruger. 'Here in Vegas? They were in Australia and wanting to go home a day or so ago, but they hadn't been allowed to, had they?—By a certain Mr. Ling.' He smiled; he had had an inkling what was going to happen and it was more or less confirmed now.

'Cheeky, but dangerous,' he muttered to himself, appreciating the fact his casinos had remained untouched. The message was being clearly conveyed. His phone rang and he looked down to see that the caller was Sam Morris.

'Hello, Mr. Morris. How's the investigation going? I have a feeling you might be needed here soon in that regard.'

'I know about it all. Don't worry. I'm here in Vegas,' said Morris. 'Does Ling know that his casinos here have been hit?'

'I think you could say that he is aware of the fact,' said Kruger calmly, as he glanced over at Ling, who was holding two phones while kicking a chair around the room.

'Look, I'm with Capone on this attack. He had to show Ling what he could do. He's still ready to make a deal. All the money will be handed back, but the team get to go back to Italy and keep the initial money that they have already got. The money from Singapore will be returned too.'

'What's your role in all this?' asked Kruger.

'I agreed with Capone that the only way to stop all this was to make Ling see sense. I wasn't involved, apart from collecting the cash. It's in front of me now. Something like twenty million. Can you make the offer to him?'

'I see, I see. Wait!' said Kruger and turned to Ling, who was sitting motionless at the bar, staring out the balcony window.

Kruger walked over slowly to him and put a hand over his shoulder. 'Just got a call. It was a Blitzkrieg,' he confirmed. Ling looked up at him and started shaking his head and mouthing some obscenities in a language that Kruger had never heard before. Kruger lingered a few seconds and then said, 'However . . . the very very good news is that you can get the money back if we agree that they can keep the money from Greece and Africa. They will go home and we'll never hear from them again. Doesn't bother me too much, but sounds like a great deal for you . . .'

Kruger watched in fascination as Ling's face transformed in seconds from a look of utter despondency to one of sheer bliss and hope.

'Please, yes, yes, yes, please!' He jumped from his bar stool and grabbed Kruger. 'What do we have to do?'

Kruger spoke to Morris, 'Done deal, Morris. How do we get the money back?'

'Well, I'm standing at the bottom floor of your private elevator, next to the doorman. He is looking a bit wary, to say the least. I'll send up the money now and that will be it? I have your word and most importantly Ling's, yes?'

'Absolutely, we just want it to be over too. We'll cover the small losses at Greece and Durban. Don't worry. The check is in the post. Quite a ride, wasn't it?!'

He spoke to the doorman via Morris's mobile and instructed him to collect the money, place it in the lift, and send it up to the top floor—reminding him there were cameras inside the lift.

When Kruger told Ling that the money was on its way via the elevator, he ran to the door and waited. When the door opened, he fell to the floor and hugged the cash like a long-lost child and then brought it into the room and started to count it.

'It will all be there, don't worry—relax,' Kruger said. 'Everything is back to normal, except two of our group and Andrews are no more. Not a bad outcome, actually . . .'

Ling suddenly looked up at Kruger in a suspicious way.

'Wait a minute! I heard you say Morris on the phone. How could he possibly have known about the money being stolen so quickly?' Ling stood up straight and walked up to face Kruger. 'He must have been in on it. He stole from me—'

'You got your money back. He and Capone were teaching you—'

'We hired him to catch the cheats and he stole from me. I'm sure he has a few million down his pants. Well, if he thinks it's all over, he and his cheating friends are very much mistaken. I'll kill—'

'I gave them my word,' interrupted Kruger slowly but very firmly.

'Fuck your word!' Ling replied with a look of dismissal.

Kruger summed things up as he looked around the room. On the table, there was about twenty million spread out. Ling had just lost all that money as far as anyone knew. He had made calls in desperate panic. That was money that was stolen, not a win for lucky punters, who would always return and give it back. Ling had sounded almost suicidal . . .

'And in the end, I am a man of my word . . .' Kruger reminded himself, moving rapidly towards Ling, who was at the bar next to the open balcony and starting to make a call.

Before he knew it, he had been picked up by his arm and collar and was out and over the balcony and down . . .

Morris, who had lingered in the Mirage lobby to phone Capone with the good news, had just walked out of the hotel entrance when the body of Ling smashed through the roof of a stationary taxi. Morris's phone rang.

The voice was very cold, business-like.

'Mr. Ling had second thoughts about our deal. I persuaded him to commit suicide. Half the money will go to me, half to the Blitzkrieg guys, and one million to you from my share. Collection of said will be organised when things have calmed down. Now, can you give me your word that it's all over?'

'To repeat an old 60's phrase from England, Mr Kruger, "It is now",' Morris replied, turning and walking firmly away along the strip, reaching for his cigarettes, intent on finding the nearest bar.

Lightning Source UK Ltd.
Milton Keynes UK
UKOW04f0432180215

246470UK00002B/188/P